Stay With Me Now

By Kaci Rose

Publisher's Note: This is a work of fiction. Names, characters, places, and incidents are a product of the author's imagination. Locales and public names are sometimes used for atmospheric purposes. Any resemblance to actual people, living or dead, or to businesses, companies, events, institutions, or locales is completely coincidental.

Book Cover By: **Covers and Cupcakes**

Editing By: **Editing 4 Indies**

Blurb

He would change the face of music... unless their love re-wrote history.

In the year 2009, Ivy stepped through the time door, not knowing what to expect. To her mind-blowing surprise, she found herself in the era of poodle skirts and soda shops.

The year is 1957, and David Miller is beginning his rise to stardom that will live on long after his untimely death. Unless history is somehow thrown off course...

The instant their eyes meet, electricity crackles between them. But his history is written, and she plays no part in it. Or does she? Can Ivy help keep his legacy intact and save him from having his life cut tragically short? Was history rewritten the moment she cracked open the door to the past?

This is a Steamy, Time Travel, Rock Star Romance. No Cliff-hangers. As always, there is a satisfying Happy Ever After. If you love steamy romances with insta love, hot love scenes, time travel, and rock stars, then this one is for you.

To those we love but are separated from by time and distance.

Table of Contents

Chapter 1

Ivy

When I woke up this morning, it was the year 2009...but I am currently standing in 1957 Nashville.

I must be going crazy.

I think back to this morning's coffee...

My best friend, Brian, is kind of a geek, and he's also my roommate. He is crazy smart, but his passion is time travel. I wrote it off as one of his quirks. Until this very minute, anyway.

Over my morning coffee, he said he found what he calls a time door. I'm not a morning person, so I kind of zoned out as he explained the geeky stuff about this door.

I do remember he said it should take me back roughly fifty to sixty years. Well, fifty-two years was about right if I am to believe the newspaper I just saw.

Even when I didn't believe half of what he was saying, I have always been supportive of him. It's just what friends do. So, the whole conversation this morning didn't come off as weird to me, but looking back, oh, what I would've done differently.

"Hey, Ivy, I did it!" Brian called as he came rushing into the kitchen.

As I said, I am so not a morning person, so all I did was look at him over the rim of my coffee cup.

He rolled his eyes at me. "The time door! I found it *and* know how to use it!"

I think I mumbled something like, "That's great, Brian."

I didn't really believe him, but if he believed it, what did it harm? Well, me, apparently.

He went on to explain how it works. I wasn't fully listening, but I did hear that you needed some sort of stone he was super excited about, and the fact we have a bunch of them in our backyard means I guess they're not that rare.

Then came the part I should have fought harder on.

"You will test it for me, right?" he asked.

"Brian, why can't you do it? It's your baby."

"Because if something goes wrong, I have to be here."

"Great," I said sarcastically.

He did have fun dressing me up in 1950s clothes. I felt like a life-size doll, and the clothes were nothing like I would ever wear in 2009. I'm a yoga pants and T-shirt girl around the house and jeans and shirt girl out and about.

So I thought he was just having fun getting me to wear something a bit fancier. I mean, we're talking high-waisted white shorts that thankfully were at a reasonable length for me. I can't stand how short the shorts are nowadays. Maybe I'm more old-fashioned than I thought.

He dressed me in a T-shirt that was a pretty shade of blue and some flats. Then I started fighting him when he went for my hair. My hair is long and deep brown in color, and I tend to wear it down either straight or with some beachy curls to it. I don't do much.

But the 1950s hairstyles? I'd never be able to recreate them myself! I wanted to go for simple, so we spent a good half hour scrolling the internet until we found a photo of Racheal McAdams with her hair half up in pin curls and just some simple curls at the bottom.

I didn't look like myself or even feel like myself, for that matter, but Brian has always been there for me. I've supported him in everything he's ever done—from coming out and telling his parents he's gay down to this crazy time travel stuff—so I wasn't going to stop now.

I watch Brian load my pocketbook with ten tiny stones.

"You should only need two stones, but I want to be on the safe side. I also put money printed in 1951 in there for hotels, food, and whatever else you need." He hands me the purse.

Nodding, I remember thinking he was sure getting into it this time, and then we were off.

We live just outside Nashville in a quiet area, but a few blocks away is a huge house that has been turned into a museum. My house is one of four on the street, and there are over twenty empty lots, so it's kind of secluded.

We walk to the end of the street, where a bunch of huge rocks make a circle. Many of the rocks are over six feet tall, and some are over two feet wide. They surround an almost ten-foot-wide area so dense you can't see through to the other side. It looks out of place, for sure, but I always thought it was a dumping ground when they built some of the buildings on the street, so I never really questioned it.

Brian swears this is where the door is, so I follow him onto the lot. We move around a few rocks, and what looks like a narrow path to the center opens. The area can't be seen from the street or any nearby areas, and I feel kind of weird being here. Then I start to feel it... a hum on my skin. It wasn't a noise, but a feeling.

Brian then gives me the details.

"Okay, you can't stay longer than two weeks because we can't take any chances that you might change history. But you need to stay at least forty-eight hours to give your body time to adjust before you come back."

I nod my head, though I'm partly distracted by the humming.

"Take in as much as you can but stay to the shadows and don't get involved in anything. Don't bring anything back that could change history. Oh, and you will have to come back via this spot. Got it?" he asks.

I just nod again.

If I believed this would work, I would have been nervous. I should have been nervous.

He keeps reminding me I've heard him talk about all this for years so there is no one else he would trust. Then he encourages me to touch one of the bigger rocks. I walk toward the rock, and I'm both relieved and disappointed when nothing happens.

But the closer I get to the rock, the stronger the humming feeling on my skin gets, and I don't know if I'm imagining it or not. When I'm just a hand span away from it, my skin feels like it's crawling. I think maybe I had too much coffee. I did have a few extra cups this morning. That must be what the buzzing through my veins is. Yup. That's it. But when I look back at Brian, he's so excited, like a kid at Christmas. And without thinking, I reach out and touch the damn rock.

Holy hell. I've never done drugs, but I would guess what happened next is what an acid trip would feel like. It lasted maybe two seconds, but at first, something was pulling me from the front, then a second later, something was pushing me from behind, and then I was weightless. There were so many colors, but everything was dimmed and blurry as though I couldn't focus on anything.

Then I felt one last huge push and landed on the ground right in front of the rock.

"Brian?" I call out frantically, looking around for him after that weird experience. But there was no Brian. Cursing him to hell because I thought he walked away, I started making my way back to the street. But the paved streets were now dirt. There were no houses, and it was eerily quiet.

Did it actually work?

Cars sound behind me, so I walk in the complete opposite direction of where my house is, or was, or would be.

I walk a few minutes out to some road I vaguely recognize. It should have been all built up with stores and restaurants, but there's barely anything there. The cars are all wrong, as though I was touring a vintage car museum. I stand there looking at all the older cars and realize that Brian freaking did it!

I stood there for a good five minutes in shock. Not one person walked by me or even paid me any attention as I just stared around me. I had no idea which way to go, so I walked to the corner where there was a little stand and looked at the date on the newspaper.

July 21, 1957.

I was in 1957 Nashville.

So, here I am. Standing on that corner, I'm just looking around in shock, wondering what I'm going to do. Thankfully, Brian gave me some money from this time, or I'd be in a lot of trouble.

I start walking to see what I can find. I figure I have to take in the city anyway, and I have at least forty-eight hours to explore. I know downtown has a bunch of hotels, so I figure I should head that way. As I walk up the street, I realize there should be a huge museum here. That David Miller, a famous singer in the fifties and sixties, has a house in this area.

He died young, in the late sixties, I think it was. From what I remember, he had a heart attack caused by his drug use. His house was turned into a museum and is one of the most visited homes in the country—well, in 2009 anyway.

I'm walking on the opposite side of the road from the famous house, and I stop when I get in front of it and admire it. There it is—Ivy Hill. This is the house I was named after. I always loved this house from when Brian and I toured it. Seeing it now makes me forget everything that just happened. How I need to find a place to stay and any concern about whether I'll make it home are forgotten. I'm drawn to this house in a way I can't describe.

It takes me a minute to shake out of my daydream when I see someone crossing the street.

"Ma'am? Are you okay?" a male voice asks.

Pasting on a smile, I look over at the gentleman. He's in slacks and a polo shirt, but the shirt stretches across his muscular body. I keep looking up, and my smile falters.

Not because he isn't handsome, but because he takes my breath away as I stare into the most brilliant blue eyes I've ever seen. He has dark black hair swept back into a classic style for the time and a strong jawline. I'm about eye level with his chin, so I have to look up a bit to see his eyes.

The look in his eyes is intense, and my heart skips a beat as he holds my gaze.

David Miller is staring at me. One look like that from the soon-to-be American heartthrob and playboy, and it's no wonder women fell to his feet.

He reaches out to touch my upper arm, trying to get my attention again. "Ma'am, are you lost? You look a little confused."

His voice makes my core clench in a way I've never experienced before. Then the fog starts to clear, and I realize I need to watch what I say. I'd sound like a crazy lady if I told him I'd never been here before because I just traveled from 2009.

I let out a small laugh. "Maybe I am a little bit. I was walking along thinking when I saw the house, and it just drew me in. It's beautiful. Is it yours?" I ask, already knowing the answer.

He smiles proudly at me. "Yes, ma'am, just bought it two months ago." He looks me up and down with appreciation in his eyes. I go to shift my weight to put some space between us and wobble a bit on the uneven ground. He catches me by my arm, and I can see the worry on his face. "Are you alright? Would you like to come in for a glass of water and sit down for a minute?" he asks.

I have to fight not to let my jaw drop. The opportunity to see the famous home I was named after before it looks like how everyone knows it now? My parents were both huge David Miller fans, and they named me Ivy after his home "Ivy Hill."

In the back of my mind, I know he's probably only asking me inside to get into my pants, but it's *Ivy Hill.* How can I pass up this chance?

With a smile, I say, "That would be nice. I bet it's just as beautiful inside as it is outside."

He laughs and holds out his arm for me to take, and I'm taken aback by how much of a gentleman he is. If the guys in 2009 were even one-fourth as much of a gentleman as men are now, dating would be so much easier.

I place my hand in the crook of his elbow, and as soon as I touch his skin, I instantly feel as though my hand is on fire, and sparks are shooting up my arm and down to my belly.

At this moment, I realize I might be in very big trouble.

Chapter 2

David

This beautiful girl on my arm just sent shockwaves through my whole body. My dad always said he knew with one look that he was in love with my mother, but the first time they touched, it was like they were burned into each other's souls. And I think that's what just happened to me.

That's how it feels now with her hand on my arm as I guide her across the road toward my house. Like my soul just linked with hers, and I didn't know I was walking around as only half of myself. But now I think I know what it feels like to be whole, and I don't ever want to give it up.

"It actually needs some work," I say, but my voice comes out much huskier than I planned. I don't want to scare her away, but I want to talk to her. I want to know every little thing about her.

"What's your name, beautiful?" I ask. She hasn't taken her eyes off the house, but when I call her beautiful, a small smile graces her lips. Pride hits me that I was able to put that smile there.

"Ivy," she says as she turns her stunning emerald green eyes on me.

"Ivy." I test the name on my lips and instantly love it. "I'm David."

We walk through the gate that's next on my list of upgrades. I need to increase security because my singing career is climbing.

My first single did better than anyone ever expected, so they are already rushing for me to put out the next. I push that thought from my head. I want Ivy to have all my attention.

"This old girl needs a name," I say, talking about the house.

"You haven't named her yet?" she asks, a little shocked.

"No, couldn't think of anything I loved," I say. Her eyebrows pinch, almost as if in confusion.

As we walk up to the door, I hold it open for her. She smiles up at me as she steps inside. Having her in my space affects me. It's almost as though with her here, it's now a home. I watch her take in the house in wonder.

"This will be the living area. It's bare now because I haven't been able to decide on a color scheme." The room currently has white carpet and red velvet drapes that were here when I moved in. It's definitely not to my taste, but I've been so busy that I haven't had time to think about what I would like instead.

"To the left here will be the dining room. The kitchen is on the other side of the wall there," I say as we head that way. I watch her eyes take it all in before I point at the stairs. "Up there are the bedrooms and where I've pretty much been living, and around here is the kitchen. This was the first room I had redone before I even moved in. I need my food." I laugh.

She smiles and takes in the kitchen. The kitchen overlooks a room that I'm sure is supposed to be a family room at the back of the house. Though I'm not sure what I will be doing with it because it sits bare right now.

At this moment, I can see Ivy in the kitchen making dinner while I sit there with my guitar working on music or maybe entertaining in the family room. I can see morning coffees sitting at the counter. I can see it all so clear, and I can't keep the grin off my face.

She walks around the kitchen, lightly trailing her fingers across the countertops like she is scared to touch them but just can't stop herself. I am now jealous of my own kitchen countertops because I want to be the one she trails her fingers across. I wonder what it would be like to feel her fingers run down my skin that way.

I start to feel the stirring of arousal and have to take a deep breath. Getting hard within the first hour of meeting this girl would send her running.

"Here, why don't you sit down and let me get you a glass of water." After she sits at the counter, she watches me move around the kitchen. Her fingers brush mine as I hand her the glass. I watch her take a few sips of water, then I have an idea.

"Will you stay for lunch? I had lunch prepared. I was thinking we could eat outside, and I can show you the rest of the grounds?" I hope she'll say yes. I just want a little more time with her, hoping she feels this connection.

She smiles up at me. "I'd love to. I'm so hungry it's like I haven't eaten in years." She laughs quietly to herself, obviously laughing at her own joke.

After asking Ivy to wait, I head to find my housekeeper, who is also doubling as my cook right now. I ask her to make lunch for us to enjoy outside since the weather is so nice.

I rush back to Ivy, not wanting to waste a second of time with her. When I get back to her, she has finished the water and is standing at the window, looking out over the backyard.

This time, I take a chance and grasp her hand in mine. Unsure of how she will react, I look at her hand and intertwine my fingers with hers, taking in a shaky breath. I always thought my parents were crazy or just special. I never thought this kind of love, love at first sight, actually existed.

Until now. Until Ivy.

Once outside, we walk the small garden my mom put in before I lead her out to where I set up a small table and some chairs so I could enjoy dinner outside. I love coming out here at the end of the day to relax, but like the rest of the house, it needs work too. We head to the table, and I pull out a chair for her to take a seat.

After sitting down next to her, I start pulling items from the basket my housekeeper left on the table for us and serve her my favorite chicken salad sandwich and potato salad along with some sweet tea.

We share glances, and she grins, watching me set out the items for us. When everything is set, I pick up my sandwich, and say, “So tell me everything about you, Ivy, and don’t leave anything out.”

Chapter 3

Ivy

My eyes widen. *Tell him everything*? He wouldn't believe me if I did. As it is, I've already had to watch what I say and think about every word before it leaves my mouth. He probably thinks I'm really shy and quiet.

"I never know what to say when someone says that. I'm better with direct questions. Besides, you don't want to know about my life. It's boring."

"That's where you are wrong, beautiful," he says, and my stomach bursts into a field of butterflies, just like it has every time he has called me beautiful today. "My parents always tell me the story of how they met and fell in love. They tell me how it was love at first sight. My dad would say he knew in the depth of his soul that my mom was his. The moment she touched him, he felt her soul burn into his. Soul mates," he says, staring directly into my eyes.

The field of butterflies multiplies, and my breathing gets heavy. His parents seem to be describing how I felt when we first met. But this can't happen. My soul mate can't be in 1957 when my life is in 2009. As if he can read my thoughts, he continues.

"That's how I felt when I saw you standing across the street today. There is something between us, and I can tell you feel it too, even if you may not want to admit it right now."

I shake my head. I can't let this happen. I'm supposed to slip in, get some info for Brian, and slip out. Not make any waves and most certainly not allow the biggest name in rock and roll to think I'm his soul mate. This is not happening.

Oh god, Brian is going to kill me.

"I bet you say that to all the girls. It's no wonder they all swoon for you." I try to joke. After all, he does get himself a playboy reputation for a reason, and I'm sure that all starts now.

I glimpse what might be anger crossing his face quickly followed by hurt. My heart clenches. I can't handle that look, and knowing I put it there is killing me. But I tell myself I'm imagining it because there is no way David Miller isn't making a play here. Right?

Before I can even speak, he is up and around the table. He kneels on the ground in front of me, so we are eye to eye. He brings one hand to my cheek and just looks into my eyes, searching for something.

His eyes plead with me as though he needs me to believe what he is about to say. It's as if he's looking past me and sees *me,* my soul, and the me I try to keep hidden.

"I haven't said that to any girl. Ever. It's okay if you don't believe me right this moment, but in your heart, you know it's true, and I will prove it to you. All I ask is that you give me the chance." He takes in a shaky breath and brings his other hand up to frame my face with his hands.

"I'm going to kiss you now, beautiful, and if you don't want that, then you need to stop me," he says barely above a whisper.

My mind races. This is crazy. We've only known each other for a few hours. I may know all about him in the future—who he becomes and how his life turns out—but he knows nothing about me. He doesn't even know my last name. But then I remember my time here is on a deadline of two weeks at most, so why not live a little and enjoy it? When I go back home, I can forget about it and move on, right?

Half my brain is yelling that I can't do this and it's a horrible idea. I should get up and walk right out the front gate and never look back. Go find a hotel room and get on with my plans.

The other half of my brain says it's only two weeks, two weeks out of my whole life. Surely, I can have a little fun? I could be one of David Miller's first conquests. My heart then weighs in like an idiot and wants to believe him. Wants to believe the words are true, that he feels this connection and truly wants to be mine.

My heart wins out, and I lean in to kiss him. I swear at that moment, the world fades away the fact that I am fifty-two years in the past and all my doubts are gone. I just know that nothing that feels like this could possibly be wrong.

When his lips move over mine so softly, sparks shoot from all my nerve endings, and it's as though our souls are connecting, and my soul is finally at home. He presses his tongue against my lips, seeking entrance, and when I open just a little, he's right there in the most passionate kiss I've ever experienced. I kiss him back with everything I have because there's no telling if I will ever get this chance again. His hand moves to the back of my head, tangling his fingers in my hair to angle my head and deepen the kiss.

Grasping his shirt, I pull him to me, and he comes like a magnet that can't stay away. His other hand grips my waist, and my heart pounds as I grow aware of every little touch of his skin to mine.

When he finally pulls back, he rests his forehead against mine, and we both try to catch our breath.

"Tell me you felt that. Tell me it wasn't just me," he begs.

I can't lie to him. Even if it's scary or I know I should.

"I felt it," I whisper.

He gives me a soft peck on the lips, then settles himself back in his chair. I can't take my eyes off him, and his gaze never leaves mine.

"That was one hell of a kiss, Ivy." His voice is as intense as his eyes.

My skin heats a bit as I look around, trying to break the connection.

"Yeah, it was," I whisper.

He clears his throat. "Eat up, this is the best chicken salad sandwich you will ever have," he says and takes a bite.

I take a bite and look down at my sandwich as I chew.

"Well?"

With a smile, I say, "It's really good." I watch a smile cover his face, thinking he won. "But it's not the best I've ever had."

His face falls, and he sets his sandwich down and wipes his mouth. "Oh, yeah? What was the best one you've had then?"

I can't tell him it is the sandwich at Panera Bread from back home because I'm pretty sure that chain hasn't even been invented yet. So I go with a version of the truth.

"There is this a soup and sandwich shop near my house, and they have this amazing chicken salad sandwich. It has grapes and almonds, and they mix it with mayo and honey and a few spices. The flavor is amazing. I have the recipe written down back at my house."

"Where is back home?"

"You wouldn't believe me if I told you."

"Try me."

I just shake my head. I'm enjoying myself, so there's no point in ruining it.

"Okay, so something a little simpler, what's your last name?"

"Collins."

"When is your birthday?"

I pause because I'm twenty-one, but I was born in 1988, but I can't say that, so I say, "October eleventh."

"What year were you born?" he asks, not missing a beat.

"Well, I'm twenty-one, so you do the math." I smirk at him.

"Only a year younger than me so 1936."

I smile at him and keep eating. We talk about simple things like favorite colors, favorite foods, and our families and friends. Before I know it, the sun is close to setting, and I realize I need to find a place to stay while I'm here.

I stand. "Thank you for lunch, David, but I really must be going now."

He stands up and takes my hand. "Let me drive you home."

"Well, I actually need to find a hotel. I just got into town this morning."

He is quiet at first and then looks into my eyes. "I have a guest room, and you are more than welcome to stay here. In fact, I'd love more time with you. How long are you in town?" he asks.

"For the next ten days or so," I tell him. Why did I say that? I should have just said two days and headed home as soon as I could. Oh, I know because my heart beat my brain to my mouth that time.

"Please, I'd love to spend that time with you. I could sure use your help planning some of the rooms here at the house, and I'd be happy to take you anywhere you need to go."

I can tell this is hard for him because he isn't used to begging for something he can just make happen. If he isn't now, I know he will be anyway.

I take a deep breath. It would make things easier to stay here, for sure, but it could complicate things too. I mean, I do have my cell phone in my pocket, for crying out loud. It's turned off to save the battery, but still, how would I explain that one?

I figure I can keep it and the rocks hidden, but I do need to get some clothes. "Okay, but I do need to get some clothes. I kind of came here on a whim and didn't bring more than what I have on me. If you point me to the local clothing store, I'll get some clothes and be back before dinner."

"Nonsense. I can take you." He starts walking with my hand still in his toward what I am guessing is the garage since that area wasn't on the tours when I went.

Then I hear Brian in the back of my head tell me to keep to the shadows. I know David is photographed every time he goes out. If I am with him, I could end up in one of the photos.

I start to panic a little bit because I need to limit the number of pictures taken of me. It could change history. "David," I say.

He stops and looks back at me. "Everything okay, beautiful?"

"Well, umm, what are the chances someone would take a picture of the two of us while we are out?"

He looks a bit confused. "There might be one or two taken of us, but I don't care. I want to tell everyone you are mine."

"No, David, please don't. I don't want anyone to be able to track me here," I say before I realize I could have said that better because he instantly looks worried.

"What's wrong? Is someone after you? You have to know I can protect you."

I need to calm him down.

"It's not like that. It's just ..." I'm franticly searching for something plausible to tell him. "This is so new, and I want to keep it ours for a bit."

He pauses and studies my face. I try not to let my eyes betray me, but it seems he can read me as well as Brian can. "You aren't a very good liar, are you?" He chuckles.

I sigh. "No, my mom used to say the same thing and so does Brian."

I watch his body tense. "Who's Brian?" he almost growls.

He is just so damn cute when he's jealous, and I can't help but smile. I walk over to him and place my hand on his chest to calm him. "Brian has been my best friend since we were kids."

"How much of a threat is he? Do I need to worry about having to put him in his place?" He still doesn't look calm. I have to admit I'm enjoying this just a bit. It's been a long time since anyone has cared enough to get jealous over me.

"David, Brian is zero threat. He is..." I think how to put this because I can't for the life of me remember how the gay community is viewed during this timeframe, but I guess I can take my chances. "Brian is gay," I say and watch him very closely.

He looks over my shoulder for a moment in thought, then he relaxes under my touch. "Okay well, let me introduce you to Nancy. She is my housekeeper and cook and the only staff I have here at the house right now. You tell her what size you are, and she will get you some clothes."

I decide to have a little fun with him. I just can't resist.

"And this Nancy, how much of a threat is she? Do I need to put her in her place?" I ask but can't keep a straight face if I tried because the corner of my mouth tilts up.

He turns all serious for a moment, then softens when he looks in my eyes. "No, beautiful, she is more like a grandma to me. If you feel threatened by anyone on my team, you tell me."

I tear up. "David, I was just playing around with you."

"I know you were, but I want to make my stance very clear, and I'm trying to do it without scaring you off."

What's scaring me is how intense this connection between us is. I have to laugh, though, at how dating or courting has changed through the years.

"If anything, it will be me scaring you away," I say just above a whisper.

"I doubt that, but we'll take it at your pace."

"David, you should be more guarded. You don't know me! I could be here after your money or just trying to get into the spotlight. You just met me. You really have to be more careful!" I pretty much scold him.

"That's how I know you aren't, Ivy." He laughs. "You don't want your photo taken with me, and you were more interested in my house than trying to climb me like a tree today. You hold your own in a conversation and aren't afraid to tell me when I'm wrong. You're a horrible liar, so I know you aren't here for my money or fame. I honestly think you are here for my house instead of me."

Shaking my head, I say, "It started off with the house, but the owner isn't half bad." I know a light blush hits my cheeks.

"Now that we both know where we stand, let me introduce you to Nancy."

I nod, and we walk inside and find Nancy in the kitchen. She's a short lady who reminds me a bit of Alice from the *Brady Bunch* TV show. She has curly blond hair that is set just perfect.

"Nancy, this is Ivy. She will be staying with us for the next two weeks."

"Of course, David! It's about time you have some guests. Oh, Miss...?" she questions.

"Please call me Ivy."

"Okay, Miss Ivy, you are the first guest here at the house, and the first guest David's had in his home in the two years I've been working with him. I am so happy to have someone to else to cook for in the house!"

I can't help but smile and look up at David. His eyes soften when they meet mine and then he turns back to Nancy.

"How do you two know each other?" Nancy asks.

"Well, we met today. She's new in town," David says, but I notice the slight shift in Nancy. It's like the protective side of her just came out.

“Nancy, Ivy needs some clothes, toiletries, and well, basically everything. Would you be so kind to run out and get them after dinner?” he asks.

“Of course!” She opens a drawer and grabs a pen and paper. “What size are you, dear?” Nancy ask me.

“Oh, a size four,” I tell her, and she drops the pen.

“Dear, my niece is a size four.” She looks me over and pulls out a tape measure.

“Okay?” I say a bit confused.

“She’s twelve.” Nancy starts taking a few measurements, moving me how she wants me.

“I’d say you’re a size ten. I will grab a few bigger things, and we can always have them resized.” Nancy nods and starts writing again.

I’m not sure I like the sizes in the 1950s. I tell her I just want comfortable clothing, and I’m not picky on toiletries, but I do love anything rose scented.

“Dinner will be ready in two hours, and then I will run out while you eat.” She nods and walks off.

David takes my hand and leads me to the stairs. I hesitate just a moment, but he picks up on it.

“Let me show you to your room. The makeshift living room is also currently up here until I finish renovations downstairs.” He rubs his thumb over the back of my hand, sending sparks to my belly and completely distracting me so all I can do is nod and follow him up the stairs.

He shows me to a beautiful guest room. The walls and carpet are white, but the bedding and curtains are a deep royal purple, and there are silver accents. I gasp before I can stop myself.

“David, who decorated this room?”

“Well, I did. I don’t know, it just felt right. Do you like it? I can change anything you don't—"

"No, I love it," I cut him off. "David, this room is what I would have chosen down to the smallest details." I walk around, taking it all in.

"Maybe I was decorating it for you, and I just didn't realize it yet," he says with a shy smile on his face, taking my hand. "Let me show you where the living room is."

"Um, do you mind if I use the restroom first?"

"You have your own. It's right through that door."

With a smile, I head in and close the door. The counter is very simple, but under the sink is a cabinet and to the side are several drawers. I open the bigger one on the bottom, and it's full of towels. Perfect. Taking the rocks and my cell phone from my pockets, I put it between the bottom two towels, figuring with over six towels in this drawer, they will be safe. I then use the restroom and step out to find David standing in the doorway between the bedroom and the hall.

Smiling, I take the purse with the money Brian gave me and decide to put it in the nightstand by the bed. I then turn to David, who holds out his hand.

My eyes never leave his while I take his hand. He gives me a real smile the kind that lights up his eyes. I watch as he points at the room across the hall.

"That's my room," he says.

"Can I see it?" I ask without thinking and immediately realize in 1957 that probably isn't a normal thing like it is in 2009.

But when I look up at David, he's still smiling. He opens the door and steps back, letting me walk in and take a look around.

His room's walls are gray, and the rest of the room is done in black with red accents. The bed is a centerpiece and large with a big canopy and all. This is the first time I've seen his room because he died in his bed, so the family never opened this room to the public.

It's like a slap in the face to know that this is the room he takes his final breath in, the room his body is found in. While it's always been a sad thought during the tours of his house in the past, the truth now grips at my chest and makes it hard to breathe.

David, of course, who can read me so well after knowing me for such a short amount of time, is at my side instantly. "What's wrong?" he asks concerned and puts his arm around my waist.

"You wouldn't believe me if I told you," I say yet again barely above a whisper.

He studies my face, and then says, "Come on." He walks me out of the room and into a room down the hall that is set up like a living room.

He sits down on the couch and pulls me down right next to him. After studying my face for a moment, he speaks.

"You have to give me some credit. You keep saying I won't believe you, but you forget I can also tell when you're lying. I don't want anything between us, so please open up and trust me," he whispers. He presses his forehead to mine, placing his lips inches from mine.

I think this through quickly. With money for a hotel room if I need it, I can go back tomorrow night at worst case because that will be close to the forty-eight-hours mark. In the back of my mind, I'm thinking it will be easier if he walks away now. If I just push him away and go home and forget about all this.

Figuring this might be the last time I ever see him look at me like this, I lean in and kiss him. I kiss him like it might be our last time because it may very well be.

He instantly takes control of the kiss by wrapping his hand around the back of my neck and pulling me in close, and it takes my breath away. He's tender and passionate, and I don't ever want this kiss to end, but before I'm ready, he's pulling away.

"I could kiss you all night, but please open up to me," he says.

With a deep breath, I wonder if this is really what I want to do? If I lie, maybe he will get angry and walk away. I'm trying to figure out where to start when his hand caresses my cheek ever so lightly.

"Please, Ivy, nothing between us. Please open up to me and trust me. Let me help you," he whispers while kissing down the side of my neck.

"I want you to know I never lied to you today. Everything I said was the truth, but I just left out some details or let you believe some things that weren't exactly true. Please remember that." I take his hand because I need the connection.

When he nods, I continue, "Things like my birthday. It is October eleventh, and I am twenty-one. I just wasn't born in 1936," I say and watch his face.

"But the math says 1936?" he asks, a little confused.

With a deep breath, here goes nothing. "I was born in 1988. When I woke up today, it was the year 2009. When you found me, I had been here in 1957 for about an hour." I wait for him to tell me I'm crazy or it's a nice joke or to stop playing around while he stands up and walks away.

Shocking me, he just studies my face and says none of that. "You aren't lying, are you?" he says. I shake my head and decide to go for broke. I launch into the story about Brian and all the details leading up to me landing here this morning.

He's silent for a long time, just watching me, and then he nods. "Okay, so I have ten days with you, and then I never see you again?" he asks, his jaw clenching.

I'm stunned, and then I just laugh because I think I'm in shock. "Just like that, you accept what I say? You aren't secretly planning to kidnap and take me to a mental hospital, are you? Please, just tell me if you are, and I'll leave you be, and you will never hear from me again."

"What reason do I have to doubt you? The only thing I'm worried about is that I really won't ever see you again."

"Well, I'm here now. I don't know what comes next, and I can't make you any promises."

He gives me a half smile, but it doesn't reach his eyes. "Why did you look like you saw a ghost when you looked at my bedroom?"

I hesitate, not planning to say anything.

"Please don't hold anything back now."

"I don't know how much I should tell you about the future to come because I don't want to have any effect on history. Brian kept drilling that into my head," I say, and he just keeps waiting for an answer.

"You do become very popular. Umm, well, the bedroom is where you died, and they found you there. Your house was then turned into a museum. This part of the house isn't open to the public, but the rest is."

He stares over my shoulder at the wall behind me.

I continue. "I've toured the house, and I've seen how you finally chose to decorate it. I also know a lot of what is to come your way. I wish I didn't, but I do."

"When do I die? And how?"

"I can't tell you that. Just know you have at least ten years before you need to worry. As far as how"—I can't help the small shiver that runs through me—"it's best you don't know."

He nods, and I'm a little shocked he believes me. I study his face, and when he turns to look at me, I see a hint of doubt, but he's doing his best to believe me. I can tell he wants to.

I take his hand. "Come here, I want to show you something."

Leading him into my bathroom, I open the drawer where I stored my cell phone and pull it out.

"This is a cell phone. It's a phone that doesn't require wires; the signal runs off towers in 2009 anyway. It's like radio towers but for phones." I turn it on and show it to him. The date shows today's date just in 2009 on the front screen. I look at him and see him staring at the phone. I keep going, showing him the icons on my screen.

"These are called apps, that means applications, and they are kind of like programs, I guess. These are minicomputers." He gives me a strange look. "Are computers a thing here?"

"Some guy at the University of Pennsylvania created one, but it's as big as a house."

"Ahhh well, in fifty years, they will fit into the palm of your hand. Each of these apps does something different. Oh, it even has a camera. Here are some photos. This is one of Brian and me taken just last weekend."

He reaches out his hand, and I notice the slight shake in it as he holds my phone and stares at it. I take in the photo he is looking at. My hair is down in beachy waves that day. I'm in jeans and a flowy purple top and a long dream catcher necklace. Brian is in jeans and a polo shirt and has his arm around my shoulders. We have an ice cream cone in our hands and are standing in what is now known as Honky Tonk Row in downtown Nashville. There are people all around us and cars on the street.

I reach over and swipe to the next photo. This one is a selfie of me and my dog, June. I smile "That's my dog, June. I keep joking I need to get a male dog and name it Cash to complete the pair." Then I slap my hand over my face. "Shit," I whisper.

"I take it I shouldn't know who those people are?"

"Well, Cash as in Johnny Cash. Have you met him yet?"

"Yeah, he and his wife, Vivian, are really nice."

"Ahh, let's just say that Vivian isn't his soul mate," I say and force a smile. He looks at me and smiles.

"Oh, I could have told you that. I'm pretty sure June Carter is."

My jaw drops, and he chuckles. "I guess I'm right, huh?"

I just nod. Then he swipes to the next photo. "You picked up on that pretty fast." I look at him as he smiles proudly.

He takes my hand and walks over to the bed. His cheeks turn a slight pink when he lies down, and he tries to sit back up. "I'm sorry, that is highly inappropriate of me. In fact, I shouldn't be in here. I keep forgetting I met you just today." He starts babbling. Kneeling on the bed, I put my hand on his chest and push him back down.

"David, a lot changes in the next fifty-two years. Women are a lot more forward, and I love that you are a gentleman, but if you want the real me, you will find a lot of what I will do will also be inappropriate in this time." I lie down next to him and place my head on his shoulder.

"This is a normal thing where I come from."

"I want the real you, not the you that you think you need to be." He puts his arm around me and pulls me even closer to him. "Promise to give me the real you, even if it's not appropriate."

I can't help but smile. "I promise."

We spend the next hour going through the photos on my phone. Everything from pictures of me around town to my last trip with Brian to Florida where we saw the Weeki Wachee Mermaids and even photos around my house. I even try to explain the internet to him.

"Think of the internet as a wealth of information. Anything you want to know is there. It's like the biggest library reference section there is, but it's all digital like the photos," I say. He nods, but I can tell he still doesn't grasp it.

By the time we were done, my phone is at 51%.

"I need to turn it off and save the battery because I don't have the charger with me," I tell him as I put it in the nightstand where I put my purse and money.

Snuggling back up to him, I wrap my arm over his stomach and just relax into him. He stares at the ceiling in silence and plays with my hair with one hand.

"If we were a normal couple in your time, and we just met today with this type of connection, what would be normal?" he asks.

Chapter 4

David

I want to know how she sees a relationship because I don't want to scare her off.

Admittedly, it was hard to take in what she said, but I know her face when she lies, and she definitely wasn't lying. I just can't seem to wrap my head around it. I mean, time travel? People talk about time travel, but I never thought it was true.

Then seeing the thing she calls a phone and looking at those photos. I don't know what to think. I just want to spend time with her and get to know her. Maybe in time, I can see where she comes from for myself and put the pieces together.

"The connection we have? This is something special, David," she says.

I smile at that because it is special.

"What about relationships? What is normal for, say meeting someone on the first day?"

"Well, having sex on the first date isn't uncommon where I'm from, but it's not something I do. But I guess dating is still pretty normal if I base it on the movie *Grease*. Dinner, maybe a movie, and a nice walk. Maybe a kiss good night. Most couples live together before they are even engaged now. Women are independent, and it's not looked down on for women to have one-night stands just like men."

I nod, taking it all in. I have never heard of this movie, but she continues before I can ask.

"Being gay isn't taboo anymore. Brian is open about it, but he just hasn't met anyone. Many people date via dating websites now." I must have given her a confused look because she spends the next ten minutes explaining online dating and profiles, and swiping left or right, and something called Tinder to me. I don't think I'm a fan of the idea.

"So, what if I said I wanted to sleep just like this tonight? Fully clothed, no funny business, but just you in my bed and in my arms. Is that crossing a line?" I ask, testing the waters.

Now that I've had a taste of her lying next to me, I don't think I could sleep without her. Especially if she is just across the hall. Her in my bed won't be normal to me, but it sounds like it might be for her time.

"No, it wouldn't be, and I'd agree, but I have a condition of my own. Please, please, please don't make me keep dressing like this while we are here at the house. This isn't me."

I almost laugh and let out a breath I didn't know I was holding. I kiss her forehead because I can, and it feels right.

"Deal. I want to know you, the real you."

"Okay, please ask Nancy to get sweatpants and T-shirts for me, not nightgowns. I've never worn a nightgown in my life. I sleep in T-shirts or sweatpants, depending on the weather. Around the house, I wear yoga pants, those black pants you saw me in when I was on my couch, and a T-shirt. And I never put this much effort into my hair, and I hardly ever wear makeup." She is rambling, so I do the one thing I know will get her to stop. I kiss her with a smile on my lips.

I kiss her slow and lazy, exploring her mouth. It's a short kiss, but when I pull away, all I think about is kissing her again.

I want her comfortable, but what she finds comfortable is a little odd to me. There is an appeal of seeing her in my clothes, though.

"As long as you are in one of my shirts, I don't care," I say because all I can see is her wearing my shirts, and I'm getting hard. Not a good situation while lying in bed with her.

"Well, some things about men never change, I guess." She laughs.

I can't help it. I kiss her again, just a short, soft kiss before we head downstairs and get ready for dinner. I also add the few changes Ivy requested to Nancy's list of clothes, and I include a nice dress because I do want to take her out.

Over dinner, we have a bit deeper conversation and talk about past relationships. We learn we both have ever only had one long-term relationship. She admits to not being a virgin, and I admit to the same thing, though she says she was only with one other person. I don't like the thought of her being with anyone, and I want to find said person and break his neck. I only calm myself by reminding myself I *will* be her last.

I ask her questions about her time, and some things she won't tell me like about my future or anything related to the stock market or sports teams.

"I don't know much about the stock market. It's not really my thing. I can tell you we have not had a woman president yet, but the first black president was just elected."

That shocks me to think the country progresses so much in fifty years that a black man is president.

"How is that possible?" I ask, thinking more out loud than anything.

"Well, in the early 1960s, segregation ends. I don't know the exact dates, but it happens, and the black community, or as they are more known, the African American community, is on equal footing in my time. They have the same opportunities, like being president."

When we finish dinner, we head up to the living room and

watch some TV. I'm still, thinking about having a black president, and how far the country seems to progress in fifty years, but Ivy knows exactly what to say to pull me from my thoughts.

"You know my TV has an eighty-inch screen, is in color, and has over one hundred channels."

"I hope to see it someday," I tell her. I can't wrap my head around so many choices.

She also tells me about reality TV. How stars like me have camera crews following them around who record their lives. It doesn't sound like anything I'd like.

When we get ready for bed, she seems hesitant.

"I want you in my bed. Nothing you don't want to happen will happen, I promise. If you want to sleep in the guest room, that's okay too, but after having a chance to hold you earlier, I know I won't be able to sleep unless you are in my arms. I have never had a woman in my bed here or even in this house," I say honestly.

I hear her say something under her breath but don't ask about it. We head to the guest room where Nancy has set the clothes on her bed. There is a bag of toiletries, and I grab it, intent on bringing it to my room. I plan to have all her stuff moved to my room tomorrow.

"Grab some clothes in sleep in and whatever else you need and bring it with you."

I watch her hesitate for a minute, then go to the bathroom. I hear her open a drawer and close it, then come out, and I see some rocks in her hand.

"What's that?"

"I need these to get home. They are very important."

I nod. She also grabs her phone and the purse from her nightstand. Then she looks at the clothes.

"What do you want to sleep in?" I ask, knowing she says she

doesn't sleep in a nightgown.

She blushes just a little, and I love that look on her.

"Well, I normally just sleep in an oversized shirt," she says.

"Come on." I take her hand and take her to my room. I set her stuff down on the couch. I open the nightstand I don't use and tell her she can put her stuff in there. Then I go to my closet and get her one of my T-shirts.

She looks at my bed again, hesitant. I get a sinking feeling now too, but I know we have to put it out of our minds. Walking up behind her, I put my arms around her waist and lean down to whisper in her ear.

"Ten years, right? I'm right here and safe, okay?" I kiss the side of her neck just below her ear and listen to her moan.

"Okay," she says breathlessly. She takes the shirt and her toiletries to the bathroom and closes the door to get ready.

I change into sleep pants and a shirt while she is in there. When the door opens, and she is standing in my shirt, I'm instantly hard.

Mine. Mine. Mine.

That thought keeps running through my head. I have trouble swallowing, but finally, I get out, "You really do look beautiful. Go get in bed, pick a side, and I'll be right back."

Going into the bathroom, I brush my teeth and take in her items mixed with mine. Her clothes on top of mine in the hamper, and the smell of her in my bathroom. The smell of roses is my new favorite scent.

This just feels right. I don't know how else to describe it. It just feels like she was always supposed to be here.

When I step back out into my room, I see she is sitting up against the headboard on the right side of the bed with her legs under the blankets.

"I didn't know what side you slept on, but I can move. It

doesn't matter to me."

I point at the clock on the left side nightstand. "I sleep on the left, so you are perfect where you are."

She smiles as I get into bed. I turn off the lights and lie down, pulling her close to me. I'm so painfully hard just being so close to her, but I'd take that and more just to have her in my arms like this. With her head on my shoulder, her breasts pressed to my side, and her legs entertained with mine, it's heaven.

I listen to her breathing as she falls asleep, and as I lie there with my whole world in my arms, I know I want this every day for the rest of my life. I just have no idea the fight I have ahead of me to make it happen.

∞∞∞

Over the next few days, I know things couldn't get any better. I wake up next to my girl, we have breakfast together, and then she reads newspapers and magazines while I work some from home, mostly taking phone calls. Then we have lunch together and hang out in the pool and in the backyard.

We do some decorating plans and then have dinner, ending our night snuggled on the couch watching TV until bedtime when we crawl into bed together, and she falls asleep in my arms.

Her second day there, I got all her stuff moved to my room, and it gets me rock-hard to see her clothes and items mixed with mine. The cold showers don't help, and neither does my hand, but I won't make that move until she's ready. I promised her no funny business in bed, and I intend to keep that promise.

On the sixth night of her being here, we are lying in bed, talking about the day, and making plans for tomorrow when I feel her lift her head to look up at me. I look down at her, and she leans up and kisses me. It starts off slow like she is shy, and I let her keep control because I want to see what she does. She shifts to deepen the kiss, and I put my hand behind her head to pull her closer.

She sits up and straddles me, all without breaking the kiss. I feel the heat from her pussy against my cock, barely separated by a few thin scraps of fabric, and I can't help but moan. I feel both her hands on my stomach and rubbing their way up my abs to my shoulders. Then she grinds again my cock, and my vision blurs. I groan and break the kiss.

"We don't have to do this. I'm perfectly okay just holding you," I say but also praying she doesn't stop.

"I need you, David, just like this, please," she begs breathlessly. And because there is not a thing I will ever deny my girl, I bring my hands to her hips and grind her down against my cock again.

There isn't a lot of light in my room, but there is enough to see she isn't wearing a bra, and her breasts are pressing against my shirt. Her nipples are hard peaks begging for my mouth. While she continues to grind on me, I lean up and take one of her nipples in my mouth over the shirt. I suck and nip and then pay the same attention to the other one. Now with the shirt wet, I have an even better view of her round breasts.

My shirt has ridden up and is bunched around her hips, so I can see her pink panties. I can even see the wet spot she is making, and I almost come right then, but I get control and remind myself this is for her.

Always for her.

I move my hand under the shirt to grip her hips and help her grind harder and faster because I'm so close already. She sits up, and I watch her lean her head back and moan. The movement pushes her chest out. I've never seen anything so beautiful in my life. It could only be more beautiful if she were naked.

I know then that any lingering doubt is gone—I'm head over

heels for this girl. She owns me, and I live for her. I was put on the earth for her. A few more thrusts and I feel her whole body start to tense up.

"Oh god, David, I'm so close. I..." she moans, digging her nails into my chest.

"That's it. Come for me, Ivy, let go." I grind her down on my hips hard, and I watch her shatter in my arms. Her orgasm has me in awe that she trusts me enough to let go like that.

I want to pound my chest because I gave her that pleasure, but a second later, she jerks against my cock, and I'm coming in my pants like a teenager. My vision blurs, and I have a hard time catching my breath. It is the strongest orgasm I've ever had.

Once my girl starts to relax, she collapses on my chest and almost purrs. "Thank you. I have no words. That was simply amazing."

"You don't need to thank me for giving you pleasure. Is it my privilege and honor to be the one who can make your fall apart like that." I kiss her again and break it off just as fast before I try to go for round two. I roll her to her side.

"I'll be right back. I need to clean up." I change my pants and underwear and climb back into bed with her and hold her tight. I have four more days, and I have no clue how I'm going to ever let her go.

Chapter 5

Ivy

Tomorrow. I now hate that word. Tomorrow is the day I have to leave. Yesterday, I walked down and found the rocks, making sure I remembered my way. I did it while David was on a phone call. He wasn't very happy I took a walk without him, but after a make-out session and an orgasm, I was forgiven.

He then insisted I let him take me out on a real date. He gave me a bit of a guilt trip to get me to agree, saying if he never gets to see me again, he wants to know he treated me right and set the bar high for any other guy to tries to gain my attention. Though I could tell the thought of me with some other guy killed him the same way the thought of him with another woman gutted me.

So we went out to dinner at a nice place. We got a private table, and then we took a walk down along the river and got some ice cream. He got stopped a few times to sign autographs, and it was great to see him with his fans. He always kept an eye on me but was very engaging with them as well.

Once we got home, he spread a blanket out in the backyard, and we laid down and watched the stars for an hour just talking. I have to say it was the best date I have ever been on. No awkward silences and no trying to figure out what to talk about; it was perfect and comfortable.

I laughed so much, and the conversation was good, and we

were just us. Just David and Ivy, not David Miller, soon-to-be rock and roll king and Ivy Collins, the time travel girl.

I plan to make the most out of today. While my heart couldn't bear it to make love, then leave, I plan to at least have his cock in my mouth today. Everything we have done has been with clothes on, so now it's time for the clothes off fun. I walk to the office at the end of the hallway and pause while he is on the phone. I know he doesn't care if I walk in.

I poke my head in and watch his face light up instantly when he sees me. I stand and watch him for a few minutes. His eyes glance up and meet mine every now and then. Seeing this side of him behind the music gets to me. He's always working with different charities and making sure the people working for him are taken care of.

In return, I see how loyal they are to him. Like Nancy. She has been watching me like a hawk, and she's so protective of him. I'm worried I'm going to slip up and say something wrong, but the flip side is I'm glad he has people in his life like that.

I close the door and walk in and go sit on his lap. He wraps the arm, not holding the phone around me, and he rests his head on my shoulder, listening to whoever is talking on the other end. I run my fingers through his hair, something I know calms him, but at the same time, his cock coming to life under my ass.

I smile, perfect. I turn and kiss down his neck before I slip on to my knees on the floor in front of him between his legs. He stares at me, but his breathing picks up as I reach for his belt. I take my time undoing it and brushing my hands over his cock more than necessary. Once his belt is open, I open his pants and push them and his underwear down enough to pull his cock out.

This is the first time I've seen it. Sure, I've felt it many times, but this is the first time with no clothes, and as I expected, it's huge. So long and so wide that I can't wrap my hand all the way around.

As soon as I try to wrap my hand around it at the base, he

quickly wraps up the phone call and hangs up.

He continues to breathe heavily as he watches me but still doesn't say a word. He is gripping the arms of his chair so hard his knuckles are turning white, and cum is dripping from his cock. I lean up and lick the cum off and give the head of his cock a kiss. His whole body jerks, and he starts breathing even heavier.

I look up at him, and his eyes lock on mine. I keep eye contact while I start to slip my mouth down his cock. He looks away, tossing his head back against the chair as he lets out a strangled moan. I work him in and out of my mouth, trying to take as much of him as I can.

"Ivy... god... so good...don't stop," he gets out in strangled gasps. Something about knowing that I'm the one making him feel like that turns me on. I reach down and push my shorts to the side and start rubbing my clit with one hand while I use the other hand to pump the part of his cock I can't fit in my mouth.

"Jesus, Ivy, you are trying to kill me." I look up, and his eyes lock on my hand between my legs, and I double my efforts, sucking harder and faster. One of his hands grip my hair, and I can't help but moan. His hips jerk when I do, and he thickens in my mouth.

"Agh, beautiful, I'm going to come," he says, trying to pull away. I suck harder and rub my clit harder, and then his cum hits the back of my throat, and he groans my name. It triggers my own orgasm, and I moan around his cock while I finish swallowing every drop he gives me.

When we both are done, he pulls me back onto his lap and kisses me long and hard.

"Beautiful, you take my breath away. That was the sexiest thing I've ever seen. You getting off on getting me off. Every time I close my eyes, I will see that picture."

He kisses me again slowly and thoroughly before pulling

away and looking in my eyes.

"I didn't know I could feel this much for someone. Please don't break me," he says just above a whisper.

"David ..." That's all I can get out before I burst into tears. He lets me cry and just rubs my back until I am done. He doesn't talk about tomorrow. He just wraps up his workday and takes me to his bed.

He calls it our bed. We lie there snuggled together and just talk.

"Tell me about your childhood," I say.

"Well, we were dirt poor and shared a two-bedroom house with my dad's brother. My parents and me in one bedroom and my aunt and uncle and two cousins in another. Both my dad and uncle worked at the local factory, taking any extra shifts they could. My mom and my aunt baked pies and sold them to a restaurant in town. Then I was about eight when my dad was injured and was out of work. My mom took a few seamstress jobs, and to keep me out of my dad's hair during the day when I wasn't at school, she sent me to a church. That's where I got into singing with the choir and learned to play the piano. What about your childhood?"

I can't help but wonder what my childhood would have been like if I had grown up at the same time as him. What would his have been like if he grew up in my time? How much of that has shaped who we are?

"Well, I don't remember much about my parents. They had me but didn't want to give up their party lifestyle. I do remember that they were big fans of your music. They died in a car crash, and I went to live with my grandparents, who raised me. No siblings, but I never missed out either. I went to college, and they insisted I move into the dorms and get the full experience. I met Brian that year. We instantly bonded at a party we were both dragged to but hated. We ditched it for this burger place we had both been dying to try. During my second year of school, my grandpa became sick and passed away, and my grandma passed a few months later. Brian was there for me through it all. We got an off-campus apartment after that, and he's the closest thing to family I have left. Tell me what you love and hate about singing."

"I love it when people tell me one of my songs helped them through a bad time. After a concert in Chicago, a man told me one of my songs stopped him from taking his own life a few months ago. He thanked me with tears in his eyes because a week later, he met his now girlfriend, and he told me he knows she is his one. Moments like that keep me going. Knowing I can take care of my parents now is a big motivator too. What I hate is the lack of privacy, the schedule while on tour, and being managed like I'm a kid."

"What are your future plans?" I ask him.

"Well, before you came into my life, I would have said I'd do this for a few years and make enough money to live on comfortably, be able to take care of my parents and my family, then shift over and help others get their start in the music business and not be on the stage so much myself."

"And now?" I am almost afraid to ask.

"Now, I'm not sure. I just know I want you to be a part of that future."

"If I could stay here, I would, but I don't even know what kind of effect my being here now is having on history. I know Brian will be watching it and digging into it like a hawk."

We have lunch and dinner in bed. And this classifies as the perfect day. After dinner, he gets really quiet, and I can tell something is on his mind, so I ask him.

"I know you leave tomorrow, but... will you come back to me?" he asks. He sounds so vulnerable, almost like a lost little boy.

It breaks my heart because I don't want to lie to him. "I will do everything in my power to come back to you, but I can't promise I will be able to."

He nods his head lost in thought. "Well, you know it's extremely unfair that you got to taste me, and I haven't gotten to taste you. Can I kiss you, beautiful"—he runs his finger over my pussy—"here?"

I can only nod. He runs a finger along my seam over my panties.

"Jesus, you are soaked."

"That's what you do to me, baby."

He sits up and slowly pulls my panties down my legs, watching me like he's waiting for me to stop him. Well, that's not going to happen. I'm so damned turned on, I might die if he stops. He tosses my panties on the ground and then runs his hands up the insides of my legs until he gets to my core.

"Open up for me, beautiful," he says. I bend my knees and spread my legs wide, and he stares down at my pussy. He runs a finger through my soaked lips up to my clit and starts to rub circles there, watching me the whole time.

He runs a few circles before he leans in and licks my whole seam, making me scream out his name. He then moans and latches on to my clit and sucks hard. My hips jerk, pressing into his face, making him moan again. He slips a finger into my aching pussy and slowly starts stroking me while he sucks on my clit. A few strokes later, he adds a second finger, and I start to shake, trying to hold off my climax, but he isn't having any of that. He hooks his fingers, finding that perfect spot, and rubs hard while he sucks hard. My hips buck wildly, and I shatter, screaming his name. He doesn't slow down. And a second climax rolls over me before he pulls his fingers up and licks them, then kisses his way up my body until he reaches my lips.

"Will you sleep like this tonight?" he asks while kissing my neck.

"Mmmm, as long as you sleep without your shirt on," I say, and instantly, he is sitting up and rips his shirt off.

We snuggle, and sleep takes both of us quickly.

∞∞∞

I woke up to David between my legs. Today, he was relentless and wouldn't stop until he pulled three orgasms from me. Then he let me return the favor and go down on him. I feel like a bowl of Jell-O, and I think his plan was to make it so I couldn't move today.

I finally have the strength to get up and get in the shower. The water is running over my hair when David comes up behind me. He wraps his arms around my waist and buries his head in my shoulder. We stand like that for several moments. When he finally lets me turn around, his eyes are red, and I know he had just been crying. That's when I lose it too. I bury my head against his chest and cry. When I finally calm down, David leans down and kisses me breathless.

Then without a word, he starts washing me. This is the first time we have showered together, and the first time we have been completely naked in front of each other. He takes extra care washing me, running his hands over every inch of me before he's done. I, of course, return the favor and wash every inch of him, committing every part of him to memory as the soap runs across his abs.

When the water turns cold, we finally step out of the shower, and he dries me off as though I am the most precious thing in the world before he towels himself dry. We get dressed, and I walk to the nightstand to get my purse, phone, and the rocks I will need. I haven't had to spend a penny of the money Brian gave me because David took care of everything for me.

David never takes his eyes off me as he opens his wallet and hands me several hundred dollars. I start to refuse before he cuts me off.

"Take it in case you need it when you come back. I've given your name to my security team so you will always have access to me, but just in case, for my peace of mind, please take it."

I nod and take the money.

"*When* you come back, bring some more of your world to show me and more pictures. Lots of pictures," he chokes out.

I agree, and we head down to breakfast. I don't eat too much, mostly picking at my plate.

"You need your strength. Please eat," he says to me.

I smile. "The more I eat, the more chance I'll throw up. It's the worst feeling of motion sickness when you reach the other side. I have one favor to ask of you."

"And I have one for you too. But you first."

I hold up my phone. "Will you take a picture with me? Just one, Brian will freak on me, I know, but..."

"Yes, as long as you let me drive you as far as I can. I don't care if it's just a minute down the road. Please."

I nod and turn on my phone.

I go sit on his lap and get the camera ready to take a selfie. He just shakes his head and looks at the phone and smiles. I snap a picture, and it's perfect.

He keeps me on his lap as we finish up breakfast. I can tell he's enjoying having me close and being able to feed me, so I let him.

Once breakfast is over, we head out to his car. We get in, and he starts the car up.

"Will you drive me around town first and show me your Nashville?" His face lights up just a bit. He takes my hand, puts on his sunglasses, and heads toward downtown.

We drive what is now Honky Tonk Row and Music Row. I tell him about how different it is, and he points out a few places where he has played as I tell him some of my favorite memories downtown. We spend two hours just driving the area before heading back toward his house. I give him directions to just past the newsstand where I read the date that first day.

He pulls over and parks the car before turning to look at me with tears in his eyes again. I take his face between both my hands and take a deep breath.

"Next year, your draft number comes up. I don't know the details of your service, but you serve for two years. Don't you dare take any unnecessary risks, but you will come home safe. When you are overseas, and it gets too much, remember how proud of you I am. How you are making a difference for me." I barely get the last part out before choking up.

I continue. "I will fight my way back to you, I promise that, but I can't promise that I will actually make it back. If I don't, you need to promise to live your life to the fullest, try to be happy, and know I'm watching from my time. I will watch every movie, listen to every song, read every story. You are going to go on and do great things, David. You will have a bigger impact in the world than you will ever know."

I kiss him then, and I put everything I have into that kiss—every emotion, every feeling, every thought. I kiss him desperately, and he kisses me back just as hard. Neither of us wants to be the first to pull away, knowing what lies ahead when we do. Tears stream down my cheek, and his tears mix with mine. When we pull away, both our faces are wet, and our eyes are red.

"I am yours heart, body, and soul, and I will always be waiting until my last breath."

I know in my heart he will marry and have a son, but I won't burst his bubble. I will reach for this moment in my darkest day.

"When you go on tour... don't..." I stop myself and shake my head.

He puts his knuckles under my chin and makes me look at

him. "Don't what?" he asks so softly it breaks my heart.

"When the guys start using drugs to stay awake, to deal with the strains of touring, don't join them. Just go back to your room and think of me this morning, think of us."

I watch his eyes tear up again. "I promise." Then he leans down and gives me a quick kiss. "Now go before I take you back home and tie you to my bed and never let you go."

I give him a sad smile and open my door and get out. Crossing the street, I turn back to look at him and wave goodbye, then turn and walk into the woods. Walking in as straight of a path as I can, trying not to cry, I force myself to keep moving forward until I get to the clearing and see the rocks. I walk over and into the center as the humming starts on my skin again.

I know I have to do this. Brian is waiting for me and probably sick with worry. People will miss me if I don't go home, but right now, all I can think about are a pair of blue eyes that I will miss more than any of them. I push forward and touch the rock before I can change my mind.

Chapter 6

Ivy

When I stumble through my front door, Brian runs up, asking a million questions. I hear none of them as I collapse on the floor and start crying uncontrollably. I cry for over an hour before I can speak again. When I do, I tell Brian he is the worst friend ever on the planet. He picks me up, takes me to my bed, and we lie there while I tell him everything, every detail, and then show him the picture and then cry some more.

I cry myself to sleep, and when I wake up, my heart hurts. But I smell breakfast, so I pull myself out of bed and find Brian cooking all my favorites.

He looks up at me. "One question. Why didn't you sleep with him? You know it would have been the best sex of your life, right?"

I try to smile. "I have no idea if I will see him again. My heart couldn't take it."

"Do you love him?"

The big questions, right? We didn't say the words, but I felt like there were right there just out of grasp. How much of what I felt was real? Will he really wait for me, or will he earn his playboy reputation and move on?

"How much of what I felt was real? I don't know."

He nodded. "Well, I've been up all night it doesn't look like there have been any ripples, so that's good. It also looks like time moves the same, so while you were on July 24, 1957, it was July 24, 2009, here." He goes on to talk some more geeky stuff as I try to eat.

"When can I go back?" I finally ask.

"At least six months," he says, and I fall apart again. "We need to make sure there are no lasting effects. This wasn't you going back and watching. You interacted with a huge music icon at that time."

"I know," I groan. But I have hope now more than I had yesterday. After I eat, I sit down and start reading everything I can on David. I stare at every photo. Then one article pops up, dated three months after I had been there. It's when he named his house Ivy Hill.

The article says it was named for someone special in his life. He says to that person he still holds every promise he made true, and he misses them every day. The picture of him is in front of the house next to the sign, and he's looking right into the camera. It's like he's looking right at me. I see it on his face; the same look he had when he says he would try to tell me how he felt, I see it in his eyes.

The press took it as someone he lost in life, but I know he means me. I show the article to Brian.

"Holy shit. So your parents named you Ivy after the house because they are huge fans, but he named the house after you?!"

"Yes! *Brian*! What the hell does this mean?!"

"I don't have the answers you want, Ivy. We need to just keep pushing forward."

I print the photo out and frame it next to my bed. No wonder so many women swoon for him. They could look at this photo and think those eyes were for them.

Over the next few months, the more I read on David, the more I find my feelings intensify instead of going away. Seeing him help at a children's hospital and then an orphanage. When he took a day to pass out food to a group of homeless men and women.

Every now and then, I'll find a picture taken, and I can see the sad look on his face. The one he hides well when he knows the cameras are there. I know that look because it's the same one I see when I look in the mirror.

∞∞∞

Seven Months Later

Every day, I woke up, did what I had to do for work, and then spent all my time digging into photos and articles of him. Every night, I'd put on his music and fall asleep to the memories of his hands on my body, that last night we spent together, and that next morning.

On my particularly dark days, I wouldn't even get out of bed but just kept playing his movies over and over again. I told myself the sound of his voice and the look on his face when he looked at the camera was all for me.

Today is one month to the day before he gets his draft call. Even though I know he will come home alive isn't helping my nerves or my heart.

Brian got so tired of my moping that he walked into my room last night and packed a bag and didn't say a word. This morning, he shoved me into the shower and got me dressed in a style of clothes I haven't seen in seven months but a bit warmer and a jacket. Then he shoved me out the door and told me not to come back for two weeks.

That's why I'm now standing in a familiar spot I never thought I'd see again. I walk down the street to the familiar newspaper stand. I check the date to be sure and smile. February

23, 1958. Perfect.

I keep walking toward the house that now holds my heart, and I feel myself coming to life with each step I take. When I get there, I take in the changes. For the most part, it looks the same. The gate and fence have been upgraded, and there is a new sign. One that I see every night before I go to bed. The sign with the name Ivy Hill on it. I close my eyes, and I can that photo of him standing next to it in this spot is there.

I pray David is home today, and that he even wants me here. There is a possibility in seven long months that he's moved on and found someone else or worse, forgotten about me. In all the research I did, I didn't see one mention of another girl, so I'm hoping against hope that he wants me here.

In the past seven months, all I did was fall more in love with him. I kept my word and listened to every song, watched every movie, and read everything I could. I've been obsessed.

The wind picks up, and I wrap my coat around me a bit more and shift my bag on my shoulder. I came a bit more prepared this time.

Crossing the street, I walk up to the speaker and hit the call button. When I hear his deep voice, a shiver runs down my body right to my heart, and tears start running down my face.

"Yes? Who's there?" he asks.

I can barely get out one word. "Ivy."

A second later, the gate opens, and I walk through toward the front door. The front door opens, and he stands in the doorway in shock. I can't tell if it's good or bad, and if he wants me there, or if I should go home.

I came this far, so I'm not leaving until he kicks me out. I walk up the steps, never taking my eyes off him, and I stand on the front porch in front of him. He grabs my hand and pulls me inside. Closing the door, he backs me up against it, wraps his arms around my waist, and buries his head in my neck.

His tears run down my shoulder, and it triggers my own tears. We stand like that, crying and holding onto each other for dear life for several minutes before he speaks.

"I've been looking for you. I hired the best detectives. They had to think I was crazy when there was no trace of you. I started to think I imagined you."

I can't help but laugh. "Silly boy, my father won't even be born for another two years and my mother for another four, so of course, there is no trail of me." For an instant, I think of my grandparents. They are no longer alive in my time, but they are right now as I breathe. But I can't go there.

He shakes his head but places his hand on either side of my face and kisses me. It's desperate, needy, and passionate like the last kiss we shared. Everything I need to know about how he feels is in that kiss. His tongue makes love to my mouth, and the sparks shoot to my down between my thighs.

His hand moves to the back of my head and tangles his fingers in my hair, pulling me closer while his other hand moves down my back and grabs my ass. He presses into me further, and I feel how hard he is for me. I grind just slightly against him.

"Ivy," he moans, and it almost sounds like a prayer. His other hand moves to my ass and pulls me up just a bit. I wrap my legs around his waist as he pins me to the door and starts kissing down my jaw and to my neck. He nips and licks his way to my pulse point where he nips me good, causing me to moan.

I wrap my arms around his neck and run my fingers into his hair, trying to get closer even though there isn't an inch of space between us.

In the distance, there is a sound of a door closing, and then someone clears their throat. I break the kiss and look up to an older gentleman standing there. Reluctantly, David lowers me to the ground. My knees are weak, but he keeps a strong grip on my hips.

He gives me another short gentle kiss before turning me around in front of him to face the older gentleman. With how weak my knees are, I can't help but lean back against David's chest and his hard cock presses into my lower back. With his hands still on my hips holding me in place, he speaks.

"Ivy, this is my dad. Dad, this is my Ivy."

The older man takes me in but says nothing.

"So nice to meet you, Mr. Miller," I say, shaking his hand a bit hesitantly.

"Nice to finally meet you too. My son has talked about you nonstop since we moved in. You can call me James."

I look over at David, and he wraps his arms around my waist and leans down to whisper in my ear. "I built a guest house at the back of the property for Mom and Dad, and they moved in about three months ago."

I smile at him. That's so David.

"Your mother is going to be so excited to meet her," James says to David. Then he looks at me. "My wife is very much a hound with a bone. She will want to know every detail about you. David doesn't let people into his inner circle often," he says as he tilts his head to the side and studies my face.

"Dad, we will see you at dinner, but I'm asking you two to leave us to catch up until then. We haven't seen each other in seven months. Also, while she is here, please don't just walk in. I won't be responsible for what you might see."

I must blush ten shades of red because his dad chuckles, and David leans down to kiss my neck again.

His dad nods. "I'll take your mother out for the day and let her know." He turns to me. "I look forward to chatting more at dinner, Ivy," he says before turning and walking out of the house.

In one swoop, David picks me up and carries me bridal style

up the stairs.

"I want to know everything I missed, every detail, but I need you in our bed beautiful, where you belong," he says as he carries me up the stairs.

We get to his room, and he sets me down, then he takes my bag and sets it on the dresser, then removes my coat and shoes. He removes his shoes, then climbs into bed under the covers with me and pulls me against him tight. It's like he's afraid I'll disappear.

We are quiet for several minutes. "I named the house Ivy Hill after you."

I smile. "I know." And he chuckles. "Want to hear something funny?" I ask.

"I want to hear everything." The butterflies I haven't felt in seven months are in full force in my stomach, and my heart that hasn't beaten in seven months is making up for the lost time.

"My parents grew up listening to your music and were huge fans. They named me Ivy after your house." I can't help but laugh.

"Wait… but—"

I interrupt him. "Brian can't figure it out, either. He has a few theories but won't share them, so I just leave him to it. He's spent the past seven months with me. I wasn't much company, so I'm pretty sure he's working his butt off to figure it out just to get me back. Now that I'm here, I feel bad for how I treated him."

Another moment of silence passes, and I speak again. "I did what you asked and brought some stuff with me and a bunch of photos."

His face lights up. "Show me." He sits up. I grab my bag and sit next to him.

First, I pull out my wallet and show him my driver's license with my birthday on it. He stares at it, then back at me. "I still can't wrap my head around all this," he says.

I smile and kiss him. He pulls me onto his lap so I'm straddling him. He is hard for me, and I rub against his cock, and he groans into the kiss.

"I've missed you so damn much. It's like half of me has been missing, and I've been walking around living my life, but it feels like it's not me. Then you walk in that door, and I'm instantly whole again. You are here in my arms, and I'm me again." He kisses me again.

I deepen this kiss. This is the kiss I thought I'd never get the chance to feel again. The kiss that haunted my dreams and would cause me to wake up out of breath, reaching for him, thinking it was real.

I grind against him, needing the friction.

He breaks the kiss. "How long can you stay this time?" he asks breathlessly.

"Same as last time, ten days."

"I'm not holding back this time. I plan to make you mine in every way starting now."

He flips me on to my back and starts pulling off my pants and underwear before I know what's going on. Next, my shirt and bra disappear, and I'm on the bed naked while he stands next to the bed and just stares down at me.

"You are even more beautiful than I remember, and I remembered you every day, my body remembered you every night, and my heart remembered every second you were gone," he says. "I missed your smell, like roses and fresh rain. I'd get a whiff of this smell in a crowd and spin around, looking for you, only to realize it was my mind craving you. My security team must think I'm crazy."

I tear up and reach a hand to him. "You have too many clothes on," I say. He moves instantly, removing everything before standing before me completely naked.

He then crawls on top of me, and his mouth is between my

legs, and he's licking me like a starved man.

"I missed this taste." He licks me again. He pushes my legs even farther apart, and he latches on to my clit, and in seconds, I'm tumbling over the edge, screaming his name, but he doesn't let up. He thrusts a finger inside me and strokes me a few times before he adds a second finger and starts stretching me out.

He finger fucks me while sucking on my clit. He reads my body and seems to know exactly when to speed up and when to slow down to draw my climax out of me. I climax so hard a second time before he starts kissing his way up my body. He gets to my neck, then kisses me, and I can still taste myself on him.

He places the head of his cock at my soaked opening, and he braces himself above me with his elbows on either side of my head. He kisses me lightly and slowly but doesn't move.

"Beautiful, I don't want anything between us. I need you skin to skin. It's been well over a year since I've been with anyone, and I've been checked. I will pull out, but I need you with nothing between us."

The passion is clear in his eyes, and I can feel everything he isn't saying as he tears up at the end. He needs to help our souls combine and our hearts to meet and become one with every part of our beings.

I nod. "It's been around two years for me, and I've been checked too. But David, I'm not on any birth control... I can explain why later, but just know I'm not."

There is a bit of confusion on his face, but he nods and leans in to kiss me. "I'll pull out, but this is us, Ivy. Whatever happens, we are in this together."

With that, he kisses me and thrusts in hard. He stretches me, and I've never felt so full. My back arches off the bed, and my eyes roll back in my head as I scream his name. He wraps his arms around my waist and bury his head in my shoulder and shudder.

He starts to thrust in and out slowly until he's seated all the way inside me.

"Wrap your legs around me, beautiful." When I do, he sits up on his knees and pulls me up so that I'm sitting on his lap, never breaking the connection.

We are face-to-face, and I wrap my arms around his neck. He firmly grips my hips and starts thrusting in and out of me in long, slow strokes. He watches every move I make, taking in every sound, and adjusts his thrusting based on what I react to. It feels so good I can't even concentrate, and the rest of the world fades away.

My nipples brush against the rough patches of hair on his chest, making them tingle and ache. My clit grinds again him every time he thrusts all the way inside me, and the feel of him skin on skin makes the connection so much more powerful.

He pulls out and thrusts in again, picking up speed. I clench my walls around him, causing him to toss his head back and moan. On his next thrust, I clamp down again, and he rolls his head forward again to look me in the eyes. His eyes are hooded, clouded in passion and love.

With another thrust, I clamp down a third time, and he leans me back just enough to take my nipple in his mouth. He sucks hard, taking as much of my breast into his mouth as he can.

He lets go with a pop and then leans down to give the nipple a nip. I arch into him, thrusting my chest in his face. He gives the other one the same attention before thrusting into me even harder.

He kisses me again before laying me back down on the bed, and I'm so close. "Harder," I moan.

"God, you were made for me." He pounds into me harder and faster. "Your pussy is so tight it's strangling my cock. Never felt anything so good in my life." He thrusts harder. "Love how those breasts bounce every time I slam into you. I need you to come, baby."

He reaches around and pinches my clit, and it sends me over the edge to the most intense climax of my life. I black out, gasping for air, and my back arches, and I clamp down on his cock. He slams into me a few more times before pulling out, and his hot cum lands on my belly. I look down to see him stroking himself with his eyes staring down at my pussy, which is still spasming, trying to find him again.

When he's done coming, he looks me in the eyes, and without breaking eye contact, I take my finger and scoop up some of his cum and bring it to my mouth and suck it off my finger.

"Ivy," he moans as more cum leaks from his cock on to my belly. He leans down and takes his hand and rubs his come onto my breasts and into my belly and all the way up to my neck. He rubs it all into my skin.

"I look good on you, beautiful. I don't think a day will go by where my come won't be soaked into your skin." He leans down and kisses me before collapsing beside me on the bed and pulling me next to him.

I catch my breath, then lean up on my elbow to look down at him. I rub my hand over his chest, playing with his nipples. I lightly pull at one, and his whole body shudders, and I watch as his cock gets hard all over again.

"On the nights when it hurt the most, do you know what I would think of?" I ask. He looks over at me with a sad expression on his face.

"What would you think of, beautiful?"

"That last morning in the shower. Every time I would shower, I'd feel your arms around me and your head on my shoulder. The first time you truly let your guard down, and you were vulnerable around me. I knew you had been crying, and while it broke my heart, that moment healed me in a way I could never explain. It was a simple way to show you felt the same way I did." I let my hand trace his abs while I kept looking at him.

"I wanted so bad to make love to you in that shower, but I knew I wouldn't be able to walk away if I did. So when the nights got hard and dark, I'd imagine what it would have been like if I had let you bend me over and take me in the shower." Another shudder wracks his body. "What if you had slammed me up against the shower wall and taken me right then?"

I trail my hand down and rub the come leaking from the head of his cock down his shaft before I get out of bed. I walk to the bathroom door before I look back over my shoulder at him. His eyes are on me just as I knew they would be.

"Baby, I don't want to wonder what if anymore." I walk to the shower and turn it on.

Chapter 7

David

The water barely starts before I'm against her from behind, my cock pressing into her delicious backside. I wrap my arms around her waist just as I did that morning seven long months ago.

"Every time I stepped into this shower, I saw that morning. I saw you standing there with the water dripping from your body, your eyes closed, and head tilted up. When I would get in the shower, I'd feel you in my arms. There hasn't been a day that I didn't step into this shower rock-hard and come into my hand just to get through the day. Most days, I'd have to finish with a cold shower too. But I refused to shower in any other bathroom. This is our room, our bathroom, our space, and when I have to be without you, this is where I am able to connect with you the most," I say and then pull her to me.

She's facing the water, and I'm standing behind her with my arms wrapped around her. My face is in her neck just like that morning, but this time, there are no tears. I'm kissing her neck and running my hands up her belly to grab her round breasts and massaging them, pinching her nipples, squeezing them together.

"What my girl wants, my girl gets, always. Now put your hands on the wall and stick that perfect ass out," I say. Grabbing her hips, I thrust home as soon as she does. Her slick heat wraps around me, and she clamps down, pulling me in.

I know I will never get enough of this, of us. No one has ever made me feel this way, and no one will because it's us. This connection makes all the difference. I know at this moment I will always wait for her between visits. No matter if it's a few months or a few years, I will always wait for her.

I'm pulled from my thoughts when Ivy tosses her head back and moans. The sound fills the room, combining with the water and the sound of our wet skin slapping together, the sound of my balls slapping up and hitting her clit with each thrust.

I run my hand from her hip up her spine and tangle it in her wet hair. Her walls start to clamp down on me. I know she's close, so I pull out, and she lets out a frustrated groan that only makes me smile. I pull her up and turn her around I lift her, wrap her legs around my waist, and pin her to the wall. I lean down and kiss her, nipping at her bottom lip as I thrust into her as deep as I can.

"Is this what you would dream about, beautiful? Me stretching you like this? Owning you?" I ask, then I lean down to her ear. "Because this is exactly what I would picture when I was I here stroking myself to images of you." I nip at her ear as she gasps. Her walls clench. Apparently, my girl likes dirty talk.

"No, my brain was never this good. This is so much better than anything I ever pictured," she says.

"Tell me, my sweet Ivy, did you touch yourself thinking of me? Did you rub your clit? Stick your fingers in you and come thinking of me?" I ask as I pinch her clit, and her whole body tenses up, her legs lock around me, and her walls clamp down on me, and she comes, screaming my name. She comes so hard her sweet cream is dripping down my balls.

It's enough to make my balls draw up tight. I thrust twice more and pull out and start coming on the wall behind her, thrusting my dick between her ass cheeks.

I still have her pinned to the wall, her legs around me when I say. "Beautiful, you didn't answer my question."

Her eyes open and take a moment to focus before she speaks, and then it's barely above a whisper. "Every night, David, every night, I'd pray for this moment. I'd picture it in vivid detail, and when I'd come, it would be with your name on my lips, but it was always disappointing. My body craved you, and my hand was a poor substitute."

I kiss her then and pour all my emotions and love into it. I make love to her mouth and try to make her understand what she means to me and what her words do to me. It's a kiss that's begging her not to leave me again. When I pull back, her eyes are a little misty, and I place a soft kiss on each eyelid before I reach for her shampoo. When she sees it, her eyes go big. "You still have my stuff?" she asks.

"Yes, having your stuff mixed with my mine made me think you were coming back, and being able to have your scent near me again soothed my soul. Your stuff will always be here. It will always be waiting for you to come back to me."

We take turns washing each other before getting out of the shower. I dry her off but refuse to let her get dressed again. I walk her to the closet and show it to her. She walks in and takes it in, her hand covering her mouth and tears in her eyes.

I look at what she sees. There is not only the clothes Nancy bought for her seven months ago but also clothes I bought since she's been gone. Things I wanted to see her in, or I thought she would like. She was always on my mind when I was traveling and touring.

"What's all this, David?" she asks.

"Every day, I thought of you. When I was touring and traveling, I would see something I knew you would like, or something I wanted to see you in, and I bought it for you, brought it home, and hung it up here in our closet. This will always be your home,

Ivy; your clothes will always hang here with mine. I have your sizes memorized, and I will always add to this closet for you. I will always keep your toiletries with mine. I just ask that you put your stamp on the rest of the house too, so I can feel you here even when you are not."

"I'm way ahead of you." She walks past me. She grabs her bag from the floor and sits on the bed. I sit down next to her and lean against the headboard. I pull her to sit between my legs with her back against me. My dick wants to come out and play again, but he's going to have to wait.

She turns to face me, and her eyes run over my face.

"I love you, David. I wasn't sure when I left, but the more I read and looked into you, the harder I fell. Today just confirms it."

I rest my forehead to hers and close my eyes. Her words are ones I would hear in my dreams and always thought they'd be just that. Dreams.

"I love you too, Ivy, so much," I whisper.

She turns forward again and leans back to rest her head against my shoulder. "I love this, the cuddling with you, your arms around me. This is home wherever we are, and your arms around me."

She reaches into her bag and pulls out two picture frames. She holds them up for me to see. The frames are a simple black but with an ivy leaf vine design around the edges. They are simple and gorgeous, but it's what's in the frames that have me choking up.

One is the photo of me the press took standing next to the sign when I named the house Ivy Hill. In this photo, I'm looking right into the camera. I remember thinking she is on the other end, and she will see this, and I wanted to show her everything I still felt for her.

The other is the photo we took of her sitting on my lap the

last day she was here. The only photo of her and me.

"These are the exact two photos I have sitting on my nightstand at home in these same two frames. I fall asleep every night looking at them and with your music playing me to sleep."

I tear up instantly but take the photos and place them on my nightstand too and then turn her head so I can kiss her. I can't seem to stop the tears that fall while I show her how much I love her with my mouth. When she pulls back, she starts kissing the tears off my face, which only causes more to fall. I close my eyes and try to gather myself, all while enjoying her lips on my face.

"I love you like this," she says between kisses

"Like what?" I ask.

"When you let your mask down and show me your vulnerable side. I see the side the media gets, which is a colder version of you. The side your fans get is a bit warmer. But this side is my favorite."

I force a smile. "Only for you. I will always have my masks down for you and only you will know the real true me. Only you will get to see my tears and know the depths of my love for you." I choke up again. "What else do you have in your bag of treasures?"

She smiles and pulls out her phone with a cord. "I brought my charging cord this time with an adapter so I can charge it. Brian said the outlet at your house is a bit different than the ones in my time, but he swears it will work. I brought a few things on my phone that I think will eliminate any doubt of where I come from."

I kiss her cheek and rest my chin on her shoulder. "Show me." She starts by showing me pictures from the past seven months. Many are in her house, and you can see the sadness in her eyes, which kills me. Then she shows me a picture of myself, but you can tell I'm older. She says it was taken the year before I die. I swallow hard.

Then she plays a song that is my voice, no doubt. But the song is one I've never heard before, much less sang and recorded. But it could very well be talking about her and how much I love her and need her.

If I still had any doubt, she pulls up a movie I apparently acted in. She says this is about four years from now, and it's me just nothing I've ever done to date. She won't tell me the movie name and only lets me watch about ten minutes of it. I know in my heart that I believe her, even if my mind still can't grasp it.

The last thing she pulls from her bag is a book. It is a book written about my life, not by me but by some reporter who did interviews of family and friends and put together a timeline of my career.

"Brian agreed I can show you a few things," she says as she opens the book.

She shows me a few things that already happened, which barely fills the first quarter of the book, but she refuses to let me see too much of anything that is still yet to happen.

She says knowing the future is a curse she doesn't wish me to bear.

"Show me the end of the book, beautiful." I want to see my death, date year, and cause, but she refuses.

"No one should know the date of their death. But I will tell you that you die in August in bed, and it will be eleven years from this year," she says.

1969.... August 1969. She won't give me any more details, and I won't press.

"Last time we were together, you mentioned I'd be drafted."

"Yes, next month."

I nod. "And I won't see you during my service, will I?"

"No, but I will do everything I can to be here when you get back."

"Two years. I won't see you for two years after this visit. I need more time. Please, I need more. Take me home with you. If you can only stay for ten days, then take me home for ten days with you, please."

She looks like she is thinking as she stares at the wall in front of the bed, so I hope it will go my way. I let her think as I put my nose to her hair and just breathe her in.

"I don't think it's a good idea. There have been enough sightings of you." She pauses. "But then again, they are looking for a seventy-year-old you, not twenty-year-old you. No one would believe it's actually a twenty-year-old David Miller. Brian will short circuit if I bring you home. I've already put him through hell these past seven months. I've been moody and not myself." Then she goes quiet again.

She takes a deep breath. "Okay, but we will be confined to the house."

I can't believe she agreed. I turn her around, so she is straddling me, and kiss her. I'm so happy right now and so hard. Without breaking the kiss, I lift her hips and sink into her. She moans into my mouth, and I make love to her mouth at the same tempo my cock is making love to her. Soft, sweet, slow, knowing I have more time with her now.

We climax at the same time, and she collapses on my shoulder. After I stop coming on the sheets, I tuck my cock back inside its warm home inside her, and I hug her to me. I rub her back, and we both just enjoy the silence. I look over at the time and see it's close to dinner.

"Beautiful, we need to get ready for dinner with my parents."

"Just a few more minutes. I'm enjoying the feel of you inside me right now and the afterglow of that mind-blowing orgasm."

That makes me proud and puts a smile on my face, so I agree. Ten minutes later, I pull out of her and help her get dressed.

"Pick an outfit for me. Something you wanted to see me in."

I look through the clothes and pull out the white capris and a white button-down shirt with black polka dots on it. It's very casual and not quite warm enough for a Nashville February, but we aren't leaving the house.

"Tell me the story behind this one," she asks as I hand her a bra and underwear.

As she gets dressed, I tell her, "I saw Marilyn Monroe wearing that outfit, and she looked so comfortable, and all I could think about was you wearing here at our house walking around bare feet and comfortable like she was."

"Ahh yeah, she's still alive, isn't she? Who's she married too? Arthur Miller, right?" she asks.

I only nod.

"I did my research of the time era wanted to know what I could. She dies from an overdose like so many stars of this time." Then she looks me dead in the eye. "You haven't tried any of that stuff, right? No sleeping pills, nothing to help keep you awake, or give you energy?"

I wrap my arms around her. "No, beautiful, I haven't touched any of it. I made you a promise."

She nods and walks to the bathroom to finish getting ready. I get dressed and follow her to the bathroom a few minutes later, and I find her tearing through cabinets and drawers with tears in her eyes. I run to her and grab her holding her to me.

"Ivy, Ivy, talk to me."

"Ten years before your death is when the first mentions of you doing drugs is." She is crying. I rub her back, unsure of how to calm her.

"That's how I die, isn't it?"

She nods and sighs. "A heart attack caused by a weakened heart due to the massive amount of drugs in your system."

The thought terrifies me. Would I really end up doing that to myself? I couldn't, I couldn't do it if it were going to take me away from my Ivy. Even the chance of seeing her years from now was better than doing that to her.

"I made you a promise, beautiful, and I will always keep my promises to you. But think about it for a minute. It's the perfect cover-up."

She sniffled and looks up at me, confused. "What do you mean?" she asks.

"Well, I'm guessing there are rehab visits where no one sees me for weeks, right?" I ask, and she nods.

"Then I die but didn't you say people think they saw sightings of me? That maybe people doubted my death?"

She nods again.

"What if I don't die. What if it's really a big cover-up... for us?" I say.

She shakes her head. "I don't have that kind of hope. David, that would mean all this was meant to be, but I don't think so. I think we are tempting fate."

"Believe in me, beautiful. Believe in us. That's all I ask. Trust me, and I promise to live my life proving I am worthy of that trust."

She takes a deep breath. "Okay." she nods. "Brian is going to kill me for telling you all this." She forces a smile.

I wipe the tears from her face and take a cloth and run some cold water and pat her face down. I wrap her hand in mine. "Mom and Dad are going to start eating without us."

We walk into the dining room, and my parents stand. My mom walks over and hugs Ivy instantly.

"I'm Helen," my mom says, and she looks at me. "I've never seen my son light up talking about someone the way he does when he talks about you. I've also never seen him so miserable when you are gone. Please tell me you are here to stay."

Ivy smiles. “I’m just as miserable without him too, but sadly, I can't stay. He did agree to come home with me for a few days to meet everyone.” She smiles up at me.

My dad hugs Ivy as well. “Nice to see you again. Let's sit and eat. Helen is starving.” They go back to their seats. I head to my spot at the head of the table and pull out the chair directly to my right for Ivy. She sits down, and I push her in before sitting down and taking her hand.

I need that touch to remind me she is really here.

“So Ivy how long are you staying?” Mom asks.

“Ten days, same as last time.” Ivy smiles as she fills her plate with food.

“Where are you from?” Mom doesn’t miss a beat. I know her line of questions like the back of my hand, and everyone who enters my life gets them. It doesn’t matter if it’s personal or business.

“A small town you have never heard of,” Ivy takes the questions in stride.

Mom watches Ivy as though she knows she’s avoiding the questions.

“What about your family?”

Ivy goes on to tell her about being raised by her grandparents and how Brian is her family.

“So you live with this Brian?” Mom doesn’t bother hiding her disapproval on her face.

“Well, yes, I own the house, and he has helped me renovate it. Plus, it’s nice not to be alone.” Ivy looks at me before Mom continues.

“Well, what kind of job do you have to be able to own a home as a single woman?”

I can’t believe in all this time I never thought to ask her this. We’ve talked more about our pasts, too scared to think of what the future holds for us.

"Helen, maybe we should let the girl enjoy her dinner." My dad tries step in.

"Well, if this girl means so much to David, I have a right to know about her."

"My mom has always been protective and even more so since my singing career took off," I lean over and tell Ivy.

"It's okay. I promise. I'm glad you have someone who is so protective of you. It's not uncommon for people to want to attach themselves to you for fame or money." Ivy sets her fork down and folds her hands. She takes a deep breath, then her eyes meet my mom's. I instantly know she is trying to find a way to associate what she does with our lives here in 1958. I make a note to ask her what she does tonight.

"Well, you know all those photos in the cookbooks of the food all done and styled perfectly? That's what I do. The styling and photo-taking."

"Oh, my!" my mom says. "What books? I want to look them up."

"Nothing too big. A lot of small books, local cookbooks, some local media for diners, and ad campaigns things like that," Ivy says in stride.

"Oh, you will have to bring some of your work one time. I'd love to see it!" Ivy nods and keeps eating. My parents share stories from when I was a kid, and they tell the story of how they met too. All the while, I only let go of Ivy's hand when I have to cut up my dinner, or when she does, then I take her hand right back. It's a little hard as I'm a right-handed person, but I make it work.

When dinner is over, my parents' hug Ivy again and me and then head back to their cottage. I show Ivy the changes around the house since she was here last. Most noticeably, the living is now in the living room. We sit down on the couch to watch TV, and she takes in the room.

"It's cozy." She snuggles up with me.

"It finally feels like home now that you are here in my arms. It only felt empty since you left."

I turn on the TV, and she picks *Leave it to Beaver* to watch. She says it's a classic in her time, and I'm kind of getting excited about my visit. I think it will help me understand her on a deeper level. Then I remember our conversation at dinner.

"What is it you really do?" I ask

She smiles. "You really can read me like an open book?" she states more than asks.

"It's my job to know everything about you."

"Well, I wasn't completely lying. I do develop recipes or tweak already made ones and style the photos and take them, edit them, and then sell the recipes and photos to online websites. Think of it as a magazine but all digital like the photos on my phone. I sometimes do crafts too but mostly recipes."

"Will you show me when we get to your house?"

"I'll show you everything, David. I'm excited to share this part of my life with you." She snuggles into me even closer.

Chapter 8

David

Over the next five days, we fall into a steady routine that I wish we could plan on for the rest of our lives. I wake up with her in my arms, we make love, and it takes my breath away every time. We shower and get ready together. She has me picking out her outfits, saying she wants me to see her in everything I pictured.

We spend the mornings in the piano room as I work on music for the new album. I would think she would get bored, but she loves watching me and even puts in her opinion every now and then. We have lunch and spend the afternoons outside. Sometimes, we hang out by the pool, and sometimes, we go for a drive. Then we have dinner and watch some TV before heading upstairs, where I make love to her again for hours until we both pass out.

Today, we are in the music room, and she can't seem to keep her hands off me. I love it, but it's distracting me too.

"Beautiful, I always love your hands on me, but I'm working on this a new song today. It's a little different than what I normally record, but I wrote it for you. Will you listen to it and give me your thoughts? It's called 'Stay With Me Now.'"

Her smile lights up her whole face. "Of course, and I'm sorry I'm being so clingy today. I'm not sure why." She scoots to the other end of the piano bench and folds her hand on her lap. Now there is entirely too much space between us.

I get a crazy idea. "Here, stand up." When she does, I take the piano bench, and instead of setting it parallel to the piano like normal, I center it and turn it perpendicular to the piano keys. I sit down and then pull her to straddle the bench and sit behind me.

"This way, you can wrap your arms around me and be as close as you want and not be in the way of me playing."

She starts kissing the back of my neck. "I love you, David Miller. I love this side of you only I get to see the most, though." I laugh, then I get my sheet music out and in order.

I start singing about begging her to come and be mine and how I'd wait a lifetime for her. Before I even get to the first chorus, she is smiling into my back, and she shocks the hell out of me by singing along with me from the first chorus on. What shocks me even more is I like her version better!

When we are done, I turn on the bench to face her and see she is still smiling.

"That is one of my favorite songs of yours. It actually becomes pretty popular in a few movies after...." She trails off.

"After?" I ask.

She sighs. "After you die," she says with a touch of sadness in her face.

"So I will be recording that one the way you sang it. I like that version better."

Now it's my turn not to be able to keep my hands off her. By the grace of God, I got her to wear a skirt today, so I pull her in and start kissing her while I run my hand up her leg. When my fingers find her core and realize she doesn't have any underwear on, I break the kiss.

"Is this why you have been all over me this morning?" Her shy smile confirms my thoughts.

I kiss her again as I run my finger through her folds. She is already soaking wet, and I'm so hard I don't want to waste time.

"Take my cock out," I mumble against her lips as I keep kissing her. She reaches and undoes my belt and my pants and pulls my cock out. She strokes it a few times, and I just moan into her mouth. Any part of her touching me feels like heaven.

Grabbing her legs, I pull them over my hips. I pull her flush against me on the bench and flip up her skirt. I move her hips just a little and slide my cock into her. As I thrust into her, her head falls back, and she moans out my name. I'm already so close I move my hand and start strumming her clit.

Her moans get even louder. "That's it, baby. Your pussy wants my come, doesn't it? I feel it gripping me so hard. Ah, fuck, you were made for me. The way your pussy takes my cock and grips it while you come. Come for me now, beautiful, come for me now," I say, and she does, hard and beautifully.

I've never talked so dirty in my life, but knowing it turns her on also turns me on. Another stroke and I pull out and come on the bench between us.

We catch our breath, and I realize this is the first time we have had sex outside our bedroom, and it was hot as hell.

"My new goal is to now take you at least once in every room of this house before we leave in a few days."

By the time we fall asleep that night, I had taken her in the living room and dining room. The following day was the kitchen, the den, and the pool.

The last day before we leave, I take her in the TV room and on the pool table after lunch. When we catch our breath on the pool table, she says, "Just one more place I want to have you in before we head out tomorrow."

"Anywhere you want, beautiful. I'll make it happen." And I mean it because these sessions around the house have been sexy, hot, and messy. Then I'm able to take her to bed that night and make love to her again, and everything just feels right.

"In your car. The blue one, it's my favorite."

After dinner, we head to the garage, and I give her three orgasms in that car before she gets on my cock and rides me to one of the quickest climaxes of my life.

After we get cleaned up, we head upstairs, and the nerves hit me. Tomorrow, we head out, and I have no idea what to expect. We are getting ready for bed when I ask, "Do I need to pack a bag of clothes or anything?"

"No, you will need more modern clothes anyway, and I like the idea of having your stuff mixed with mine." She winks at me.

"How long does it take to get from here to there?" I ask.

"You mean from the house to the rocks or from 1958 to 2010?"

"From 1958 to 2010."

"Haven't timed it but it's only a few seconds. Do you get motion sickness at all?"

"No, why?"

"Well, I generally feel a little sick after. You feel like someone is pulling you, then like they are pushing you; everything is a blur, but there is light. Wear comfy shoes and clothes that are okay to get a bit dirty. We are walking there and then we are walking to my house. It's not terribly far but best to be comfortable."

I nod as I take it all in.

That night, I can't seem to stop needing her. We make love three times.

"Baby, we need our sleep. As much as I'd love to go another three rounds with you, I promise we still have more time," she says.

I hold her as she sleeps, but it's still another few hours before sleep finally claims me.

∞∞∞

I wake up the next morning to her mouth on my cock and her hand playing with my balls. I gasp, and a minute later, I'm coming down her throat while she sucks me dry.

Catching my breath, I say, "Fuck, beautiful, that's one hell of a way to wake up."

"I know you were worried last night and having problems sleeping, so I wanted to make sure we started the day off right."

"I want to start every day off with you just like that."

"Trust me, I'm trying to find a way."

So I kiss her because I do trust her, and then we get up and shower and get ready. We eat breakfast, and my parents come in to say goodbye.

"You kids be safe. Oh, is there a number we can reach you at?" Mom asks.

Ivy looks at me. "Well no, it's a drive into town to use the phone."

I can see it a brief second where my mom doesn't like what she hears, but she pastes on a smile anyway.

"Mom, I'll be fine," I try to reassure her.

"Well, we want to hear all about your trip when you get home, son," my dad says as he hugs me.

My mom follows it up with one of her mama bear hugs before they head out for the day.

Ivy comes over and takes my hand and kisses me.

"Are you ready?" she asks.

She grabs her bag, and when I nod, she hands me a hat and sunglasses I watched her grab from the closet earlier, and we head out. We walk down the street to the area where I dropped her off last time. The street is fairly deserted when we duck into the woods.

"I'm beginning to wonder if I should be worried you are bringing me out here to murder me," I joke.

"Nah, I wouldn't murder the guy who gives me the most amazing sex of my life. You need to be more worried I'd tie you to my bed and have my way with you for the rest of your life," she jokes back.

"Somehow, I think I'd be okay with that," I joke just as we enter a clearing. The area has massive rocks as tall as me or taller. We head to them, and before we walk in them, Ivy hands me a couple of the rocks I always see her with.

"It only takes one but best to have extras."

She takes my hand again, and we walk around some rocks toward the center of them. I feel my skin start to hum and almost crawl.

She looks over at me. "Do you feel it?" she asks.

"Yes," I say, still a bit shocked.

"Okay, hold my hand, and we touch the rock at the same time, on three?" She points at the massive rock in front of us.

I take a deep breath and nod, never taking my eyes off her.

She starts to count, "One... Two... Three..."

I reach out and touch the rock when she does.

Chapter 9

Ivy

The world finally steadies, and I look over at David. He's looking at me with what I have dubbed as my look. It's a look of wonder, awe, and love.

"You okay?" I ask him.

"Yes." He looks around with wonder in his eyes.

I nod, and I take his hand and start walking out of the rocks and down my road. A few minutes later, we reach my driveway, and he stops. He is staring up at the house.

I'm proud of my house and being able to buy it on my own. It's got four bedrooms, a finished basement, and a big fenced-in backyard. In the driveway is Brian's car, a sharp contrast from the car styles he's used it.

"What do you think so far?" I ask. He just smiles at me. We walk to the front door, and I unlock it and enter. Brian comes running up with a bottle of wine and a pint of ice cream.

"I'm prepared this time, sugar and alcohol. How was your visit? Did you sleep with him? How did he take it when you said you wouldn't go back until after his Army time? And HOLY SHIT!! IVY, WHAT DID YOU DO?!"

That would be the moment Brian saw David. I shrug my shoulder.

“This is Brian. Brian, this is my... boyfriend doesn’t seem strong enough of a word.” I laugh. “This is my David.”

David holds his hand out to shake, but Brian just stands there with wine in one hand and ice cream in the other, and his mouth wide open, and his eyes huge just staring at David.

“Okay, then.” I take the ice cream from him. “Maybe, let’s not waste this.” I grab David’s hand and bring him to the kitchen. I put the ice cream in the freezer and turn around to see David standing in the middle of the kitchen just looking.

I point at the microwave. “Did they have microwaves back then? I didn’t see one in your kitchen.”

“Yeah, my mom has been talking about them nonstop and begging me to install one.”

I then look in the fridge and see the pizza Brian had ordered. I pull out a slice, put it on a plate, and put it in the microwave for a minute. When the timer goes off, the pizza is warm but not hot, and I hand it to him. He touches it, amazed, and picks it up to eat it, and his eyes go wide.

“This pizza is amazing!” he says.

“Well, David Miller likes Pizza Hut, huh?” Brian says now that he’s finally composed himself.

“Brian, make yourself useful. David needs clothes. You know what I like, so do your thing.” I wink at him.

Brian's eyes light up, and he goes to grab his tape measure and takes a few measurements. I hand him my debit card and tell him to pick up David’s toiletries too, and he’s out the door.

I watch David slowly walk around the kitchen, taking it all in much as I did to his house that first day. He opens my dishwasher and shakes his head.

“A lot different than the one you have, huh?”

“Nancy would go crazy over this. She loves that dishwasher and won’t let anyone, even me, touch it still.”

"Oh, I know I got the talk." I laugh.

I follow him into the living room as his eyes land on my large forty-inch TV, which I turn on, and his jaw drops at the color, quality, and that there are, in fact, over a hundred channels.

"I know you said a hundred channels, but..." He trails off.

"I know. It's hard to imagine."

I watch him nod, and he just looks around. I show him what a CD and DVD are, and my computer before I pull him to my room and lock the door.

He sits down on the bed and looks at the two framed photos on my nightstand that now match his. I come up and stand between his legs, and he rests his head on my chest and wraps his arms around my waist.

"A lot to take in, isn't it?" I ask.

"Yes, but seeing you here in your world, your eyes lit up today, talking about this stuff."

"David, my eyes lit up because I got to share it with you, and I got to watch you take it all in. None of this means anything without you, though, I'd give it all up in a second to just have *you*."

He looks up at me with his arms still wrapped snugly around me. "How can I help? Can I leave you some money in my will or hell, leave you my house? Please let me take care of you."

"Baby, you can't be linked to me. How would you explain leaving money to someone whose parents haven't even met yet at the time of your death? It would raise too many questions. Your house is going to be a museum dedicated to your career, and your fans will be visiting it. Millions a year will come and see where you lived and visit your grave and your parents' graves. It will provide hundreds of jobs for this community, and we aren't changing that."

He squeezes me tighter. "Our house, beautiful, that isn't my house. It's *our* house."

That makes me smile. I wish it could be true more than anything, but I take what I can get.

"I will find a way to take care of you. Mark my words, I will find a way."

I laugh because somehow, I know he will.

"So, we have ten days?" he asks.

"Yes, what do you want to do while you're here?"

"I want to go for a drive and see your Nashville."

I think about it. We can take Brian's car because he has tinted windows, and if we stayed in the car, and he wore a hat and sunglasses, it could work.

"Okay, but we do not get out of the car, and you have to wear what I tell you."

He nods and agrees.

"Baby, I need you." I run my hand over his already hard cock.

I stand and slowly strip, giving him a show once I'm naked. I move to him and help him take his clothes off. Then I crawl into bed, and he's right beside me.

We lie on our sides facing each other, and his eyes never leave mine. He grabs my leg and pulls it over his hip, then slowly slides his cock into me. His strokes are unrushed but firm. His hand comes up to cup my breast, and his thumb rolls over the already hard peak and strokes it in time with his cock moving in and out of me.

He's so sweet, and it breaks my heart. Between kisses, he tells me how much he loves me and how his life held no meaning until I walked in. How he lives for me, how he doesn't care if it's in my world or his, but he will find a way for us to be together.

I love his dirty talk, but this sweet side of him is just as much of a turn-on, and I'm already so close.

"My sweet, sweet Ivy, I'm going to spend the rest of my life living for you. I'm going to make you so damn proud of me, and everything I do will be for you. I love you more than words could ever express. Come for me, my sweet girl."

He kisses me and moves his hand down to stroke my clit. I shatter in his arms with my heart full and my body locking up and clamping down on him. He thrusts a few more times before pulling out and coming on my thigh without ever breaking the kiss.

When he's done coming, he slides his cock back into me. It seems to be his favorite thing; he loves falling asleep with his cock inside me. But this time, we just lie there staring into each other's eyes, neither of us wanting to break the spell. I tell him how much I love him and how my heart and soul are his for always.

After a bit, we hear Brian come home. The door closes, and we hear him yelling, "My eyes are closed. I don't know where you ended up, but I promise I can't see a thing just... OW!" I hear him run into a wall and can't help but laugh.

David has a huge smile on his face too. "I think I like him," he says, making me smile.

"Ivy, are you here? MARCO!" Brian yells.

I laugh. "POLO! We are in my room and will be out in a few. Your eyeballs are safe!" I yell back.

"Oh, thank god! I'm going to unload my car!" Brian yells back.

I turn to David, who is still looking at me with so much love on his face I tear up.

"Let's get dressed and go see what he got for you. Then we can spend the day exploring the TV, okay?"

His eyes light up, and he nods. We get cleaned up and dressed. I dress in my normal clothes, yoga pants, and a racerback tank top.

"That's what you wear around the house?"

"Yes," I say a bit hesitantly

"Beautiful, that is so damn sexy. How am I ever going to get enough of you?"

"I hope you never do because I couldn't bear to lose you," I say honestly.

"I couldn't agree more." He kisses me on the forehead.

We walk out to see Brian standing around a pile of bags, and I groan. "How did my bank not call and say my debit card was stolen?!"

"Girl, because you go on worse shopping sprees than this, just with food!" he says, and I laugh. He continues. "The girl at the counter thought I was crazy as we hunted down his scent bath products, but because I'm awesome, I found them! Oh, and look at this," he pulls a shirt from the bag.

It says, "I'm not old, I'm vintage," and I bust out laughing.

"Wait, one more!" Brian says, looking so proud of himself. This one says, "Rock and Roll Hall of Fame." My eyes tear up instantly.

"Beautiful, please, you have to tell me why you're upset, so I can fix it." His thumbs are brushing away my tears, and I faintly hear Brian saying how freaking perfect he is.

"The Hall of Fame, you get inducted into it. It opened after you died, and you were one of the first people they inducted at their opening along with Elvis, Chuck Berry, and a few others."

David looks back at the shirt, and a slight smile crosses his lips, but he looks a million miles away before his eyes land back on me.

We spend the rest of the day with me cooking and Brian showing him all about the TV. I put his clothes in my closet with mine and his stuff in the bathroom. I get now what he means about his stuff mixed in with mine. At one point, when I brought out some more snacks, David grabbed me around my waist and pulled me onto his lap.

"Sit with me, beautiful. My skin is crawling from having you so close and not touching you." He kisses my neck.

An hour of snuggling later, he asks, "When will I see color TV in my time?"

I pull out my phone and google it. "Early 1960s," I say, and he nods.

We have dinner, and I show him a bit of what I do with the food and pictures and some of my work. Brian agrees to let us take his car out tomorrow so long as we stay IN the car, and we agree.

Then we spend the night making love soft and sweet just like we did that afternoon.

∞∞∞

In the morning, Brian helps me get David ready to go out. We used a hair spray color leftover from Brian's Halloween costume to dye David's hair and assured him it would wash out tonight. Then I have the best time dressing him. I put him in a pair of medium wash jeans and a button-down shirt the same color blue as his eyes. I roll the sleeves up on the shirt, and I don't think I've ever seen him look more handsome.

"You look so freaking sexy. I don't want to let you leave this room, much less the house." I run my eyes down his body.

"Stop looking at me like that beautiful, or you will never get me to go back home when our ten days are up."

"Looking at you like what?"

"Like you're fucking me with your eyes."

"That's because I totally am," I admit, and he growls at me. After a day of TV, he is talking a bit more like Brian and me; it makes me smile to myself. I wonder if he even realizes he's doing it. His words are a bit more relaxed and not so properly spoken.

I sigh and take his hand. I put sunglasses on him, and we get out the door and into Brian's car. Before I can even back out of the driveway, I see him fidgeting in his seat.

"What's wrong?" I ask, and I pull on to the street.

"This is wrong. I should be driving you around."

"This isn't 1958, David. Us women like to drive ourselves, thank you. We aren't helpless, you know," I say a bit harsher than I meant.

His head snaps to mine, and he takes my hand. "No, not like that, beautiful, I just like taking care of you, and that includes driving you around so you can relax. I trust you completely, I just..." I squeeze his hand and interrupt him.

"I'm sorry, I understand." I take a deep breath.

Taking him downtown, I drive many of the same roads he took me on and point out some of my favorite places. We drive down Broadway, and there are a few places with statues of him, Elvis, or Johnny Cash outside. I point them out, and he just shakes his head.

"It's just hard to wrap my head around it. I never expected to be anybody. I loved to sing, and it just took on a life of its own. But here. I've been dead how long?" he asks.

"Just about forty years."

"Forty years, and I'm still such a big name like this? I just can't wrap my head around it is all."

"Well, I think a part of it is you died in the height of your career; people speculate where you would have been if you lived. Johnny Cash was a huge name in your time too, and he stayed popular all his life and is still pretty big now seven years after his death, but the hype around you is even bigger. Many people from your era made a huge impact on music and what it is today. Elvis, Dean Martin, Patsy Cline, Bob Dylan, Frank Sinatra, Chuck Berry, and later, The Beatles, The Rolling Stones, and The Beach

Boys."

I continue. "If that isn't enough, you go on to star in some of the most iconic movies. I think I read you starred in over twenty movies! Two of the most popular being the one in New York and the one in Hawaii, and baby, when you are filming in Hawaii, think of me and bring me back Hawaii as best you can. It's been a dream of mine to visit there someday."

He leans his head back against the headrest, taking it all in, then he rolls his head to the side to look at me.

"I will get you to Hawaii, beautiful. I'll use a fake name if I have to, and we will make love on the beach. Give us both something to look forward to."

"I want to show you something even though I probably shouldn't."

We drive down by Ivy Hill. We can't get close unless we get out of the car, and we can't do that, but he can see the buildings across the street that holds his awards and cars and all his memorabilia. He can see the signs and his fans walking around.

"This is what has become of your house. They proudly display all your awards, outfits, cars, and your home is open for tours."

He nods. "Is the blue one on display there?" he asks.

My face flushes as I think about what exactly we did in the back seat of that blue car. "Yes, it is."

He groans. "We need to talk to Brian. I want to see all this. Please, I'll wear a wig. I don't care, I just... I have to see it," he begs.

"Baby, I will do anything for you. Just let me find a way, okay? Now one more stop before we head home."

We stop at Panera Bread and get several chicken salad sandwiches for dinner. "Remember when I said I've had a better chicken salad sandwich? Well, this is it, and it will be dinner."

His eyes light up. "I can't wait to try it."

We get home, and Brian isn't home from some work meeting yet, so David pulls me to the couch and kisses me long and hard.

"Thank you for today. As hard as it is to be away from you, seeing how important my staying in 1958 is helps. It's one thing to hear what my legacy does, but another thing to see it. I'm not sure I fully grasp it, but I understand it a lot more now. For that reason, I will live my life in 1958, but only if you promise to visit as much as you possibly can."

"Of course, I will, baby, and I promise to be there when you need me at every event in your life. I will make sure of it." I smile at him. He lays me down on the couch and kisses me as he lays on top of me, and we have a good old fashion make-out session.

That's how Brian finds us when he gets home.

"Oh, god! Couldn't you have at least put a sock on the door?!" he screeches.

Laughing, I sit up and adjust my shirt, and David adjusts himself.

"We weren't doing anything, and besides, we aren't in college anymore, so no sock on the door, but we do have something to ask of you."

"Anything if it means I don't walk in on that again." Brian makes a fake disgusted face.

So, I go for the shock factor. "Well, I want to go back when David does just for two weeks. I'll come home the day before he gets his draft orders. I think it's best I'm not there for that."

I see David's eyes go wide, and a huge smile spreads on his face. He leans into me and kisses me. "So I will get two more weeks with you?" he asks with so much hope in his eyes.

Brian looks at me, then shrugs his shoulders. "I don't see why not."

David's face lights up, and he kisses me again.

"One more thing. David wants to go tour Ivy Hill while he's here."

"*WHAT?! NO*!" Brian screeches.

"Wait. Hear me out, okay? What if he dyed his hair AND we had him in a baseball cap, sunglasses, AND he grew out a beard? There are next to no pictures of him in a beard, and that wasn't until he was older. Come on, they have the impersonators go there all the time, all dressed up who *actually* look and sound like him. He will fly under the radar, and if he doesn't, we'll bolt. And they chalk it up to the crazies having another sighting, but how would they explain a sighting of twenty-three-year-old David when he should be close to seventy-five by now?"

Brian pinches the bridge of his nose and closes his eyes and takes deep breaths. "Okay, how about I promise not to go into the depression like I did last time I came home? It will be two years this time. I can't promise I won't have bad days, but I promise to be myself and reinstate weekly movie nights and going out and being your wing-woman to find you, Mr. Right. Please, please, please?" I try to bribe him.

His eyes soften, and he looks over at David and then me. He hugs me tight. "Okay, but just so you know, I was never upset at you over the past seven months. I love you, Ivy, you're my best friend, and more than that, you are family."

Then he pulls back and looks at David. "Okay, buddy, one week. Don't shave, and we will be dying your hair, and you won't be talking while we are there. Oh, and Ivy, teach him to use an iPad. They use them for the tours there. I'll plan an outfit that won't draw attention. And whatever you two do, please keep it to your bedroom, and I promise to call you on my way home from now on and announce myself coming in the house." He forced a whole body shudder out.

I laugh and get out the bag with the chicken salad sandwiches in it for dinner, and we three all sit at the table.

"Okay, so the first day we met, we had lunch together, and he serves chicken salad sandwiches and claims they are the best he's ever had," I tell Brian.

"In which case, she takes a bite and says she's had better and tells me the little deli by her house makes them." David holds up his sandwich.

Brian laughs. "Okay, take a bite, and let us know what you think."

Then we watch David take a bite. "Don't think I've had people watch me eat so intently before," he says before taking another bite.

He nods his head and swallows. "Well, as always, my woman is right. This is much better than what I served her. I need this recipe for Nancy."

I laugh. "Oh, this will be one of many recipes you add to your collection I plan to rock your food world over the next three weeks."

David just smiles at me and gives me my look. The one that tells me everything I need to know.

Chapter 10

David

This past week has been amazing. Ivy has shown me her work. I have to say I love watching her work, and the food I get to eat afterward is amazing. We haven't left the house since my tour around Nashville, but I haven't wanted to either. When Ivy isn't working, I haven't let her out of my arms. We have snuggled, watching a lot of TV, or we are in bed having some mind-blowing sex.

My soul is bound to hers, and I have to say I always saw singing as my passion, but this life here with her fits. It feels comfortable, and it just feels like home. I don't care about the money and fancy home, cars, and clothes. I care about this, waking up with Ivy in my arms every morning.

I've asked Brian about working on a plan to make it happen. He says he's working on it but won't give me details. Of course, I'd rather it be today and not in ten years, but I'll take what I can get.

I look at Ivy as she sleeps in my arms. She is beautiful with her hair messed up from our lovemaking last night, and my little love bites all over her chest, belly, and thighs. Today is the day we go tour Ivy Hill as it is now. I'm a bit nervous, to be honest, but I know the best way to cure that nervousness.

I move down the bed, taking the covers with me until I'm

between Ivy's thighs. I push her legs apart and lean in and give her pussy a long lick up to her clit. She starts to stir a little, and I smile. This has become my favorite way to wake her up. I suck on her clit lightly at first and then slowly increase pressure.

I use both my thumbs to spread her lips wide before I dip my tongue inside her warm pussy, and I am rewarded with a moan. I start making love to her with my tongue when she gasps and reaches down to grip my hair. Her hips start to buck, and I know she is close, so I move back up and suck on her clit while I shove two fingers inside and start to stroke her sweet spot. After only a few strokes, she comes in my mouth. I lick up every drop as she says my name over and over again.

When she finally starts to relax, I move up her body, kissing up her belly and sucking both nipples before kissing her neck and finally her lips. She wraps her arms around my neck and her legs around my hips, and I place the head of my rock-hard cock at her soaking wet opening.

"Good morning, beautiful."

She smiles and looks up at me.

"It is a good morning when you wake me up like that." She sighs, then wiggles under me, trying to lift her hips. I kiss her again and then thrust home. I start my thrusts slowly, pulling out all the way before sliding back in. She raises her hips to meet my thrusts.

"Baby, I'm so close already. Don't go easy on me this morning. Give me that sexy cock hard and fast." She groans, and I nearly come at her words. But like always, what my girl wants, my girl gets. I start pounding into her fast, and listening to her moan is the sweetest sound in the world.

I reach down and rub her clit because I need her to come before I do, and she screams out her orgasm after only two strokes of her clit. Her pussy clenches, trying to suck me in deeper. I barely manage to pull out before I come all over the sheets.

I catch my breath and have to ask. "Beautiful, why don't you get on birth control? You told me before you'd tell me why, but we've been pleasantly distracted." I kiss her neck and down to her shoulder.

"Well, there are a couple of types of birth control now. Most common is the pill. I was on it for a year, and it made me really sick. As soon as I got off it, I was better. We tried the shot too, and I had the same reaction. It just made me so sick. I wasn't with anybody then, so I just stopped taking any birth control and haven't had a reason to until now. I guess I can talk to my doctor again but—"

I cut her off with a kiss. "No, I don't want you doing anything that will make you sick. I would love to come inside you, and god, the thought of getting you pregnant makes me so hard. But I won't leave you to raise our child alone, and I am perfectly fine pulling out."

I watch her nibble on her bottom lip, and I can tell she is thinking.

"What's on your mind?" I ask her as a nuzzle her shoulder.

"Well, my friend Angela has the same problem, but she is married, so she and her husband use what's called the family planning method. This app tracks when she will ovulate, and then they just avoid sex during that time. She's been really good at it. Other than those days, they have sex daily, and she hasn't gotten pregnant in years. I can have her teach it to me while you're gone, and then we can use it when you get back. Think of it has your welcome reward."

"God, beautiful, I'm going to be hard all the time thinking about that. It's all I will be able to think about." I can't wipe the smile off my face.

She smiles at me and runs her hands over my beard. It feels weird to me, but she seems to like it, especially when I have my face between her legs.

"I'm going to miss this when it's gone. It's another side of you only I get to see," she whispers.

"I promise to find ways to grow it out around you." I kiss her pulse point on the side of her wrist. "Only you."

We finally drag ourselves out of bed and get ready. When we step into the kitchen, Brian has a coffee cup in his hand and is glaring at us.

"I don't need to be woken up to your screaming orgasms," he jokes with a smile on his face.

Ivy laughs. "Well, consider it payback for the ones I had to listen to when you were dating that jerk, Ray."

I just smile and shake my head as we have breakfast, and then Brian sets out to dye my hair. I guess it's a washout color, so it will only be for today. He has me change into jeans and a sweatshirt, and he hands me what he calls a baseball hat and sunglasses and says not to take the hat off even inside. I start to protest, but he says it's common now to wear hats inside.

Common or not, it's still disrespectful. But being I'm walking into my house, who am I disrespecting? Myself?

Then we are off to Ivy Hill. Brian is driving, and I'm in the back with my arm around Ivy, but the nervous energy is back, and I can't help bouncing my leg a bit. I listen to them talk, and they tell me how the upstairs bedrooms are blocked off as the family keeps it private since that's where I died. They also debate about skipping the memorial garden, so I don't see the dates of death for my parents and me. And finally agree we should skip it.

Ivy goes on to tell me a bit about how Elvis's family did much the same thing with his house in Memphis.

"I visited him at Graceland a few months ago. I thought my house was extravagant, but it doesn't hold a candle to Graceland." I laugh.

"I've always liked Ivy Hill better." Ivy smiles at me.

We get there and park and then head in toward the visitor center. Ivy and I walk hand in hand, and I lean down to whisper to her.

"Technically, this is our first date here in 2010." I smile.

"It is, but I'm not sure how we could ever explain this first date to anyone." She laughs, and I do too.

Brian heads over to the counter to buy our tickets while Ivy and I go and look at all the photos on the walls. Let me tell you, there are no words to describe how weird it is to see pictures of your future self doing things you haven't done yet.

One of the photos is of me standing next to the Ivy Hill sign when I named the property. The same one Ivy has framed on her nightstand and gave me to put on mine. I lean down to whisper in her ear. "I was thinking of you when that photo was taken, hoping you would see it and know how much I loved you."

She looks up at me with tears in her eyes, but a smile on her face as she leans in and gives me a quick kiss.

Once Brian joins us, he says we have to take a bus over to the main house. The museum and a welcome center are on the far side of the property, and with so much to see, they bus people over to the main house. I take a deep breath and nod. Ivy squeezes my hand and smiles at me.

We sit at the back of the bus with me against the window. I look across the aisle and see two girls about Ivy's age who are looking and giggling at me. I tense up a bit and look out the window, trying to hear what they are saying.

"Isn't he cute?" the blonde says.

"Yeah, I love that beard on him. He looks super sexy," the brunette says.

"Who's the girl? I bet it's his sister," the blonde says again.

Just to shut them both up, I look over at Ivy, put my hand under her chin to get her to look at me, and then I kiss her hard.

I get so lost in the kiss that I don't realize the bus has already stopped in front of Ivy Hill, and the girls are standing up to get off.

Ivy smiles up at me. She knew exactly what I was doing.

We get out of the bus, and I look up at my house. I remember buying her not that long ago. My first big purchase with the money I had made directly after that, I bought that blue car Ivy seems to move so much.

Looking at the front door, I remember opening it just three weeks ago and seeing Ivy standing there. I never thought I'd see her again, but there she was. I felt whole, like I could breathe again. I was no longer drowning; I was flying.

I look at Ivy, and I can tell she is thinking about that moment too. So I lean down to whisper in her ear. "I had never seen anything so beautiful as you standing there a few weeks ago."

She turns and whispers in my ear, "I feel like I'm giving you the keys to the time machine because most of the house looks nothing like it does now," she says, and I smile.

We walk in, and I keep my head lowered as we get handed the iPad Ivy has been showing me how to use. We walk into the living room and see the piano room just beyond it. I see a slight tinge of pink on her cheeks, and I know she is thinking about what I did to her in that room just recently. And now I am too. The room is different, brighter, and I love it. It feels like Ivy.

I look up the stairs, which are blocked off, and honestly, I like that a part of us is private. I wonder if Ivy's things are still mixed with mine in my room. If the bathroom still smells like her.

The dining room is next on the tour, and it hasn't changed too much, but all I can think about is how I ate Ivy's pussy on that table for lunch. In the kitchen, I see her sitting in the counter and me between her legs.

Closing my eyes, I have to take a few deep breaths to get my cock to calm down. He doesn't understand why we can't toss her back down and recreate that afternoon.

The tour takes us to the backyard, and I see a building I don't recognize. It turns out, I built it as an office for my dad, who helps manage me, and I love that idea.

We see the pool, and then Ivy is pulling me away from the crowd in another direction, and I realize it's what she called the memorial gardens. From here, I can see the metal plaques covering the graves, but I can't read anything. I stop in my tracks and stare. I see a sadness in Ivy's eyes.

I lean down to her ear. "Is it just me and my parents buried there?" I whisper.

"Yes, I just pray it's not really you in that grave. My heart couldn't take it."

My heart breaks, and I pray it's not me too because the thought of breaking her heart like that shatters mine.

We head back across the street to see the museum. I take in all the photos and clothes, but she must see something because she goes tense and pushes me in another direction. "Please trust me. It's better you not know some things about your future until they happen, okay?" she whispers, and I nod.

We get to the car area, and there she is. The blue Cadillac I took Ivy in on the back seat. The one I drive her around Nashville in every time we go out, and the one I drove to say goodbye to her with the last time she left. I take a shaky breath.

We finish our tour of the museum by seeing a massive twelve-foot-tall wall covered in gold records, and I realize they are awards for my different songs and albums. There is a whole section on the missing first gold album and speculation on where it is or who I could have given it to.

I have that album hanging up in my office in Ivy Hill, so I'm not sure what happens to it between now and then. There is a spot saying it would be worth over ten million dollars now since it's the first one of my career. I realize none of that will mean anything if she isn't by my side when I accept them.

All of this is amazing, and I realize many people dream of this, but when I look in Ivy's eyes, I know I'd give it all up for her. It means nothing without her. I'm going to fight for her until my last breath.

Chapter 11

David

Two Years Later

I look around at the guys on the bus with me. We just landed Stateside a few hours ago, and we are heading back to the base. When we get there, I get to officially sign out and head home. I am done with my military service.

Just as it has many times over the past two years, my mind drifts back to my Ivy. Those last two weeks she spent with me at my house, she cooked so many amazing foods for me, saying the Army wasn't going to feed me well, and she wasn't kidding. We made love on pretty much every surface of the house. If her face was blushing when we toured Ivy Hill that day, it would be redder than a tomato now.

She went home the day before I got the letter in the mail about where I was to report. That day, she took my heart and soul with her. Watching her disappear into that stone was the worst thing I've ever seen.

I went home and got so drunk, but it did nothing to dull the ache for her. I spent so much time in our room in the days before I had to leave. Once I was sworn into the US Army, I started counting down the days until I'd see her again, and it's so close now.

We pull on to the base, and I finish everything as fast as I can. I walk out and see my mom and dad but no Ivy. I try to hide my disappointment by giving my parents a huge hug. I have missed them, and I know these past two years weren't easy on them. I'm still in my uniform that I traveled home in. I didn't want to take the time to change, and a part of me wanted Ivy to see me in it.

On the drive home, my parents talk about the things I've missed with family and friends, but I don't hear much of it. I just stare out the window, thinking about Ivy and hoping I see her soon.

We get home, and I walk through the door and drop my bag when I hear a loud "SURPRISE!!!" I look around at all the people closest to me in my life there to celebrate my return. I know I'm blessed, and I realized how much so while I was overseas. But I still don't see those piercing green eyes that have haunted my dreams. My heart breaks because I need her like I need my next breath.

Face after face is in front of me, and all I can think about is the one person I've been keeping from them. The one person I want on my arm to finally introduce to everyone.

As I scan the crowd, I see a few people move. I start pushing people out of the way to get to the back of the room, and I see her standing at the bottom of the stairs.

She looks even more beautiful than I remember. My eyes lock with hers, and I just keep moving forward. When I reach out to wrap my arms around her waist, my hands are shaking.

"Welcome home, soldier." She wraps her arms around my neck. I lean in and kiss her hard. I kiss her with every emotion I've felt over the past two years. The rest of the room fades away, and it's just me and her—my reason for being, my reason for living and breathing. My heart that has been aching every second of every day for the last two years has been healed and is racing like mad.

I've never been so happy to be home.

∞∞∞

Ivy

I stayed behind when his parents went to pick David up from the base. I wanted them to have that time alone with him. I waited in the back of the room filled with people of importance to him. While I waited, the past two years flash through my mind.

When I left him, I gave myself forty-eight hours to cry in bed. Then I picked myself up and took Brian out to dinner and then to his favorite club for drinks. Despite what I was feeling, I'm so grateful to Brian for bringing David into my life.

That night at the club, I was asked three different times to dance, and I turned every one of them down, but Brian met Kevin, and they have been together ever since. He's so happy, and Kevin has become such a good friend to me as well.

I kept my promise and picked up my life and tried to stay out of the depression I let take over me last time. I still internet stalked David, and I had a few bad days when I just couldn't get out of bed over the years, but here I am.

I'm pulled from my thoughts by the sound of everyone shouting surprise. I see David walk through the door, followed by his parents. He looks so handsome in his military uniform. I rub my thighs together. I thought I was turned on before, but after seeing him in his uniform, I want to drag him upstairs and send everyone home.

I see him look around, and a look of disappointment crosses his face before he masks it and starts saying hello to people, but his eyes keep scanning the room. Then his eyes lock with mine, and everything spins. He walks toward me, and my heart races. It's no mystery why he was labeled a heartbreaker in his time. I'm sure girls would kill to have him look at them like this. I see his hands shake as he puts his arms around my waist. I wrap my arms around his neck and smile.

"Welcome home, soldier," I say right before his mouth lands on mine. That kiss is everything. My nipples harden and ache for his touch. I let him control the kiss, and it goes on forever but ends too soon all at once.

He smiles down at me. "You're here." He strokes my cheek and rubs my arms.

"I promised you I'd be here, didn't I?"

"You did." He takes my hand and doesn't let go of it for the rest of the night. He drags me from one person to the other and introduces me to every one of them proudly and with a huge smile on his face. We talk about everything from his time in the Army to what's next in his music life.

Hours pass in what feels like minutes, and people start saying goodbye. Once he has said goodbye to everyone, we sneak away to our room.

As soon as the door closes, he locks it and has me backed against the door, and his hands and lips are all over me.

"I missed you so much, beautiful. I thought about you every night, and in my darkest days, the images of you were what got me through. I need you so badly I can't breathe. I love you, sweet Ivy. I love you so damn much." He kisses me before carrying me to our bed.

"I missed you too, baby. I have so much to tell you, and I want to know everything. Right now, I need you just as badly. It's been too long. I love you too, David, more than I know how to put into words."

With that, he pulls my dress off over my head. And my bra and panties are gone in an instant.

"Lie down on the bed." He starts to remove his boots and his uniform. Once he's naked, he's on me with his face between my legs, and he wastes no time.

I'm already so turned on from missing him and seeing him in his uniform that he gives my pussy one lick and sucks once on my clit, and I'm coming apart, screaming his name. He doesn't let up until I give him two more orgasms.

When he finally pulls away, he looks me over with a growl and then attacks my mouth in another soul-searing kiss.

I gasp when the head of his cock is at my entrance. "David, baby, please don't be gentle tonight. I've missed you so much. My body has craved you, so show me exactly how much you have missed me." He slams into me so hard it takes my breath away.

I claw at his back. I know I have to be drawing blood, but I can't stop. I wrap my legs around him and thrust my hips to meet his thrusts.

"Fuck, beautiful, this tight pussy is trying to siphon the cum from my balls. I'm not going to last." He starts to rub my clit.

I'm so close I figure it's time to deliver his homecoming present. I grip my legs tighter around his hips. "Don't you dare pull out of me tonight," I whisper in his ear. His whole body shudders, and his hot cum starts to coat the inside of my pussy, setting off my orgasm. He covers my scream with his mouth and keeps thrusting, causing another orgasm to follow the first.

He doesn't stop coming until I start to relax and come down off my climaxes. He collapses on top of me, breathing hard. After a minute, he rolls us to the side, keeping his cock buried inside me.

"God, beautiful, I've dreamed about coming inside you every night I was gone," he says, cupping my tits and lazily playing with them.

"I started that family planning method I told you about. I've been tracking everything for the past two years, and it's fate this week is the perfect window for us."

He smiles at me. "Tell me everything I missed."

So I pour my heart out. I tell him about taking Brian out that night and him meeting Kevin. I tell him about work and what happened in my world. He listens to every word and asks questions.

He's quiet for a minute before he speaks. "I have to know, Ivy, and no matter what the answer is, nothing changes, but were you with anyone while I was gone? It..."

"No, baby, no other guys even interested me. There hasn't been anyone, and there never will be."

"It's okay if there was. I know two years is a long time. I want you just the same but—" I cut him off with a kiss. And flip him over on his back and then sink down on his cock.

"Does it feel like anyone else has been in this pussy?" I ask, and he shakes his head. "No, that's because it's yours, and I didn't let anyone touch what's yours." I rock slowly on his cock. "Now, same question to you. Was there anyone else? As you said, two years is a long time."

He grips my hips hard and thrusts up into me. "Fuck, beautiful, did you not feel the amount of cum I just released into you? You gave me back-to-back orgasms because it's been so damn long, and you are all I thought about. Sitting in my cot with your memory turned me on hotter than any girl I saw over there. Now stop being so gentle with me and fuck me properly."

He thrusts into me as hard as I slam down on him. He holds my hips so hard I know there will be bruises, and he maneuvers my body up and down his cock.

"This image is one I came in my hand to so many times," he says, and god, is it sexy. I toss my head back as my eyes roll into the back of my head, and my body locks up with my climax. He leans up and sucks hard on my nipple, and I fall right into another orgasm before I hear him groan and feel his hot release inside, which triggers another mini orgasm before I collapse on to his chest.

Once we both we gain our breath, I shift to my side next to him, and I say, “Your turn, solider, I want to know everything.” At the same time, I run my finger through his chest hair and over a new scar on his shoulder.

He starts from the beginning and tells me about how he barely got out of bed until the day he had to report for duty. He tells me about training and then being shipped over to France and about some of the guys he met.

I keep on tracing the scar, and he sighs. “I had two close calls, which I’m sure you know about.”

“Actually, I didn’t read about your Army time. I knew you came home alive, but I didn’t care to know the details until I was able to hold you in my arms.”

He goes on to tell me about the close calls, which were during practice when one guy showed up drunk, and he and another guy got injured trying to take him down. Another close call was also at practice when shrapnel went flying and hit his shoulder there. He said other than a few stitches, it was no big deal, and there is no lasting damage.

Leaning over, I kiss the scar and run my tongue along it, and his whole body shudders.

I lie back down with my head on his shoulder, running my hand through his chest hair again. “So, tell me about Anna.”

His whole body tenses, and when I look up at him, his face has paled.

Chapter 12

Ivy

I keep rubbing his chest, and I lean in to kiss him over his heart. Nothing he tells me will be new information. I know a fight is coming with what I will be telling him. This is 75% of the reason I refused to read about his Army time because I hate this.

He takes a shaky breath and pulls me closer as though he's afraid I'm going to bolt.

"David, baby, look at me." I wait for his eyes to meet mine. My chest squeezes at the sadness and fear I see there.

"I already know the basics of what happened, but I need your story, then I will tell you what is going to happen. But through all this, I'm not going anywhere. I love you, baby."

He closes his eyes and takes a deep breath, and I see a tear run down his cheek. I lean in and kiss it away.

"My first few months in France, I tried to drink my loneliness away. The guys I was stationed with would have parties and hang out at bars. About four months in, one of the parties was at one of the guys' houses. Not anyone I was stationed with, but one of the guys who I'd been hanging out with knew him, so we went. It would be the first chance at homecooked food since we got there. That house was Anna's parents' house."

He is trembling, so I pull the blanket over us both, and I reach up and start running my fingers in his hair to help calm him. He still has his eyes closed as though he can't look at me.

"I drank a lot that night, but I remember everything. Anna was sixteen, bragging about turning seventeen soon. She knew who I was, and my music, and our designated driver said she was flirting pretty hard. I know she flirted a few times, but I blocked out a lot of what she said because I was thinking about you. I remember that I was thinking of our tour of Ivy Hill and how you would blush when you looked at the spots where I had made love to you, and it made me so damn hard. All I could think about was getting back to my barracks so I could have my nightly time with you, even if it was just with my hand. No matter how lonely I was, that was still how I ended every day, and I loved it."

"I guess she noticed how hard I got and thought it was because of her. So after we left that night, she told her parents we had been flirting. Well, the following week, there was a company event, and Anna and her parents were there. She kept flirting, but I wasn't drinking that night, so I know I firmly told her no, and I had someone back home I loved. She said it's okay she never had to know, and that thought made me sick. She started showing up at different events and get-togethers and flirted every time. At one point, I started walking away from her. Then I just stopped going out for a while."

As he's talking, I see a stack of mail on his dresser. I know where this is going, but I just need him to get it out and be the one to tell me.

"Then two months ago, her dad got promoted and was officially my superior. He invited me over to dinner, and I couldn't say no. From what Anna had told him, I had been inappropriate with his underage daughter, who now was eighteen, and he made it clear he expected me to follow through and make an honest woman of her. The whole time, Anna had this evil smirk on her face. I don't know what she told her father, but it wasn't good. I refused to go out any more or do anything until we left, so I didn't chance running into her. I plan to get my manager on it and scare the crap out of him to make it stop. But I swear to you I never touched her, and I never flirted with her. Ivy, I swear it!" he says with tears in his eyes.

I lean down and kiss him. "I know you didn't, baby."

Then I get up to go through the mail. Finding the pink envelope is easy, but finding the second one I am looking for takes a minute.

I turn back and get back in bed with him still naked, but he is sitting up against the headboard and has pulled the blanket over his waist. I smirk and pull the blanket away. "Don't you dare cover up what is mine. I haven't seen you in two years. There is no way I'm done looking at you," I say, and he forces a smile.

I hold up the two envelopes, and anger crosses his face.

"I already know what these letters say. This one," I say, holding up the white one, "is from Anna's parents threatening you and reminding you about what he said at dinner. And this one"—I hold up the pink one—"is from Anna. She admits to lying to her parents about what was really going on between you two. She basically confessed everything but begs for a chance with you. It's everything you need to get her parents off your back." I watch relief cross his face. I set the envelopes down and get on my knees next to him, bringing my face level to his.

"But you won't. These letters don't come out to the public until after your death."

He grabs my hand. "Like hell, I won't."

"David, listen to me. You will marry this girl," I say, and my eyes tear up.

He jumps out of bed and starts pacing and pulling at his hair. "No, there is no way I'm marrying anyone but you. I have never been unfaithful to you, and I won't start now. You are the love of my life, my soul mate. How can you think I would marry someone else? Especially someone like that?!" he says, raising his voice.

Sitting on the bed, I remain resting on my knees but turn to face him. "Baby, we can't be legally married, and we can't change history. It's imperative that we don't! Now listen to me. Okay?" He stops pacing and faces me but stays on the other side of the room.

I have been dreading this conversation, and it's been keeping me up at night. Brian and I have talked at length about what I need to tell him and what I can't. I chickened out twice coming here, but I missed him so much, and that pushed me on.

"You *will* marry her, you will bed her, and she will give you a son. He *has* to be born. He is alive in my time, and he does some amazing things in your memory and gives you two grandkids. You will stay with Anna until she files for divorce when your son is three. As soon as she is pregnant, you go live in California away from her and knock out one movie after another. The papers will say you are having an affair with pretty much every one of your co-stars, and Anna will have an affair."

His eyes are wide. "That's four years!! You want me to be married to another woman for four *years*?! No, I can't do it. The thought of even kissing someone else makes me sick to my stomach."

I take a deep breath and fight the burning at the back of my throat. I've been trying not to think about this and the detail behind it. The thought of him in bed with someone else kills me, but I knew from the start that he'd be married to her one day, and I couldn't change it. It was easier not to think about it until I had to, but now it's tearing me apart.

"David, your son has to be born."

"Okay, I get that, but what about us? How will you find me in California?"

I take a deep breath. "I won't. During this time, I won't interfere in your marriage because it's vital she is the one who has an affair and files for divorce. We can't risk it," I say with tears running down my face.

He falls to his knees and buries his face in his hands and starts crying. He folds himself over until his face is in the carpet, and his sobs are wracking his whole body. Getting up, I grab his shirt and pull it over my head before I kneel beside him and pull him into my arms.

Tears are running down my face, but at my touch, he just starts to sob harder. We stay that way for a good half hour. I will stay there and hold him as long as he needs it.

Eventually, he rolls over on his back and lies down and just looks up at me. His eyes are red from all the crying. His face is still wet, and he just looks broken.

Then it's like a spark goes off. He gets up on one knee and frames my face in his hands. "Marry me."

"Baby, we can't in either my time or yours."

He shakes his head. "I don't care about the marriage certificate. It's just a piece of paper. Marry me and be my wife in all the ways that matter, in my heart, body, and soul. I will love you until the day I die, Ivy, but I'm going to fight like hell to make sure that is fifty years from now and not eight. Marry me. We can bring Brian and my parents and have my dad marry us. Please, beautiful, I need to bind you to me in every way possible."

He's offering me everything I want, and the fact that he mentioned bringing Brian here shows he knows me better than anyone. "I love you, David. Yes, I will marry you." The second I say yes, his lips are on mine, and he has me on my back on the floor. He pulls his shirt off me, and before it even hits the floor, his cock is inside me and filling me up.

He's not in a hurry. He's lazily thrusting in and out of me just like that day in my bed. Again, he's pouring his heart out to me, telling me how much he loves me. How he doesn't know what he did to deserve me and how it will only ever be me.

His sweet words wash over me, and before I know it, we are both coming at the same time, and it's just magical. This is what they truly mean by making love.

When we are done, he pulls out and scoops me up and lays me back down in bed before walking over to his bag and pulling something out. He comes back to bed and takes my left hand and places a ring on my finger. It's a simple ring with diamonds in a swirl pattern.

"I saw this when I was overseas and bought it for you. The swirl makes me think of the time passing when we move from now to your time. I knew then I wanted to marry you, and I wanted this to be your ring." I burst into tears, and he holds me tight as we both fall asleep.

∞∞∞

The next morning, his parents pull me aside and say they want to do a little something for his birthday since it was a few weeks ago. They ask if I can get him out of the house for a bit, and I agree.

I find David in the piano room sitting on the bench but not playing. I sit on his lap, and he wraps his arms around me.

"So, you promised me a real date when you got home. I'd like to cash that in now." I smile at him.

"Oh yeah, what did you have in mind?" His eyes rake over my face as though he is trying to memorize every detail.

"I was thinking of lunch at one of my favorite spots."

"Where might that be?"

"How about you drive, and I'll give you directions."

He smiles. "Deal."

We get in the car and head west out of Nashville to Loveless Café. It's much smaller now, but it will grow over the next fifty years.

David parks the car and gets out and opens my door. He takes my hand, and we walk in. I brace myself for what I know is coming.

We step inside the door, and everyone recognizes him, asking for an autograph. He looks at me with a strained look on his face, and I just laugh. "You can do what you do because of the fans, so you better sign those autographs, buddy."

He signs twelve autographs, and I take two photos of him with fans before we can be seated. He pulls out my chair for me and everything. Once we are seated, he just looks at me.

"What?" I ask.

"You are amazing, that's what. I haven't dated much, but any time I did, a situation like that didn't end well."

"What do you mean?"

"Well, one girl wanted people to pay attention to her, and when they didn't, she told them she was my fiancée. I corrected her real quick and left her there alone. The other girl got so mad at me for signing autographs on a date. But you get me. You were perfectly content to help them take photos and form a bit of a line so I didn't miss anyone."

"I guess I just see things differently. Your fans are everything. The moment they go away, you become irrelevant. I know this is your dream, so I'm going to do everything to support you in it."

"You are amazing. I love you, beautiful." He takes my hand with the ring he put on it last night and kisses the palm, then kisses the ring.

"I love you, baby. You have no idea how much."

After lunch, we stop by a jewelry store to find a ring for him.

Something simple but a little more than just a plain gold band. It has to be fate because we find the perfect one that kind of matches mine with the swirl design, and it's his size so we can take it home tonight.

"I also want you to have the dream wedding dress, so I'm going to have my mom take you shopping for one, but I'll handle everything else, okay?" he says on the way home, and I agree.

When we get home, both his parents are waiting for us by the front door, and they wish him a happy birthday. They take us out to the backyard where they have a table with gifts from family and friends and a small table with a guitar cake. They have him sit down, and they sing "Happy Birthday."

When his mom asks me to take his photo since I'm the photographer in the bunch, I instantly know what this photo is going to look like. I've stared at it several times over the past two years, trying to figure out when and where it came from, but no one seemed to know. He sits down beside the cake, and I get the camera ready. He takes two fingers and tries to sneak some icing, but I catch him with his finger in his mouth, and he's giving me *my* look. The one filled with love, lust, and passion. I snap what is to become an iconic photo before handing the camera to his mom and going over to sit on his lap.

I shoot up a little prayer of thanks that my grandfather taught me how to use his old cameras growing up. He instilled a love of photography in me but always preferred his old cameras to the new point and shoot ones.

"I've stared at the photo I just took at least a hundred times in the past two years trying to figure out when it was taken. Baby, it's going next to my bed, and I want it blown up and on the wall in our room," I whisper into his ear.

"Okay, beautiful, anything you want," he says and kisses me.

A little bit later, she is off to the side, talking to his parents, and I'm just staring off to where the memorial garden will eventually be. Thinking how hard those two years were and whether

I could do fifty or more with that kind of pain. How does a person put one foot in front of the other, knowing they will never see the love of their life again? At least I knew he'd be there in my arms, in my bed, in me still, at the end of the two years.

I'm pulled from my thoughts when I hear his mom give a happy squeal and hug him. When I look over at them, I see her rushing over to me, and she pulls me into a hug. "I can't wait to take you dress shopping. I knew when I saw you that day that you were it for my David. He looks at you the same way his dad looks at me," his mom says.

Then she pulls away and looks at my ring. "Oh, it so beautiful," she says with tears in her eyes.

David and his dad walk over to me and hug me.

"Tomorrow, we are heading out for a few days and bringing back her family, then you can go shopping," David says.

"Oh, I can't wait to meet them. Please let us work on the details while you are gone!" his mom says. "Any special requests?"

"No, I just can't wait to be married." I smile up at David.

Chapter 13

Ivy

The next morning, we are trying to catch our breath after coming through the rocks. We left early, so the road was deserted. We walk hand in hand to my house, and I smile up at David in his hat and sunglasses. He smiles back and runs his finger over my ring. It seems to comfort him. He has been doing it more and more since yesterday.

We walk in the door of my house, and I yell, "Honey, I'm home!"

I hear a muffled, "Oh, shit," and two thumps as Brian and Kevin fall off the couch.

"Oh, shit." I pull David around, so his back is to the guys. "Kevin's here," I whisper to David. He still has the hat and sunglasses on, so I doubt Kevin has a clue.

We stand there and don't move until Brian comes running up. "Kevin asked me to marry him, and I said YES!!" he screams.

David and I laugh, and I hold out my left hand and say, "David asked me to marry him, and I said YES!" I say just like he had, and his face drops.

"Ivy, you can't!" He starts, and I put my hand up.

"It won't be legal on paper, but it will be in every way that matters. He knows about Anna, but he'll do it. We need this," I say more hushed. "Now, what do we do about Kevin because I came here with plans to drag you with me to be at the wedding in a few days!"

"We tell him," David says. "He's important to Brian, which makes him important to you, which makes him important to me," David says to me, and I melt.

Brian's hand goes over his heart. "He's really amazing, isn't he?" Brian sighs, and I laugh.

Then I take a deep breath. "Okay, let's do this."

The three of us walk into the living room where Kevin stands. David holds my hand in his again, rubbing his thumb over my ring.

I smile at Kevin and just dive on in. "So, other than what I've said, what has Brian told you about the guy I'm seeing?" I ask.

He shrugs. "Just that he's super busy so you guys don't get to see each other often, and he just got back from overseas. He says you are crazy in love with him, and he treats you like a princess, and that's all I need to know."

"What we are going to tell you cannot *ever* leave this house, okay?" I tell him. I give him my hard look.

"She's not kidding. No one would believe you anyway," Brian says.

Kevin nods and walks up to Brian. "I just asked you to spend the rest of your life with me, and you said yes. Your secrets are mine; your burdens are mine. Don't keep me in the dark. I want all of you," Kevin says to Brian.

I look up at David, and even though he still has his sunglasses on, I can feel his eyes on me. He leans down and whispers into my ear, "The same goes for you, beautiful. I want all of you, even the dark parts." Those pesky butterflies are going crazy again, and I'm pretty sure I'll need to find a new set of panties soon.

"Okay," Brian starts off by taking a deep breath. "Well, you know my obsession with time travel, so that's no secret. Almost three years ago now, I had a theory and wanted to test it. Ivy, being the kick-ass friend she is, agreed with my crazy plan. In the process, she met the love of her life."

Kevin nods and looks at David. "And that would be you?" he asks, and David nods.

"The thing is they can't ever truly be together because my theory worked," Brian says, and Kevin starts to look confused.

"Kevin, do you believe in fate?" I ask.

"Of course, I do. It brought me Brian and you."

"I didn't until that day Brian is talking about. Do you know why my parents named me Ivy?"

He shakes his head, so I continue. "They named me after Ivy Hill," I say.

He smiles. "I guess they are huge David Miller fans, huh? But I mean, who around here isn't?" Kevin says.

"It's okay, baby, take off the hat and sunglasses," I look over at David and say. He nods, and ever so carefully, David removes his hat and then his sunglasses and looks up into Kevin's eyes. We all watch Kevin. At first, he doesn't react, then he laughs.

"Oh, this is a good joke, guys. He looks so much like David too. You guys did good on this joke."

Not one of us moves or laughs, and Kevin notices that.

"It's not easy to wrap your head around it. I get it. I couldn't until Ivy brought me here the first time," David says, and Kevin's eyes go wide. David has a classic voice that is very recognizable.

"It's hard when Ivy tells me things that will happen that I don't like, but she always soothes it over with the good that comes after. I don't know if I truly die on that August day or if I find a way to be here with my heart and soul, but I plan on fighting until my last breath to do so."

"When I stepped through the rocks that day, I ended up in 1957. Fate took hold of me, and before I knew it, there was David. We spent ten days together, and when I had to come back home, my heart and soul stayed in 1957. Shortly after I left, he named the house Ivy Hill. Brian and I spent hours making sure there were no ripples in history, and seven months later, I got the chance to go back. We got to spend a whole month together between my time there and him coming here. I came home, and a day later, he got his Army orders."

I pause and take a deep breath before continuing. "He got back just a few days ago, and he asked me to marry him. It won't be legal. It will just be us and our vows and our rings, but I need you both there. You are the only family I have, and that means everything to me."

Kevin finally turns and sits down, and Brian sits beside him on the couch, rubbing his arm. "But he gets married and has a kid?" Kevin asks.

David sits down and pulls me on to his lap. "I promised Ivy I won't do anything to change history, so I will marry her on paper only. My son will be born, and the second she is pregnant, the marriage is done. I won't touch her again. I'll do what history says and head to California and make movies to keep busy until she files for divorce. The only thing that I still need to work out is Ivy. She is refusing to see me for those four years, but I don't know if I can take it," he says and gets choked up.

Kevin nods. "I get it. She doesn't want to be the other woman, and it will be too hard to see her in any way. Think about how you would feel if the situation was flipped? Would you be able to see her and act like she isn't the love of your life?" Kevin says.

"No, I wouldn't," David answers, taking in a shaky breath, and he starts rubbing my ring again.

"Please, will you guys come to the wedding? It's just a few days, and it might help with the final plans. It's going to be small, just you guys and his parents in his backyard, but you can see Ivy Hill in the before state of what it is now."

"I'm pretty sure this is still some massive joke, but I'll go along with this. I'm okay to be proven wrong." Kevin nods, but

I can only imagine the conversation he and Brian will have tonight.

I jump up and hug him. “Okay, now so Brian, the cake photo? It was celebrating his birthday a little late just yesterday. Oh, and I was the one who took that photo.”

Brian laughs. “That explains the look on his face!”

“Yes, I want it printed out for my collection. Now I’m going to feed you all while Kevin and David get to know each other, and then tomorrow, I am stealing Brian to help with some super-secret wedding-related things.”

“Sounds good. When are we planning to go?” Kevin asks.

“Day after tomorrow. We will leave once it’s dark,” I say. “Also, Brian, did you find out who owns that lot with the stones?”

Brian and I had a last-minute thought before I left this time. We wanted to buy the lot with the stone and the time door so we could be sure it was left untouched. Brian promised to do some digging while I was gone.

Brian’s face goes pale. “You won’t believe me.”

“Just tell me.”

“I do,” says David. “I bought it after I got home from visiting you here. I wanted to make sure there wasn’t ever anything to stop you from visiting me.”

“Okay, then what happened to it after he died?” I ask, cringing.

“Well, it was placed in the trust with all his other assets. I did a little digging, and apparently, there are strict orders that it is never to be sold or even touched. They have no idea why, but I guess they plan to honor David’s wishes.”

“Well, that’s good.” I turn to David. “I had planned to buy it, but I guess you beat me to it.” I laugh.

We spend the rest of the evening talking and laughing. I look around, really taking it in. Everyone important to me is in one room, and I never want this day to end.

∞∞∞

The next morning, Brian and I get ready to head out. "Are you sure you will be okay?" I ask David for the third time.

"I promise, beautiful. I won't leave the house. Kevin and I are going to talk and watch some TV." I see the twinkle in his eyes.

"Men and their TVs," I grumble playfully.

I take a deep breath and hand David a cell phone. It's a prepaid phone Brian and I keep in the house for emergencies ever since he dropped his and ran over it with his car.

"What's this?" he asks.

"It's a phone. It has my number, Brian's, and Kevin's in it. I want you to keep this on you at all times, okay? And when I text you, please answer back. Kevin can give you a rundown of how it works."

Pulling out my phone, I send him a quick I love you text. His phone dings, and he looks at it, and his eyes soften. "I love you too. I know you and Brian are going to be out doing wedding stuff, but having this link to you still means everything." He leans in and kisses me. "Thank you."

Then Brian pulls me away, and we get in the car. "Where to?" he asks.

"I need the sexiest white lingerie for my wedding night we can find. And then I need to have something custom made from a friend of mine."

"On it," he says, and we head to the store.

Then I text David.

Me: God, baby, I miss you so much already!

I wait to see those three little dots come up and let out the breath I didn't know I was holding when they do.

David: Me too, beautiful. Kevin and I are watching some show called American Pickers.

Me: Oh yeah, we are all kind of obsessed with that show. The stuff they find would be new to you.

David: Yeah, it's amusing to watch.

Me: I love you. We are pulling into the store now. I'll text you again in a bit.

David: I love you too, please stay safe.

Me: I will. I promise.

As we walk in, Brian asks, "Looking for anything specific?"

"Well, I want it to be white, and I want it to be super sexy. Not like anything he would see back home. I did a quick online search, and the lingerie in the 1960s looks like what we'd wear as nightgowns now. Not what we consider sexy."

It only takes us thirty minutes to find the perfect outfit. It's a white lace bra and thong that leaves nothing to the imagination. It has a matching see-through lace, what they call a nightgown that goes to the floor. You can see through the whole thing, and it's open in the front with a belt kind of like a robe that hides nothing.

We grab some lunch. Then we head over to my friend Ginger's place. I've worked with her a few times over the years doing photos for her websites. Ginger makes custom wood signs and always has a section of finished wood on hand and a steady hand, so I know she can pull this off today.

I tell her what I want and that it's a gift for someone but more of a private joke. She shrugs and gets to work. It only takes her an hour to get it done, and then she uses a hair dryer to set and dry the paint.

When we are heading out, Ginger wraps the sign up in some burlap for me, and I pay her double. She starts to refuse, but I insist. It's my way of saying thank you.

We head home and spend the evening with our men. David makes love to me that night, and something just feels different. It feels right and perfect.

∞∞∞

The next day, we are all packing our bags. Kevin and Brian spend the day getting a few outfits together that wouldn't be out of place in 1960. I pack up my items, and once night falls, we head out.

We get to the rocks, and Kevin looks a bit leery. I look over, and say, "We will go first, okay?" and he nods.

I look over at David, and he gives me one long kiss and takes my hand. "On three?" he says, just as he has every time we have gone through before.

I nod. "On three."

Then he counts. "One... two... three." And we touch the rock and are pulled and then pushed into 1960 again. We move off to the side, and I fall to my knees, dizzier and weaker than I have been before.

"Ivy, what's wrong?" David asks, a bit panicked. He's on his knees beside me and holding me in an instant. I focus on taking deep breaths.

"Please talk to me. Are you okay, Ivy? God, please talk to me," he says as he rubs my back.

"I'm okay. Just give me a minute," I whisper. He doesn't relax or let me go.

I hear Brian and Kevin land, and David says, "Brian, over here."

Brian is on the ground at my other side in an instant. "I think she just jumped too close together. This is her third time in less than a week. I think she needs to stay here a bit longer this time and let her body adjust," he says. I start to feel better and sit up a bit and lean on David.

"That's exactly what it is," I say.

"Well, you won't ever hear me complain about getting more time with you. In fact, I plan to take you on our honeymoon after we are married. I was going to try to convince you to give me more time anyway," David says.

"Fate steps in again." I smile. All three guys chuckle. Then a weird thought pops into my head.

I look up and notice Kevin looking around and bouncing on the balls of his feet.

"What's on your mind, Kevin?" I ask him to take a few more minutes to rest.

"Well, not going to lie. I didn't believe this whole time travel thing. I don't know what just happened, but if we are in 1960, I feel like I should have asked a few more questions."

"Like what?" I ask him.

"Well, being gay is a crime in 1960..." Keven trails off as Brian grabs his hand.

"David, how will your parents react to Brian and Kevin being a couple?" I ask.

"They will accept him and love them both because they are your family, and you are about to become my family. My uncle, my mom's brother, is gay. We don't visit him much now. We don't like to draw attention to him, but they accepted him and his partner, and I know they will accept Brian and Kevin too."

"Ivy, what do David's parents know about you? Why do they think you can't legally get married?" David asks.

"Oh, ugh well, we told them we were having problems with

my birth certificate and all. I think his mom was excited to throw a party, but she has been giving me this look, so just be careful what you say, okay?"

They agree, and I take a deep breath.

"Okay." I sigh. "Time's a wasting, and I want to lie down."

David chuckles as he helps me up, and he keeps his arm around me the whole walk to Ivy Hill.

We walk in, and his parents are in the kitchen drinking what looks like coffee. His mom rushes over to hug us.

"Oh, you're back. I can't wait to fill you in on everything. Honey, you look pale. Are you okay?" she asks me.

I smile. "Yeah, just a long day traveling. I'm a bit motion sick, so I will be turning in early."

"Oh, you poor dear, of course!" Helen says.

I introduce his mom and dad to Brian. "This is Brian. He's my best friend, and he has been like a brother to me. And that is Kevin, his fiancé. They are my only real family," I say, then watch his parents closely.

Brian kicks in. "We know we can't legally be married, but we are doing like Ivy and David. We will be married in every way that matters."

Helen and James smile and hug them. They congratulate them and welcome them into the family just as David said they would.

"Let me get you guys upstairs to your room so I can get Ivy to bed. She needs her rest because tomorrow, she is going to go pick out her dress, and then we get married in just forty-eight hours."

I swear I've never seen him so happy.

He grabs my bag, and we head upstairs. He shows them to a suite at the other end of the hall and then picks me up and carries me to bed. He takes care of me as if I'm the most precious thing in the world, and I'm going to break. He removes my pants, shirt, and bra and then slips one of his shirts over me. He then strips down to his underwear and climbs into bed with me.

He pulls me up to his side, and I snuggle up with my head on his shoulder. "Baby, please don't go in my bag. I have something for you for our wedding, but I want it to be a surprise, so no snooping," I say as I close my eyes.

"I promise. While you, my mom, Brian, and Kevin are out wedding dress shopping, my dad and I are going out. I have a few surprises for you too."

"Mmm, make love to me, baby," I say and reach down to wrap my hand around his cock.

He sucks in a ragged breath. "Beautiful, I will never deny you, but you needing rest is more important tonight. I was also thinking, maybe we don't have sex again until our wedding night. It's only two days, and I want to make the day perfect for you."

"Mmm, okay, but you will have to be the strong one here. My willpower isn't that great around you."

He laughs. "Go to sleep; I got you." That's the last thing I hear before drifting off.

Chapter 14

David

I'm standing next to my dad, and I can't seem to stand still. Always waiting on this woman, and I will happily do it every day of forever. Today is the happiest day of my life; my sweet Ivy agreed to marry me, to be my wife, the keeper of my heart and soul, and in turn, she will trust me with hers.

Her, my mom, and Brian went wedding dress shopping yesterday. We wanted to keep it quiet, so I pulled a few strings by saying a family member was getting married. Ivy gave my mom an idea of what she wanted, and my mom had twenty dresses set aside in a private room for the three of them. My mom says Ivy fell in love with the third one she tried on.

Kevin went with my dad and me to set up some last-minute things for Ivy and run some errands for my mom, like picking up the flowers and a small cake. My mom did an amazing job setting up this back part of the garden for the wedding.

I'm taking it all in when I see Ivy and Brian walk out of the house, and I can't breathe. She is in the most beautiful dress I've ever seen. Tight at the top and loose and flowy at the bottom and only a small amount of tulle, but what I love is the lace all over and how it flows into a short train. Her hair is done in a hairstyle that I recognize from her time. It's curled and pulled over one side of her shoulders. She looks like an angel, and I've never seen her more beautiful.

I don't even realize I'm crying until she is in front of me and reaches up to wipe my tears away.

"Ivy, my sweet Ivy, you look so beautiful it hurts to breathe."

"This this how I will always remember you. The look on your face, the tears in your eyes, and how incredibly sexy you look in this suit," she says. I've heard the camera's shutter, so I know my mom has taken a few photos. Then my dad performs the ceremony, and we say our vows.

I slip her wedding ring on. It's a simple band with a swirl design and a few diamonds. Then she slips my wedding ring on with the same swirl design. I vow to her and myself that no matter what comes our way, I will never take this ring off.

We spend some time celebrating with our family. There are a beautiful cake and my mom's amazing cooking. My mom keeps taking photos of Ivy and me, and I can't wait to get my hands on them. We celebrate until the sun goes down. My mom and dad eventually head back to the cottage, and Brian and Kevin head to their room.

I can't seem to keep my hands off her, but when we get to our room, she pulls back.

"I want to give you your wedding presents first."

I nod, getting a little choked up and nervous about the ones I have for her.

She goes into her bag and pulls out a small box the size of a shoebox. She seems a little nervous, so I know this means a lot to her. She hands me the box, and I open it.

"These are all the letters I wrote to you when you were overseas."

I get choked up and kiss her, but then I laugh.

I hand her a box too. "I guess we had the same idea." The box is full of letters I wrote to her. There is one from almost every night.

She smiles. "I'm going to save these to read until I get home." I agree to do the same.

She reaches into her bag again and pulls out a flat item covered in what looks like a potato sack. She hands it to me, and when I open it, I tear up and start shaking. It's the perfect gift she could have ever given me.

On a piece of painted wood is hand-drawn wording that I can't stop staring at. "David and Ivy Miller" and at the bottom "est. 1960."

"This is the closest I could get to taking your last name."

"It's perfect, so perfect, and I will hang it in here next to some photos of us," I whisper, and she leans in and kisses me so tenderly my eyes tear up again. I am always crying around this woman. Only for her.

I pull out my second gift to her. It's the cake photo she loves, and I framed it for her. Pointing at the nightstand, I show her I have a matching one there.

This time, her eyes water. "I have one last gift for you."

"Beautiful, this is too much. You have given me the best wedding gifts possible."

She has a wicked smile on her face. "Oh, this one is just as much for me as it is for you." She turns around so her back is facing me, and says, "But you have to unwrap it first."

I'm instantly hard and can't unbutton her dress fast enough. I have to see what she has on under it.

When I'm done with the last button, she turns back to face me. Taking a deep breath, she lets the dress fall to the ground.

For the first time ever, I come in my pants without so much as a touch. My orgasm is short and almost buckles my knees. After a minute, I can fully take her in.

Under her dress is the sexiest white lingerie I've ever seen. I'm sure this is from her time because I don't think they make anything like it now. She is in a sexy tight white bra covered in lace, and I can see the outline of her nipples through the bra, and it's trimmed in the same color blue as my car.

I run my eyes down her body and stop on the barely-there white lace panties. She turns to show me what she calls a thong. It frames her luscious ass perfectly. Fuck, I've never seen anything so sexy in my life.

As she steps out of the dress, I walk toward her and lean in to kiss her. She instantly takes control of the kiss, and I'm happy to let her. She pushes me backward a bit and only breaks the kiss to take my shirt off. I unbutton my pants, and as they fall to the ground, she keeps pushing me backward.

The couch in our room hits the back of my legs, and she pauses long enough to pull my underwear down and then pushes me down on the couch, giving me another up-close look at her, and my god, I will never forget this sight for as long as I live. When we are apart, I know this is the image I'll think of when my fist is doing a poor job of fucking my cock.

Ivy still has on her sexy outfit when she gets on her knees in front of me. I try to pull her onto my lap. "It's your turn to come, beautiful."

She shakes her head. "All still a part of your wedding present, so sit back and enjoy, baby."

Then her mouth is on my cock, and I toss my head back as my hips buck into her mouth. I could come again already, but I fight for control because I want to enjoy this. The head of my cock hits the back of her throat, and my hips jerk again. She slides her mouth back up my shaft, and her tongue slides on the bottom of my cock.

I groan. "Ivy, my sweet Ivy, your mouth feels so good, beautiful. Oh, god, I'm so close." I clench my jaw. Then she starts sucking harder, and she tugs at my balls. My hips jerk again, and I'm coming down the back of her throat, screaming her name as my hips buck out of control.

Once I'm done, she gives my cock one more hard suck before letting it slip out of her mouth and looking up at me.

"Fuck, beautiful girl, that was amazing. Thank you for that."

With a smile, she stands and then sits down to straddle me. She kisses me as I run my hands up and down her sides. Even after two orgasms, just being able to touch her like this is getting me hard and ready for her again. After a few minutes of kissing, she reaches down and moves the scrap of fabric doubling as her panties to the side and slides down my cock slowly. I have to grip the side of the couch so as not to grab her hips and slam into her.

She is enjoying being in charge tonight. I see it on her face, and I want to give her this. When she's fully seated on my cock, she leans down and kisses me again, and she tightens her pussy around me. "Fuck, baby, that tight pussy of yours has a death grip on me!" I groan out.

She slides up and down my cock slowly. "Baby, you feel so good. I can feel every inch of you in me. And ... ahhh," she moans against my neck. I wrap my arms around her waist and pull her as close to me as possible, not wanting an inch of space between us.

I angle my hips to hit her clit on every thrust, and then she tenses up and shatters around me. Her pussy locks on to my cock and pulses, and my climax crashes into me. I yell out her name and come deep inside her.

At that moment, I wish so badly my seed would take hold and give us a child. I want that with her, a piece of us, but I could never leave her to raise that baby alone. Since neither of us can spend more than a few weeks in either time, how would that be fair?

∞∞∞

The next day, Brian and Kevin say they are going to explore Nashville before heading home that night, and I take Ivy on our honeymoon. We get the airport, and we head toward a private plane a friend of mine is letting us borrow. Ivy loves it, and I love that on the several-hour ride, I got to have her three times. Ivy made some joke about officially being members of the mile-high club now.

I take her to Hawaii just as I promised I would. I rented a private cottage on the beach and a car for us to get around in. We spend a week making love and visiting many of the sights that she has always dreamed of. Then we flew to California because my girl wanted to go to Yosemite National Park and see the Wawona Tree. It's a massive tree carved out where we can drive through it. We are even able to get our photo taken by a sweet couple with the car under the tree and us leaning on the front of the car.

Ivy tells me that tree will fall in 1969 in a bad storm, just nine years from now. We then drive to Calaveras State Park and see the Pioneer Cabin Tree, a smaller version of the Wawona, and we get our photo taken there too. I love seeing her face when she gets to see something she never would be able to in her time. There is no greater feeling than being able to provide that for her. I've been wearing a disguise most of the honeymoon, and we haven't been recognized, so it's been our heaven.

We are now in Maryland sitting at a park watching a couple with a newborn baby. My Ivy has tears in her eyes, and it's not from the baby they are playing with. The couple is her grandparents, who raised her and have since passed in her time, and the baby is her father.

We are sitting on a bench, and I have one arm around her and the other in my lap. I'm holding her hand, running my thumb over her wedding ring. I do this because I still can't believe she is mine, and that she's here. I just need that reassurance that it's real.

Her grandparents get up and walk by us, and her grandmother notices the tears and sees the wedding rings. "Don't worry, sweetheart. You will have your own soon. It can take time."

Ivy smiles. "Oh, we just got married. I just thought it was so sweet to see you two playing with your son like that. I don't think my parents even cared enough to, and I can't wait to do it with my kids."

"Oh, sweetheart, how long are you two in town for?" her grandmother asks.

"We leave tomorrow. We have to get back home," she says.

Her grandma looks over at her grandpa, then looks at me again. I know then she recognizes me.

"Well, if you don't have plans, I'd love to have you over for dinner," her grandma says.

Ivy takes a shaky breath and looks at me. I know she wants to, but she's scared I'll be recognized.

"We'd love to," I say since I know they already know who I am. Ivy's eyes get big.

"We are that red car there. Would you like to follow us over? I have a roast in the oven now," her grandma says.

I smile. "Sounds perfect."

Ivy and I get in our car, and I follow them while Ivy lays into me.

"What are you thinking? They will recognize you if they haven't already. Oh god, David, we are in so much trouble! They never once mentioned having dinner with you! We can't change history!"

"Yes, she recognizes me, but I also know how much having

this time with them means to you, so I think it's worth it." I won't admit I wasn't thinking about history and send up a silent prayer that this doesn't blow up in our faces.

Ivy groans. "Oh god, she said she has a roast in the oven. It's fate. I love this recipe so damn much, but I never got it from her before she died."

I can't help but smile. This honeymoon has been perfect.

After pulling into the drive behind her grandparents, we follow them inside. I watch as Ivy takes in everything in the house. She lingers on a few items, so I know she remembers them.

They go to put their son, Ivy's dad, in his crib for a nap.

I walk beside her, and whisper in her ear, "Is this the house they raised you in?"

"Yeah, almost everything is in the same place too," she whispers back, but I can still hear the emotion in her voice.

They join us in the living room, and we all sit down. After a moment of silence, I take a deep breath and take my sunglasses off. "I know you guys know who I am, but I'm asking please not to make this public. We aren't legally married, and the press doesn't know about Ivy," I say.

Her grandparents and Ivy look at me.

"Well, first, you should call me John, and this is my wife, Cecille. You can trust we won't say anything," he says.

Ivy looks at them with tears in her eyes again. "My parents... weren't great, and they had me at home and never filed the paperwork. I had no idea until we tried to get married, and there is no record of me. We are working on it, but for now, we had our own ceremony with vows, the dress, and just a few family members."

John and Cecille nod. It's the best way to make them understand, but I know when the news of Anna and me getting married breaks, I'll have to come back and set things straight with them. For Ivy.

We talk for a bit, and Ivy has questions and listens to stories I know she has heard before. I share stories with them from touring and my music. When her grandmother goes to the kitchen to finish making dinner, Ivy goes with her. I know she is excited to cook with her again. I watch her walking into the kitchen with the biggest smile on her face, and I know I'm wearing one too.

"You love that girl, don't you?" John says.

"Yes, sir, with all my heart. If she asked me to give all this up today, I wouldn't even think twice. I'd be done."

John looks at me for a minute. "But she hasn't asked?"

"No, and she won't. Ivy always reminds me my fans are why I am able to do what I do. She encourages me to sign autographs and take photos and talk with them and is content to watch from the background."

John nods. "You know, when I saw you two, I had to do a double take because she is the spitting image of my mother. What is her last name?"

I think quickly, knowing I can't tell him the truth, and say, "Vaughn," giving him my aunt's maiden name.

"Are you having a lot of trouble getting the paperwork done for her?" he asks.

"I'm sure I wouldn't if I put my name to it, but she wants to do this quietly. She doesn't want to alert her family of where she is just yet. I guess you can say it's a bit complicated."

We sit down for dinner, and Ivy was right. This roast is amazing. She has this dreamy look on her face all through dinner as we talk about anything and everything. After dinner, she walks over to a table in the entryway and stares at it. John notices and tells her the story about how his mom saw it in a store and wanted it. His dad picked up odd jobs and saved up to get it for their anniversary.

Cecille hands Ivy the recipe for the roast and gives us both big hugs.

"Come back anytime. No notice is needed," Cecille says, and John agrees.

We get in the car, and we make it down the street before Ivy bursts into tears. I drive back to the hotel, rubbing her back. When we park, she is still crying, so I pull her onto my lap.

"That was the best thing anyone could ever do for me," she says. "Thank you, David. I love you so much."

"I love you too, beautiful. You are my whole world." I put on my hat and sunglasses and get the room key and then carry her to our room.

We spend the night making love.

∞∞∞

The next day, we get back to Ivy Hill. On the flight, Ivy tells me stories from her grandparents and of her childhood. She avoids her parents, and I won't force the subject just yet. I know they are dead, and knowing they can't hurt her is all I need.

I also ask her who else she wants to meet or talk to or see that she can't now, and she gets a wicked smile and says Johnny Cash. I let out a growl, and she laughs.

"He's not my type, baby, but I love his music, and his and June's story too. I'd love to hear him sing in person. He died before I could go to a concert of his."

I agree to make it happen.

"There is one more thing."

"Name it, and it's yours."

"There is a photo of your time in the Army. You're sitting on a stool in uniform, playing the guitar, and you are looking off to the side?"

I nod, remembering that day.

"I want that picture blown up and framed to be placed in Ivy Hill."

"Done." I smile. My girl is easy to please.

When we get home, the picture of me eating my birthday cake a few weeks earlier is waiting in our room. I stare at it, and I know why she loves it. The look I was giving her is like I was fucking her with my eyes. She shows me where on the wall she wants it hung, and I make it happen.

We have one week left together, and I try not to think about that and just live in the moment. I take her out to dinner twice, and we do some shopping. We spend the days out by the pool and make love on every surface of the house again.

Chapter 15

Ivy

It's now the day before I have to go home, and we just finished dinner. He picks me up and carries me upstairs, which makes me squeal and laugh. I love it when he does this. He sets me down on the bed and kneels in front of me and just puts his head in my lap. We sit there for several minutes, me playing with his hair, and I soak up every detail.

After a few minutes, he looks up, and I see all the same emotions I feel shining back in his face—love, pain, passion, need. Without a word, he stands up and takes my shirt off and then takes his off while I remove my bra.

He just stands in front of me, allowing me to take in my fill of his toned chest while I'm sure he does the same. He takes one shaky breath and then removes his pants and underwear before gently laying me down to remove mine. We move to the center of the bed and lie on our sides, facing each other with our legs entwined. My hand rests on his cheek and his hand on my hip. We stare into each other's eyes, not saying a word.

He gently pushes some hair out of my face and leans in to kiss me. It's so tender and sweet, and I get lost in his kiss. His hand moves down my side to my leg, then pulls it over his hip. He scoots even closer to me and then gently slides into me, causing me to gasp.

I lock my leg around his hip, and he cups my breasts. He

continues to thrust in slow, firm strokes while his thumbs run over the hard peaks of my nipples. He never breaks eye contact from me unless it's to kiss me. His eyes tell me everything I need to know—how much he loves me, how much he needs me, and how happy he is that I'm his.

His hand makes its way down to my clit and starts stroking it slowly while he tells me how much he loves me in the sweetest ways, how much I turn him on, and how much I mean to him. But that's not what sends me over the edge.

"Every time I see you, I fall in love with you all over again. But this moment here inside you and you staring into my soul is the one I will never forget. This is the moment I know you were made for me," he says and then kisses me with a rough passion.

"I need you to come for me, beautiful, because as much as I love being inside you and having your pussy squeeze my cock like this, I love to watch you come and give yourself to me even more."

He pinches my clit, and that's when I fall over the edge. Grabbing his shoulder, I arch my back toward him, and my legs lock around him as I come. Just as I'm coming down from my climax, he tenses and spurts his cum inside me, and I come all over again. I swear even when I'm relaxing, he's still coming. It's so much that our mixed juices are leaking out of me, covering my thighs and running down his cock.

It was so sweet that I hadn't realized I'd started to cry until I feel the wetness on my cheeks and see the same on his. I reach up to wipe away his tears, but they keep coming.

"I can't marry Anna. How do you expect me to kiss her or even share her bed?" he whispers.

"You will." I frame his face with my hand and wipe away more tears. "For me, you have to until she becomes pregnant, which happens on your honeymoon." I try to force a smile. "She will give you a son, David. He's a great guy, and he needs to be born."

"I'd rather have a son with you." He is still whispering.

"I need you to promise me, baby. I want you to myself, I do, but it's so important we don't change history. Please promise me."

He nods.

"I need your words."

"I promise."

"Stay on friendly terms with Anna and see your son as much as possible, okay?"

More tears run down his face, and it breaks my heart.

"Will you come back before we are married? Please promise me you will," he whispers again

I lean in to kiss him gently. "Yes, that wedding is a good year away, so I promise I will be back. I wish I could stay, but people will miss me. I have to build our life back there so maybe, just maybe we can pull this off."

He takes my face in his hands and kisses me passionately. I feel more of his tears on my cheek. "*You* are my wife in every way that matters. You own my heart, my body, and my soul. *Nothing* will change that. Tell me you know *nothing* can change that."

I force a smile. "I know."

"She will only be my wife on paper, and that is it. Please come to California to visit. I'll get a house out there for us. I'll get a plane, and you can use it to get from here to California."

I'm shaking my head before he finishes. "I can't, David. I won't interfere with your marriage; I won't be the other woman."

"But *she* is the other woman. You came first!"

"If the situation were reversed, how would you feel walking into my marriage, having to see that guy, hear people talk about my husband, and know it's not you?"

"I don't know which would hurt more, that or not seeing you

for four years. Four *years*!! Those two years were the worst, and I almost didn't make it!"

"I know it won't be easy, but once this is done, you will be mine for good, okay? Brian and I will throw ourselves into research and planning our future. I promise to watch everything you do. But in return, I need something from you."

"Anything, beautiful, anything."

"I need you to keep your promise and not do the drugs. It's going to be hard. We will both be in a dark place, but if I gave you a date for the next time I'm here when those four years are over, we can count down together. I just need you to stay away from the drugs."

"I promise, baby. If there is even the slightest chance we can pull off our forever, I won't do anything to stop it." He kisses me again.

"You know so much of what I see in my research of your future makes sense now. I'll be digging into it all again."

We both fall asleep clinging to each other, willing our time not to be over yet.

The next morning, I wake up and stretch only to find myself alone in bed. I sit up and listen to see if maybe he's in the bathroom. When I hear footsteps in the hall, and the door opens, I look over to find him shirtless and carrying a tray of food.

"I thought we'd do breakfast in bed," he says, setting the tray on the bed. "And I have this for you." He pulls out the framed photo I had asked for of him playing guitar in his Army uniform.

A huge smile spreads across my face as I stare at the photo. "I love it. I want to put it downstairs on the wall by the stairs so everyone can see it. I am so damn proud of you, and that photo represents how strong we are."

He smiles. "I agree, beautiful. Now let's eat."

We make love and shower together, which seems to be our tradition when we are getting ready to part ways. He asks to walk me to the stones, and I agree. I give him some of the stones he needs to travel and tell him it's only for emergencies, but I want him to have a way to me if he needs me.

We get to the stones, and he stands there, hugging me.

"I know we were meant to meet. There are too many things that make sense once it happens to us. We are meant to be. I just know it," I tell him

With a nod, he starts to rub my wedding ring.

"I promise never to take it off."

He smiles with tears in his eyes. "I won't ever take mine off either. You put it there, so it stays there." He pushes me back up against one of the smaller rocks, which isn't saying much because it's still as tall as he is.

He presses into me and kisses me hard. Reaching between us, he unbuckles his pants and pulls out his cock. "I need you, baby. I need you going back home with my cum between your thighs, knowing you're mine."

He raises my dress and grabs my ass, lifting me and pinning me to the rock. I wrap my legs around his waist, and he slams into me. I moan, and he starts thrusting in and out of me hard and fast. Kissing my neck, he licks my pulse point.

"You are mine, Ivy, and *nothing* changes that. Tell me you know that nothing can change that you are mine, and that. I. Am. Yours," he says, punctuating each word with a thrust of his cock.

"I am yours, David, forever and always. You are mine; we will make it through this and be together again. I know it."

He kisses me, bruising my lips, and when my climax hits, he

covers my mouth with his to take my scream. When his climax rolls through him, he moves his mouth to my neck. The strength of his bite stings my neck, and then he kisses away the pain.

After he catches his breath, he pulls out of me and moves my panties back in place. He pats them against me, soaking them in his cum before he puts my dress down, and then he gets dressed.

Then he just holds me with his head on my shoulder.

“I love you, Ivy. You promise you will come back before the wedding please,” he begs.

“I love you too, David, and I promise I will be back. I’m not sure when exactly, but I will be back.”

He kisses me again. “Okay, go now before I carry you back to Ivy Hill kicking and screaming.”

My eyes fill with tears, and so do his. I take a deep breath and turn to walk to the stone as my skin starts to hum.

When I look back one more time, David hasn’t moved, but tears are rolling down his face, and they match mine. I don’t say a word because I can’t. I turn and walk through the stone.

Chapter 16

Ivy

3 Months Later

It's been three months since I walked back through the stones. Three months since I've seen David, and as I stare at the counter in front of me, I realize it's going to be at least eight more months before I can go back to see him. I burst into tears again for the third time today. Sinking to the floor, I can't stop myself from crying.

Brian finds me on the floor in my bathroom, crying and unable to stop. Kevin comes rushing in, and I know the minute they see it. They gasp, and I instantly feel two sets of hands on me, rubbing my back.

"It's going to be okay, Ivy. We are right here and not going anywhere," Brian says. Picking me up, he carries me to my bed and lays me down in the middle, then crawls in to face me. Kevin gets in bed behind me, and with their warmth enveloping me, I finally start to calm down.

Who knew a little stick with a plus sign could turn your whole world upside down?

Brian and Kevin are in the middle of planning their wedding.

They don't need this. I plan to kill Angela as soon as I get the strength to move. Her family planning method sucks.

Well, at least there is one positive. Kevin is a kick-ass midwife.

"Kevin, you will be my midwife, right? I want to have this baby here at home, surrounded by as much of its dad as possible. Brian, I need you on video duty. I want the whole thing recorded. I want it documented so that when I tell him, I can show him too. I need your guys' help to document everything."

"We are here for whatever you need, and I'd be offended if you let anyone else deliver this baby," Kevin says.

"I don't want you guys making a single change to your wedding plans, though. Promise me."

"We promise," Brian says after a moment.

"I have a huge favor to ask of you two. Would you consider living here with me after you are married? I don't use the basement, and it opens to the backyard. We can renovate it, and it can be your space. We can put a kitchen down there if you want, so you guys don't have to leave if you don't want to. But I am scared to do this on my own."

They are quiet for a moment, and I know they are doing some communicating over my head, but I don't have the strength to look up and watch.

"That sounds perfect, Ivy, but no kitchen needed. We don't want things to change. We love your cooking," Kevin says.

"Kevin?" I ask.

"Yeah, babe?"

"How long after the baby is born before I can go see David?" I ask.

He takes a deep breath. "Well, you would have your follow-up appointment at six weeks, so I would say at least that long. You will be cleared pending no complications after six weeks."

"When can I start exercising?"

"You can do light exercising now and during those six weeks unless I tell you not to, okay?" Kevin says.

I nod.

"What's going through your head, Ivy?" Brian asks.

"I can't tell him about the baby. We are getting ready to be apart for four years, and if he knows, it will change everything, and I know he won't give a shit about keeping history the same. Also, I don't want too many changes to my body...."

"Why?" Brian pushes.

"Well, I've read in interviews that people heard David say he could never be with a woman who has had a child, and a mother's body turns him off." I start crying.

"Where did you hear this?" Brian asks, clearly angry.

"In some of the interviews I've read."

"After Anna had her baby?" he asks, and I nod.

"I'm willing to bet that's something he said to push Anna away. This is David. He's crazy about you, and you told me he said a few times he wishes he could have a child with you."

In my heart, I know that's true, but I can't help but wonder and worry.

I nod and start crying again. "I know, it's just..."

"Hormones," Kevin finishes.

They get me up and lead me to the kitchen for something to eat, and I start to feel like I can do this.

Later that day, Kevin takes me into his office and gives me a checkup, and as promised, Brian records the whole thing. I find I'm about twelve weeks along. I hadn't had my period, but I was so depressed after saying goodbye to David again that I hadn't noticed. I thought it might have been the stress or time travel knocking my cycle a bit off.

I spent the rest of the day thinking and planning. This is a curveball I didn't see coming.

∞∞∞

Five Months Later

I am 35 weeks now, and Brian and Kevin have been doing pretty much everything to keep me off my feet. I'm pampered and loved, but I'm bored as hell.

Brian and Kevin got married and went on their honeymoon last month. They ended up buying a cabin in the mountains about two hours from here and spending a week there. They have told me I am welcome to use that cabin anytime, and I'm sure I'll be taking them up on it.

The basement remodel is finished. It didn't need much. We moved the washer and dryer up to the main floor, put in a full bathroom down there for them, and tore out the carpet to add wood floors. They painted and had fun decorating it. They have a decent-sized bedroom and bathroom, an office for Brian, and a huge living space.

They made a library in one corner and a traditional living room in another and a little breakfast area and finally gave in when I insisted on a mini kitchen, at least. It's small, but I got them a sink, stove, and fridge with some cabinets. They have huge windows along the one wall and French doors going out to the backyard. There is so much light that you would never know it was in the basement.

The whole basement is bigger than the two-bedroom apartment Brian and I shared in college.

Brian and I have been working nonstop, digging into everything surrounding David's death. Every little detail, reports before and after, has given us an outline of a plan for bringing David here, but nothing's concrete yet. Brian keeps talking about having to create a profile for him and doing it slowly so as not to raise any red flags.

I've been researching David and the key events of his life while we will be apart those four years. After an hour, I flip to a video of an interview I've been watching at least five times a day since I found it last month.

David is asked why he has two rings on his finger where his wedding ring is. He got this dreamy, faraway look on his face for a moment and then gave a half-smile.

He points at the first ring, and says, "That's my wedding ring with Anna," and then he points at the second ring, our ring. "This ring represents a promise to a family member, someone who means everything to me. I promised never to take it off, and I never have, and I never will. The promises this ring represents haven't been broken."

"Will you elaborate on that?" the interviewer asked.

"No," David said.

"How does Anna feel about someone else's ring coming before hers?"

"Does it really matter how she feels about it? Wasn't it you who reported she was having an affair with her tennis partner?" David said.

The interviewer got all flustered and went back to asking about his movie. But at that moment, David looks at the camera, and I see it. He looks like he's looking right at me, as though he knows I'm going to watch this video. He smiles and gives the camera *my* look, and I know we will make it through this okay.

Four Weeks Later

It's the middle of the night when I wake up, and I feel like I just peed myself. Lovely. I go to the toilet only to realize I'm leaking. I'm pretty sure my water just broke. I waddle over to the basement steps and open the door and call for Kevin. A minute later, he is upstairs.

"I think my water broke," I say and show him the bed. I have been having irregular contractions for a few days now, and at least one of the guys has stayed by my side. Kevin has Brian trained on what to do if I go into labor, and he isn't here, and we have practiced everything.

Brian comes up and helps get my bed changed and covered in the plastic, so it's ready. At this point, a contraction hits, not hard, but I know they will get worse. I stare at the photo of David eating the cake from his birthday. That look is the one that has gotten me through everything. Once the bed is ready, I lie back down.

My labor is quick for a first-time mom, but it's not painless. Having the baby at home means no drugs, but it's the tradeoff I make to have the baby born as close to David as possible. I have one of David's movies playing in the background, and his music playing softly. Pictures of him are everywhere. Brian is filming and taking photos.

Once it's time to start pushing, I'm holding our baby boy in my arms after only four hard pushes. I'm crying, and I'm a mess. Once it sinks in that we have a baby boy, I start laughing about how fate likes to mess with us, and of course, we have a son. I name him Adam David, and I cringe, giving him my last name since he is a Miller, but it is what it is.

Adam is a healthy seven-pound, six-ounce baby and has David's natural blond hair and his blue eyes. Brian says he has my smile.

I am having such a hard time letting him go for others to hold him. It's the closest thing to David I have. A true piece of him. As much as my heart hurts at the thought of David, Adam can heal it.

While Adam will eventually have his own room upstairs, the corner of my room is set up for him, so he's with me for now. I've been talking to Brian about moving my bedroom upstairs when Adam moves to his own room, but that's months away.

Brian and Kevin joke about how I'm going to spoil the baby by letting him nap on me, and all I say is damn right I will be spoiling this child.

Chapter 17

David

Eight Weeks Later

I'm sitting in the piano room trying to work on new music, and like every day, I'm praying today is the day my Ivy comes to visit. The wedding is in two months, and she promised she'd be here. It's been a year since I've been able to hold her in my arms, and I've been going crazy. How the hell am I going to do four years like this?

I think about that day on this piano bench when I made love to her and can't help but smile. I start to get hard, but the sound of Anna's voice kills my good mood. It's like nails on a chalkboard to me.

"David, baby, we have the cake tasting today."

I cringe, the anxiety of having to marry Anna is wearing on me, and my parents have even pointed it out a few times, though it's the nicer of the conversations I've had with them recently.

"Anna, I've said it before. Don't call me baby." I hate it when she does that. Only Ivy can call me that. I watch Anna roll her eyes. "And this is your wedding; you pick the cake."

"David, stop, this is our wedding. You need to be a part of this."

I've tried to pretend and be nice with Anna like Ivy asked, but a year in and the pretending stopped at month four.

"Anna, let's call a spade a spade. This is your wedding, one I'm being forced into. Pick the cake, pick the colors, and pick the damn decorations. Just tell me when to show up," I say, not hiding my anger.

At month four, I snapped at Anna. She was clinging all over me and trying to kiss me constantly, and it made me sick to my stomach. We had it out about her lies and how her father was forcing me into this marriage, and I made it clear I didn't want it. She cried and said she would make me fall in love with her. We just needed time together. I told her not to hold her breath.

She's been trying ever since with things like the wedding planning and dates "for the press." It drives me crazy, and I can't wait to leave and head to California.

Anna's parents moved to Nashville once the news of our engagement was announced. Once married, Anna will be moving into Ivy Hill, and the thought makes my skin crawl. I don't want her here; this is Ivy's home. I had three deadbolts installed on Ivy's and my bedroom door. I don't want her in there for any reason while I'm gone. The staff and what will be Anna's security have been informed she is not to be in that room.

Anna is here doing wedding planning, and I can't wait for her to leave tonight. She insists on being here every day now, and I don't know how much more I can take. We fought just yesterday because she wants to go on a two-week honeymoon, and I refused, saying I only had time to take her away for a weekend. I had to remind her yet again how I didn't even want to do that.

I can hear Anna in the kitchen, so I go back to looking for music and working on a few songs. An hour passes, and I feel it. The house comes to life.

My breath catches. Am I going crazy? Maybe I've finally lost my mind. I stand and turn around, and Ivy is standing in the living room, watching me. I take a second to take her in. She has more curves than the last time I saw her, and I can't wait to get my hands on them. Her hair is longer, and she looks exhausted, but I've never seen her more beautiful.

Out of the corner of my eye, I see Anna standing by the stairs, staring at Ivy. I don't care. Let her see. She has this dream in her head that she can make me fall in love with her. Let her see my heart is already claimed.

"Ivy, my sweet, sweet Ivy. You came," I get out barely above a whisper.

"I promised you I would," she says. Neither of us has moved, and at this, I rush toward her and pick her up and swing her around in a circle. She is laughing, and when I set her down, I grab her face and kiss her hard and then rest my forehead on hers.

"I'm never going to make it through this."

"Yes, you will in flying colors."

It's like she finally realizes there might be other people around, and she takes a step back, but I'm not having it and take a step toward her. She looks around and sees Anna, who looks beyond pissed, and Ivy's face drops. Oh, I won't be having that.

"Ivy, this is Anna; Anna, this is Ivy. You will treat her with the utmost respect." I direct toward Anna.

"I won't allow you to bring whores into my house and into our marriage, David. How will that look to your fans?" Anna says. I attempt to lunge at her for calling Ivy a whore, but Ivy steps in front of me. She is calm, and how she does it, I don't know.

"Anna, I know who you are, and I know all about the lies you told and the threats your father made. See, in doing so, you are ruining more lives than David's. This is *my* house. It was named after me all those years ago. You'd do best to remember the only reason you will be living here is because I told David you should be." Ivy smiles at her as though they are best friends.

"I'd also be very careful before spreading any of these rumors about him and me to the press. Anything other than the perfect family will be grounds for not only divorce but also your letters and your father's letters to go out to the public, and the fact that you have been supplying David with drugs before the wedding has even happened will all get out. Can you imagine how your life will be with all of David's fans against you? You'd never be able to leave the house! Oh, and the terms of your prenup will kick in, making it so you get absolutely nothing in the divorce," Ivy says with a smile on her face.

I can't help but smile. Of course, Ivy knows about the prenup. I have a rough copy but wanted to talk to her about it before finalizing it. I want to make sure everything is covered.

"I'm not signing a prenup!" Anna screams.

"Oh, yes, you are, or there is no wedding. My lawyer will have it to you by the end of the week. You will have one week to sign it, or the wedding is off," I say. I watch my parents, who have seen all this unfold, and they turn white and are staring wide-eyed.

My mom goes to open her mouth, but I give my head a slight shake, and she closes it while giving me the mom look. I know this is going to be a conversation sooner rather than later.

Anna stomps off, gathers her things, and turns to leave.

"Oh, and one more thing," Ivy says. "I suggest you stop trying to redecorate my house and moving my photos." She points at the wall where my Army photo was. "I will be putting that photo and all the others back."

Anna, not realizing the best thing to do would be to shut up and leave, says, "Our wedding photo is going there."

"No, it's not," I say. "It won't be going up anywhere in this house."

With that, she stomps off and slams the door behind her.

"Well, that could have gone better." Ivy laughs. She then turns to my parents. "I won't stand in the way of their wedding, and I won't be back after they are married, so don't worry."

"Why don't you stop this?" my dad asks.

Ivy gives a sad smile and says the truth. "You can't change history, no matter how much you want to."

My parents look at each other. They've picked up on things Ivy would say or do, and they'd make comments here and there, but it's like that statement was the confirmation they needed.

"And how long does this sham of a marriage go on?" my mom asks. "Don't lie to me, Ivy."

With a deep breath, Ivy tells the truth. "Four years. She will give you a grandson, and all the rumors of his drug problems and all the women he's with will be a lie. That is all I can give you."

My mom stares at Ivy for a minute, then nods her head. "Well, come sit down and have lunch. I think it's time we learn about the real Ivy, don't you?"

Ivy looks scared, and my heart is racing when my mom looks at me.

"David Adam Miller, I am your mother. If you can't trust me with something like this, then who the hell can you trust?"

"It's not a matter of trust, Mom. It's a matter of whether you will believe it."

My mother looks me dead in my eyes. "Try me."

Ivy is here, and I want nothing more than to take her upstairs and not let her leave our bed, but I know my mom won't let it go. So, we sit down for lunch, and we are quiet for a moment before Ivy looks up at me.

Ivy reaches into her purse and pulls out her ID from her wallet. I nod my head, letting her know it's okay. Ivy squares her shoulders and says, "My name is Ivy Cecille Collins, and I was born October 11, 1988." She hands her ID over to my mom, who takes it while keeping her eyes on Ivy.

My mom and dad look over the ID front and back and then

hand it back to Ivy. Ivy puts it in her wallet and pulls out her cell phone.

"This is what phones look like in my time. With no wires, they go anywhere and are like minicomputers. They take photos and video and let you call people and even video chat with them. It's like a phone call but with video. It won't work here because cell phone towers haven't been built."

She puts the phone away and looks at my parents.

"Keep going," my dad says, his voice flat.

She starts with how Brian found the rocks to her first visit here down to my visiting there and ends with her visit today. She tells them how it's important that history isn't changed, which is why I have to marry Anna.

When she stops, she takes a drink of water, and my mom pours herself a third glass of wine.

"So that is why you couldn't get married legally and why David couldn't find you when he looked," my mom says, and Ivy nods.

"Also explains all your little quirks we have been picking up on," Mom says more to herself than to us. "What happens if David doesn't marry sleazy Anna?"

Ivy laughs, and it puts me at ease. It's great to hear her laughter again.

"Well, to be honest, I'm not 100% sure, but I do know it will have a huge impact on history. Their son won't be born, which means his children, David's grandchildren, won't be born, and that will trickle down. All his charity work won't happen, which will affect thousands of lives. Who knows how it will affect Ivy Hill, his museum, and how he's remembered."

Ivy pauses, and I can tell from her biting her lip that she is thinking about what to say before she continues. "But I can tell you Anna gets what's coming to her. After David's death, she releases a book trying to say it's a tell-all of their life, and she is berated for lies and trying to tarnish his memory. His fans don't like her one bit. It comes out later from the doctor Anna has been using that she was .... well, she had a huge role in his death." Ivy trails off.

"Tell me," my mom says in her mom voice.

Ivy sighs. "Reports say he dies of a drug overdose, and it comes out later that Anna was the one supplying him the drugs."

Mom shoots me a death glare. "I haven't taken a single one, I swear. Please let Ivy finish, and you will understand."

"There is a huge conspiracy around his death. Random sightings afterward and lots of information Brian and I are sorting through. But our plan is to let the public think he is doing drugs, that he is cheating on Anna, and when the time comes, to let it look like he overdoses and bring him home with me for good. Brian has been working with a friend, and he can set up a new identity for him. No one will ever know a thing."

"And his family?" my dad asks.

"Well, we can set it up so you can come to visit anytime, though you need at least a forty-eight-hour window, or you can get sick. I learned that one the hard way. Once David passes, you, John, will be in charge of his estate and running it until his son becomes an adult. The house gets turned into a museum for fans to visit, and several buildings are built across the street to showcase his awards, outfits, cars, and more. It will supply hundreds of jobs and not only make the estate millions a year but bring in millions in tourism to the area."

Both Mom and Dad just stare at Ivy, and her grip on my hand tightens. She is waiting for their reaction just like I am.

"You know how crazy this all sounds, right?" my dad says.

Ivy looks down at the table and takes a deep breath. I squeeze her hand this time, trying to offer comfort.

"I know, Dad. In time, I'll prove it to you, but I need you to trust me. I know that's asking a lot, but I promise when we can explain, it will all make sense."

John nods. We continue eating lunch with my mom asking odd questions like what happens to certain stars and what certain things are. She asks Ivy questions about things said and done since she has been at Ivy Hill. She even asks her some of the same questions, and I know it's to see if Ivy is consistent in her answers. She did this to me as a kid a lot too.

Once we finish lunch and the table is cleared, Ivy says, "Well, since we are all here, we need to discuss the prenup with you and Anna."

I nod, and my mom gets up to get a pen and paper for me. "I will go talk to my lawyer first thing tomorrow," I say.

"Okay, here is how this is going to work. She can stay here at Ivy Hill until the baby is born. This way, your parents can help watch her and make sure she is staying healthy and off drugs while pregnant. From everything I've read, she does, but we can't be too careful." I agree and so do my parents.

"Once the baby is born, and she gets the all-clear from the doctor in six weeks, you will buy her a house over in Memphis. Not a mansion but just a slightly larger than normal three-bedroom home with a good yard. You buy it, but it's to be in her name. She moves in there and gets that in the divorce. She will get child support and alimony. Child support will stop on the day of your son's eighteenth birthday, and you will set up a trust fund for him for when he is twenty-one and graduates from college," she says.

I don't even flinch at the number she gives me because there is no question that I will take care of my son. I continue taking notes.

"She will get a lump sum plus child support and alimony. Any adultery will cause her to waive her right to any and all income and property at the time of divorce."

Ivy pauses and stares off into the distance. "There needs to be a clause that she gives up any and all rights to Ivy Hill and all income Ivy Hill generates in the future, and that clause needs to include when it's passed down to your son. We won't talk about your will now, but all that will go to your son in a trust John will manage. This might sound petty, but I don't want her redecorating here. It's just..." Ivy looks at me.

"Our space." I finish for her, and she nods.

After we talk a bit more about the prenup and wedding, my parents head back to the cottage, and I take Ivy upstairs.

She looks at me a bit funny when she sees all the locks on our door but walks over to the photo on the nightstand and just stares at them.

I come behind her, and she says, "Kind of sucks these are going to get packed up."

"Like hell, woman, did you see the locks on that door? She is not stepping foot in this room." I grab her hand and pull her down the hall to the other end of the house and show her a room half the size of mine that also has an attached bath. Anna has already started to decorate it. I think she thinks I will be staying here too. She is so wrong.

"This will be her room while she is here, and I will not even touch her in this house. This is our place and ours alone. All the stuff will remain where it is in our room, your stuff mixed with mine, though I plan to take some of your stuff to California with me."

She rolls her eyes. "Oh, I bet she'll love that."

"I don't care. This marriage is only happening because history says so and because you say so. Because of the lies Anna told and the threats her father made. I've told Anna as much, but she thinks the more time she spends with me, the more I'll fall in love with her." It was my turn to roll my eyes.

"Don't you go falling for her now, David Miller. It would break my heart."

"Don't even talk like that," I growl. I grab her waist and toss her down on the bed, and in a flash, I have my cock out, and her skirt flipped up. I rip her panties out of my way and line my cock up with her soaked opening. I slam home and lean my weight on her, pinning her to the bed.

"You have my heart," *thrust* "my soul," *thrust,* "you own me, sweet Ivy," *thrust* "don't ever doubt that." I hear her moan and try to arch her hips to meet my thrusts, but she can't move since I have her pinned to the bed.

"God, beautiful, I missed you. If you think you are wearing clothes for the next two weeks, you have lost your mind."

"David," she moans. She is close, and I feel it. We both have all our clothes on, but we need this quick fuck to calm this need. To reconnect our souls so we can talk. I felt a wall between us, and I can't have that.

Her pussy squeezes my cock like a vise, and her warm, slick heat is almost more than I can take. I'm so close that when she comes undone screaming my name and digging her nails into my back, her release triggers mine, and I come inside her. I come so hard I fill her up, and it leaks down between us on to the bed. I bury my head in Ivy's neck and smile at the thought of our combined juices soaking what will be Anna's bed. I don't think I'll have this room washed. We will leave it just as it is.

When I regain my strength, I sit up and tuck myself back in and flip her skirt down. I pick up her ripped panties and grab her hand. This time, she's the one who rubs her thumb over my ring.

"In case you're wondering, I won't be removing that either," I say as we walk down the hall. "I'll tell anyone who asks it's a promise I made, and I will keep, and it doesn't come off."

When we get to our room, I point at the locks. "I installed these to keep her out of our space. I've instructed the house staff and her security that she isn't to go near this room. I will also tell her if she tries to get in, she will be kicked out of Ivy Hill on the spot."

Ivy nods as we head into our room. Once inside, I close and lock the door and walk over to her. I run my hand over her new curves.

So much has changed in a year. What's it going to be like for the next four years? How much am I going to miss?

"Your body has changed," I say. She stiffens, but I continue before she tries to talk. "I love these new curves, beautiful. I can't wait to get my hands on them."

My hands slide up under her shirt, and she pulls away. We can't have that.

"When I got home, I got a bit depressed. Pair that with the research I helped Brian with and eating a ton of ice cream, and I put on some weight. I lost most of it, and I promise, the next time you see me, I'll have my body back."

I growl and grab her hips and yank her toward me. "You will do no such thing. I love these new curves, and I love you. As we grow, our bodies and our hair color will change, but what I love about you will not because I love your heart, your mind, and your soul. To me, you will always be beautiful."

Grabbing the hem of her shirt, I look her in the eyes as I pull it over her head slowly. I take off her skirt and stand back to look at her. Her breasts are bigger by at least a cup size, and she has some stretch marks near her belly and hips, and my cock is leaking from just staring at her.

Staying where I am, I strip off all my clothes and grab my cock slick with my own cum. It's red and angry because it only wants to be between her legs.

"You see this? You did this; your body is so fucking sexy. Remember our wedding night when I came in my pants just from looking at you? I almost did the same thing just now while staring at your sexy curves. Do you understand me? You are fucking beautiful."

She has tears in her eyes and nods her head. I lay her on the bed and kiss her hard. Then I kiss down her neck and down the valley of her breasts.

I take the nipple of one into my mouth and lick and suck it hard, then give it a little nip before I lean over to give the other one the same treatment.

I kiss her down to her belly, and I take my time and kiss every stretch mark. I kiss my way down to her hips. Shouldering her legs apart, I kiss my way over her mound down to her clit where I latch on and suck hard. That is all it takes for her to shatter around me. Her thighs lock around my head, holding me in place as I lick up her warm honey. When she relaxes, I don't stop, and I force another orgasm from her before kissing my way back up her body.

"Do you believe me now, beautiful, or do I need to do that all over again?"

"I believe you, David, but if you don't get inside me now, I might die."

"Well, we can't have that," I murmur against her neck, and in the next moment, I thrust into her.

I know I won't last long after hearing her climax with my head between her legs and getting no relief for my cock. I grit my teeth and angle my hips to hit her G-spot on each thrust. I'm deep in my woman, and all I can think about is staying here for the rest of my life and never leaving. I want to fill her up over and over again.

She is letting out the sexiest moans, and I lean down to suck her nipple into my mouth. After a few more thrusts, I move to the other nipple, and then her walls start clamping down on me. God, it feels like heaven, and I watch her fall over the edge. It's the sexiest thing I've ever heard. And that sound of her coming is one I hear every night in my dreams. It sets off my climax before I collapse on her. When I finally stop coming, I roll over to my side.

"I have a favor to ask you. Something I want to do while I'm here."

Well, now she has my attention because she knows I'll give her anything.

Chapter 18

Ivy

After that round of lovemaking, there is no doubt left in my mind that he loves my new curves. I feel guilty about lying and not telling David about Adam, but I know in my heart it's for the best. It would only make these next four years even worse for him.

"What do you want to do, beautiful?" he asks me while rubbing his hand over my belly and hips, tracing the stretch marks. There aren't too many. I put on minimal weight and exercised like crazy during my pregnancy and after. I used lotion and stretch mark cream religiously.

"I want to see you perform at a concert. I've seen some videos, but I want to see the real thing."

"Done. I'll talk to my manager in the morning. I have to talk to my lawyer anyway, so I'll head out and take care of that tomorrow morning. You stay here with Mom and Dad, and after the concert, I plan to take you to a cabin I bought in the mountains for a week. I'll tell Anna I have to work, and you are going home. She comes here way too often for my liking."

He does just that. The next morning, he is gone for a few hours and comes home and insisted I fill him in on everything he missed over the last year. We stay in the TV room, and I tell him about Brian and Kevin's wedding and them agreeing to stay with me, the remodel of the basement, and our hunt to find a way to bring him to me and cover up his death.

"Oh, and to give us both a light at the end of the tunnel," I say. "September 11, 1965, is when your divorce will be final, and I will be here."

Then we hear a bunch of doors slamming and footsteps stomping down to the TV room. David tenses, and I have a feeling it's Anna. "You shouldn't be scared in your own house," I whisper.

Anna appears and doesn't hide the rage on her face when she sees me. "You went through with the prenup?!" she says to David.

"Yes, you will learn I mean everything I say, especially since my gut tells me you and your family are nothing but a bunch of gold diggers."

She has the audacity to look like she's been slapped.

"The day after tomorrow, I have a last-minute show here in town, and then I have to go away on business for a few days, few meetings to take," he tells her.

"So close to the wedding?" she whines. God, I can't stand this girl. I want to grab David and run away with him. I can't help but feel I am causing this pain, and not for the first time, thoughts run through my head of what if I changed history. But I know in my heart I can't. So much would change and not for the better.

"Yes, the world and my career don't stop because of you. Now, I have company. I will call you when I get home from my trip, so I suggest you have the prenup signed and filed by then. I don't wish to see you until you do."

Her eyes water, and she runs out of the room. We sit still and listen to her leave the house.

"I don't even feel bad about what we did to her bed," I say, then I climb over to him, and we do the same thing on the couch.

∞∞∞

It's the day of the concert, and he says he has a surprise for me, and I can't wait. He says the show is almost sold out, which is crazy for how little notice they gave. We get there, and he takes me backstage. I meet his manager, and he introduces me as simply his family. It's true, and no one needs to know the details. He sets me up with a member of his security team and a chair at the side of the stage so I can watch him play.

Just before the show, he comes over and kisses me.

"Now, I want the full experience. Don't you hold back, you hear me?"

"Yes, ma'am." He gives me a devilish smile.

He goes out and sings three of his more upbeat songs, then he dedicates one to me. But he does it in a way his fans could think he's talking about his soon-to-be wife by saying it's for the woman he loves and holds his heart. Yet he looks right at me when he says it.

After that song, he says he has a surprise, and if I hadn't been sitting down, I might have fallen out of my chair when Johnny and June Cash walk on stage. Well, I guess she is still June Carter right now.

I have tears in my eyes. He remembered. They all sing a few songs before Johnny takes the stage on his own for a few songs.

When the show is over, I get to hang out backstage with Johnny and June and David. If anyone understands that the road to love is a difficult one, it's them, and they don't judge us for what is currently going on. They are fighting their own uphill battle.

I have to be careful about the questions I ask to make sure they are in line with the year, but it was great to talk with them.

After a few hours, David whisks me off to his cabin, but when we get there, I stand in open-mouthed shock.

"This is not your cabin."

"Yes, it is. Why wouldn't it be?"

"This is the cabin Brian and Kevin bought and spent their honeymoon in!!!"

"No way." He looks at me with wide eyes.

All I can do is laugh; it's just another sign that fate brought us here. If only fate could take care of Anna, then life would be perfect.

For the next week, we don't leave the cabin other than for our nightly walks down to the stream at the far end of the property.

Our last night here on our walk, our talk turns serious. "You know what you are asking of me is unfair," David says.

"What do you mean?" I ask.

"Well, you asking me to be unfaithful to you while you get to remain faithful."

I can't help but laugh. "I think you might be the only man ever who is upset your wife is giving you permission to be with another woman. Four years is a long time, and I won't be upset if any of the rumors of women you are with are true. Just be honest and tell me which ones are."

He looks upset. "I will not be sleeping with anyone except Anna, and I plan to do that only once."

We walk a bit in silence. "Do you plan on dating over these four years?" he asks quietly.

"No, believe me, I understand your statement of the thought of it makes you sick. Just, I know I sound like a broken record, but no drugs, please. Brian's and my plan is contingent on that, okay?"

"I promise, beautiful. I will not break any promise I have made you, ever!" He pulls me to him in a fierce and passionate kiss.

That night, we make love so sweet we both cry, then he takes me so hard and rough, saying he wants me to feel him between my thighs for days. He doesn't let me sleep. Anytime one of us gets tired, he slams into me again. We both get a few hours of sleep before waking up to our ritual shower.

Before we get in the car, I hand him a stack of letters.

"Don't open these until the date on each envelope. This is my way of being there for different events in your life, okay?"

"I promise, I also plan to write to you every day."

"So do I. I will keep a journal, and I want to know everything. Every detail. And I'll do the same."

We sit next to each other in the car holding hands on our way to the stones.

Walking through them this time will be the hardest thing I've ever had to do.

Four years and counting.

Chapter 19

Ivy

Four Weeks Later

All I can hear is that Britney Spears' song "Oops, I did it again…" going in my head. Yeah, another stick with another positive sign. I sigh. I get another piece of my David, and he gets something else to be mad at me about.

"Girl, you just need to get on birth control next time you go see him or take some condoms. Jeez!" Brian jokes.

"Wouldn't dream of it. These two pieces of David are going to get me through the next four years."

June 21, 2013

David,

I hope you won't hate me, but I found out I'm pregnant again. Yes, again. Our son Adam David is our honeymoon baby born just four months ago, and now coming back just before your wedding, I'm pregnant again.

I have chosen not to tell you because I feel it will make our separation harder, and I'm terrified it may be too hard and drive you to the drugs anyway. That is my greatest fear.

Brian is recording everything, so we will have hours of video for you to watch. I'm really hoping this one is a girl this time.

I love you with all my heart.

Ivy

July 12, 1961

David,

I know yesterday was one of the hardest days of your life. The wedding and the wedding night. I know traditionally I should congratulate you, but I'm sorry I won't.

I hope you will forgive me for putting you through this, and it doesn't make you resent me or love me any less.

I also have this striking feeling to remind you not to let her mess with my house. I love it the way it is. As you are preparing to head out to California, I hope you still plan to take some of my things with you. Make sure to check the pockets in the red coat of mine in the closet. You're welcome.

I miss you terribly, baby, but the good news is there are 4 years, 1 month, and 2 days until I see you again. That's 1,522 days. I know it seems like a lot, but so far, we are 2 months, 51 days down. We can do this, baby.

When you get to California, remember I will be watching every movie. It's what I fall asleep to every night. Your voice lulls me to sleep.

I love you more than words can say.

Ivy

July 12, 1961

My sweet, sweet Ivy,

You're right. Yesterday and last night were hell. I had our vows adjusted to say, 'will you take this woman to be your legal wife.' Nothing more, no till death do you part. She was fuming, but I refuse to disvalue our vows.

Then last night.... I had to get so drunk, and even then, I had to think of you the whole time. Afterward, I locked myself in the bathroom and cried. I showered long after the water got cold, scrubbing every inch and washing with your shampoo and body wash to get your scent back.

I could never love you less or resent you. I hope you will forgive me for last night for being unfaithful.

Oh, and thank you for that pair of underwear in the red coat. It still smells like you. Those little Ziploc bags are amazing.

You are the love of my life, and I can't wait to start our life together.

David

February 2, 2014

David

Our sweet baby girl was born today. She has your eyes and hair, just like her brother. Clara Cecille is her name after our grandmothers. She loves to cuddle, and I can't seem to put her down.

Confession: I let Adam sleep in bed with me more than I should. Holding a piece of you helps me sleep. I don't see him or Clara being out of my bed anytime soon.

I pray every day you will forgive me for this secret. I love you so much.

I tell the kids about you daily and play your music and movies for them. They will know you always.

All my love,

Ivy

April 20th, 1962

David,

Congrats, Daddy!! The photo of you looking at your son. I'd love to know what you are thinking. The love there, the press ate it up.

Remember to spend time with your son Scott as much as you can. Maybe not the diaper-changing time, but cuddle that baby and love him with all your heart. He will have a rough childhood, and none of this is his fault.

He grows up to be an amazing man and does some great things. You will be so proud of him. Next time you visit, we can look him up and show you.

Also, congratulations are in order for your movie premiere just days before your son was born. I've been falling asleep to that movie every night for the last week. I'm guessing Brian is saying, "Woman, pick another movie!" by now while Kevin just laughs at us.

Give that baby a kiss for me. Despite his mom being Anna, he is a piece of you, which means he will always hold a piece of my heart.

Knowing we have hit the year mark, I thought I'd give you a little something to make your nights a little spicier. I hope you enjoy the photos.

3 years, 4 months, and 22 days. 1247 more days.

I love you to the moon and back.

Ivy

April 20, 1962

My sweet, sweet Ivy,

I know I promised I would never lie to you. I imagined it was you having my baby that whole day. But you are right; I love my son so much.

In those photos, I was thinking about how lucky I am to be

blessed with this little boy, and I'm pretty sure at one point I was thanking God it only took one night and one time for it to happen.

I have to say I laughed, thinking of Brian telling you to pick another movie. I can see it clear as day in my mind.

You, my beautiful girl, are an evil, evil woman. I will say I have to buy you new panties because I've been using them around my cock when I come thinking of you. But those photos? I haven't been able to get my cock to go down since I saw them three hours ago.

My favorite is the one with both your fingers in your pussy and leaning up to look at the camera. God, I can't stop looking at it. Oh, be right back. Need to take care of my cock again.

My hand just isn't the same, baby. I will apologize now because the next time I see you, I plan to be in your pussy for twenty-four hours straight.

All my love,

David

December 10, 2014

David,

Today, I broke. I'm not as strong as I thought I was. Your concert in Atlanta? I was there. I had to see you. God, watching you on stage is mesmerizing.

You are the sexiest thing I've ever seen. I know why all the women swoon after you.

You sang our song, and I remembered our time on the piano bench. My panties were soaked, and all I wanted to do was go up to you and drag you off to the closest door. But I knew I had to be strong for us.

I love you.

Ivy

Dec 17, 1962

David,

Just a quick note. 999 days. We made the triple digits. To celebrate, I have one more photo for you. Remember how much I love you and included in this envelope is another envelope with no date to open it. Save it for when being apart is unbearable, and you don't think you will make it another day.

Congrats on your new single, and I love you.

Ivy

Dec 18, 1962

To the evil women who owns my heart,

You are truly evil.

I love you.

I had to cancel work yesterday because I couldn't get my cock to go down.

Evil woman.

Don't ever change.

David

May 16, 1963

David,

OH MY GOD!!! Congrats on your first Grammy award last

night!!

It was such a huge event. I hope you celebrate some! I want to celebrate with you.

Now tonight, go to bed at 9 pm, lie back in bed, close your eyes, and think about me. Open the attached letter only then.

2 years, 3 months, 26 days. 849 days.

See you at nine, my sexy husband.

Ivy

May 16, 1963

David,

Tonight, we are going to celebrate together. I am already in bed thinking of you wearing the black lace outfit in the photo.

Take your cock in your hand and picture me spreading my legs for you. I'm pulling my panties aside for you to get a view that is only for you. Only you have been in this pussy since the day we met. I'm soaking wet, thinking of you lying in bed stroking your cock.

I'm now rubbing my clit, baby. And don't you dare come until I tell you and don't you dare skip ahead.

I'm dripping wet, baby, all for you. Take the cum leaking from your cock and spread it over the tip and give it a few tight strokes.

My other hand is playing with my nipples, and I just plunged two fingers into me and moaned your name. I'm pulling my fingers out, and they are soaking wet. I stroke my clit again and buck my hips.

Keep stroking your cock, baby, just like I would, but don't you come yet.

My eyes would be staring right at your cock and the leaking cum, and I'd be licking my lips. Dying to taste you. Dying to have you in my mouth.

I'm so close, baby. I want you ready to come with me. I'm plunging my fingers in and out of my pussy, and my hips are bucking as my other hand reaches down to stroke my clit.

Oh god, baby, I'm coming. Come with me, baby.

Congratulations on your big day. I hope I made this award night special for you.

I love you with all that I am,

Ivy

May 16, 1963

My beautiful Ivy,

My god, that was the best way to celebrate. I haven't come so hard since the last time I was inside you. Just thinking you were there with me doing this for me was hotter than hell.

My sweet, sweet, Ivy, I love you so much. You have no idea how much I needed this, needed you tonight. I was happy to accept the award, but my heart just needed you there. I do all this for you. My sweet, amazing girl, you are my everything. There is nothing I wouldn't do for you. Even this crazy four-year stint, I do it for you.

849 days until we start our forever.

I love you and you alone, my Ivy girl.

David

September 12, 1963

David

Earlier this week, you started your adventure in Hawaii. This movie you are shooting is one of my favorites and not just because of its location.

I want you to enjoy your time there, and for our anniversary, I want you to rent that same house and spend a weekend remembering all the dirty things you did to me there. My favorite was our night in the hot tub.

We are getting so close! We are under two years now. We have done two years before, so this is a cakewalk for us. We got this!

1 Year, 11 months, and 29 days. 730 days.

I love you like a fat man loves chocolate cake.

Ivy

September 12, 1963

My sweet, sweet Ivy,

Hawaii is beautiful, but you should be here with me. Thinking of our time here, I figure it's as good a time as any to tell you none of the rumors to date of the girls I've been with are true. I haven't had a single one of the drugs they are reporting me to have used either.

I did a show in Maryland last weekend, and I stopped in to see your grandparents. I know they have no idea who you are, but I felt I owed it to you to explain.

Your grandfather almost closed the door in my face, but I begged them to let me explain. I told them about the letters from Anna's family and how you told me to do this while you got everything sorted out.

I don't think they like me very much, but they are at least speaking to me. We had dinner together. They asked about you and want to see you again. I love hearing the stories they tell that you have probably heard many times over.

I did as you asked, and as soon as Anna got the okay from the doctor, I moved her into her own place, and she has no access to Ivy Hill anymore. Other than visiting with my son, I haven't seen or heard from her. Last I heard, she was having an affair with her tennis partner. Poor guy.

I miss you every day, and my body craves you every night. My heart beats for you, my sweet Ivy.

I love you.

David.

November 11, 2015

Today, I went to see you again. You were in Charleston, South Carolina, doing a show. Just seeing you on stage and watching you perform turned me on so desperately.

I think you might have seen me tonight, but I bolted, and you never caught me. I felt horrible, but I needed to be closer. I needed to know you were okay.

I love you, David. Please forgive me.

Ivy

January 1, 1964

David

I know the music single you released today is about me. I smile every time I hear it and think of you.

Remember that time we spent together in California on our honeymoon, the night in the bathtub? Think of that tonight because I will be.

My sexy husband, you are only getting better with age. I love you.

1 year, 8 months, 10 days. 619 days.

Happy New Year. We got this baby.

I love you.

Ivy

January 1, 1964

Sweet, sweet Ivy,

That song is about you, about us, and my love for you.

I spent yesterday with my son. He's an amazing kid, and I love him so much. I hope one day we have kids. I'd love to see a little girl just like you running around.

You, my sexy wife, are such a turn-on. I can't wait to see you again and be inside you again. I love you with everything I am.

David

June 16, 1964

David,

If you are reading this, it means times are too hard right now. I want you to cancel your plans for the next few days and go back to Ivy Hill. Come home so I can take care of you. I love you. On your plane ride home, I want you to think about that first day we met.

Why did you invite me in to give me a tour of the house? I accepted because I always felt a draw toward Ivy Hill. I was named after it, but it was more than that. I think it was you before I even knew you. I always felt at home when I toured the grounds. Little did I know.

Think about that first night we slept in each other's arms. It finally felt like home.

Think about our first kiss.

Think about the time in the back of your car. That memory still makes me smile and blush.

When you get home to Ivy Hill, go to the guest room across the hall from our room where I was going to stay that first visit.

In the bottom right of the tall dresser is a box for you. I left it there on my last visit. Open the letter first.

Remember, David, we can do this. Our love is greater than time and space. I love you enough for both of us right now. I need you, baby. See you soon.

Ivy

June 18, 1964

Welcome home, baby.

Go lie down in our bed and surround yourself with me. Our wedding photos are there. That was one of the happiest days of my life. Now I want you to open the box and do as I say, okay? First, take out the card with the recipe. If I was there, this is what I'd make you right now. Take it to Nancy and have her start cooking. Tell her I miss her.

Next is my favorite shirt. It's yours, but I would always wear this when I was missing you the most. Put it on, baby.

Now for the phone. It's your phone, so plug it in and let it charge.

While it's charging, I want you to look at that photo the day you named Ivy Hill. When I look at this photo, I know we are meant to be together. The bumps along the way suck, I know, but I just know it was meant to be.

Check on the phone, baby. If it is charged enough, turn it on, but keep it plugged in. Go to the photo section. I recorded a few videos for you. The first one is to go with this letter. The others are just me going about my everyday routine but talking to you while I do. I hope this gives you a taste of our future.

I love you. When it gets too hard, watch these videos. It's what gets me through. I love you, baby. I can't say it enough.

Ivy

Chapter 20

Ivy

June 19, 2016

Brian and Kevin took the kids out for the day. I just needed a break. My heart hurts, and I can just feel something isn't right. I've been stalking the news, looking for changes, looking for photos close to David's date today. Nothing. There is nothing.

I make a cup of coffee and walk around the house, trying to calm myself when there is a knock on the door. I freeze. Brian and David don't knock because they live here. No one just shows up, who could it be?

I put my coffee down and open the door, and I can't help but gasp. Oh god, this isn't happening. We have one more year.

David pushes his way in, closes the door, and sinks to the floor crying. I pull him into my arms and let him cry, then I remember the kids, oh god.

Me: Keep the kids out. David showed up, and he isn't doing good at all.

Brian: Take him to the cabin for a few days. We got the kids.

Me: Good idea! Text you when we leave.

"Baby, please talk to me. I can't help you if you don't talk to me. I love you, David, this is killing me." He finally looks up, and I can't help but think he still looks as handsome as ever, but he looks more worn down, tired, and like he wants to give up. I can't have that.

"Ivy, my sweet Ivy, I'm so sorry," he says, then takes another deep breath. "I was missing you badly, and Anna, she has been... not nice, lots of threats even though she was caught with her tennis partner."

"And she's having an affair with her dance instructor now," I add.

He shakes his head. "Your letters have been the best part of my life. I live for opening the next one, but after dealing with Anna the other day, it was too much, and I lost it. I wasn't thinking. I was going to take one of the pills just to sleep the day away. It was in my mouth, then I saw your letter for when things get too hard, and I spit it out. I didn't take it. I swear to you, I didn't take it!"

"I know you didn't, baby. I believe you." I run my hand through his hair.

He tucks a piece of hair behind my ear. "I came home to Ivy Hill just like you told me to. I watched your videos so many times and knew you were so close. I didn't care anymore. I was here before I could change my mind. I need you; I need us. I know there is still a year left, but please give me a week."

I straddle his lap right there on the floor. I take his face in my hands, and he leans into my touch.

"I can't give you a week," I say. His face falls, and he closes his eyes. I kiss a few tears away. "I can give you two weeks," I say, and he hugs me so tight and takes in a shaky breath.

"Thank you, sweet girl," he whispers into my neck.

"Let's pack a bag and head out to Brian and Kevin's cabin, have some time with just us, okay? We can come back here whenever you want."

He nods and follows me into my room. He is looking around the house, and I know he sees all of Adam and Clara's stuff and the baby photos. I know I have to tell him. I just hope it's what pulls him through the next year and not a cause for him to downward spiral.

Once in the car, I text Brian that we are leaving. We have a two-hour drive, so I figure now is as good a time as any. I hand David my journal and take a deep breath.

"This is the journal I promised to keep. I need you to know how much I love you. I did what I thought was right. You are going to be mad, and I get that, but we will spend a few days in the cabin working things out before we head home, okay?"

"There is not a thing you could do that I won't forgive you for."

I smile. "We will see about that. Get reading."

Ten minutes later, I see him trying to control his breathing, and I know he's mad.

Oh god, I might lose him over this.

"Please keep reading," I whisper. I poured my heart and soul into that journal, so I need him to read it all.

He finishes reading just as we pull on to the road for the cabin.

He's quiet and looking out the window. My heart is beating so fast and loud I think he can hear it. I put the car in park and unbuckle my seatbelt and turn to look at him. He looks over at me and moves so fast I gasp. Instantly, he has me sitting on his lap and his arms around my waist and tears in his eyes.

"Yes, I'm mad I missed time with my kids, and I'm sad you felt you couldn't tell me, but I love you even more. You gave me two kids, two pieces of us combined, and my heart is so full. I want to spend some time with you here and reconnect, but then I want to meet my kids. Please."

I nod, and he kisses me so tenderly. We get out of the car and head inside the cabin.

No sooner do I close the door than David has me pinned to the door.

"Talk to me, beautiful. I want to know why you didn't tell me about our kids." He chokes up for a minute. "I know there is more than what is in that journal."

This man could always read me so well from day one. I take a minute to think about what I'm going to say but decide to lay it all out in the open. This is David, this is us, and we have nothing between us.

"Well, when I had Adam, I was scared. I knew once he was born, I would go back and see you, and I had read several accounts of you saying that a woman who had a baby was a turn-off, and you could never be with a mother, not even the mother of your own child."

He rests his forehead on mine. "Ivy, Ivy, Ivy, my sweet, beautiful Ivy. I *love* your curves, your stretch marks, all of it. Did I say those words? Yes, but to Anna. To get her to leave me alone, I said a few things worse than that as well. But you as a mother?" He presses into me, and his rock-hard cock digs into my belly.

"You feel that? God, thinking of you round with my baby is such a damn turn-on. I'm pissed I missed it. I want that with *you* and only you. Now, keep going. I want to hear it all."

"Well, I knew this time apart wasn't going to be easy. Case in point, we are here now. I figured if you knew about the kids, you wouldn't stay away, and it could risk everything. Hell, I couldn't stay away. I've gone and watched you play a few times just to be close to you."

"Yes, you did." He smiles at me. "I did see you that night in Charleston. I thought I had finally lost it because it was so real, but when I went after you, you just vanished."

I kiss him slowly and soft before pulling back. "I'm sorry. I knew I wasn't supposed to be there, and I couldn't mess anything up. Brian doesn't even know I went. I told him I had a work meeting so they would watch the kids."

"Beautiful, I need you," he says and reaches between us to unbutton and pull down his pants. "My heart and soul need you." He wraps my legs around his waist and pulls up my dress. "But after I'm done taking you, I want to know all about our kids, okay?" He thrusts into me hard, making me scream his name and claw at his back.

He isn't gentle, and I know it's partly because of being separated and partly from his anger of me keeping the kids from him. All I can do is hold on while he slams into me balls deep before pulling out and slamming into me all over again.

He pulls down the top of my dress so he's free to watch as my tits bounce up and down as he continues to slam into me. He reaches down to stroke my clit.

"Dammit, beautiful, come for me now," he growls into my ear before he sucks on my earlobe, sending me over the edge. I tense around him and scream out his name just as he bites into my neck. He pulls out and then moans into my ear.

After we catch our breath, I ask, "Why did you pull out?"

"Because I'm not chancing you getting pregnant again. The next time I come in you will be when we are together for good. Then I will be trying to get you pregnant."

He set me down, and we both readjust ourselves. "Beautiful, go lie down in bed, and I want you naked. I'm going to clean this up, then I'll join you."

I head over and grab my bag, then head to the bedroom. I do as he says, and I'm lying naked on the bed beside a box when he walks in.

"What's this?" he asks, walking over to the box. I smack his hands away.

"Ditch the clothes, then you can have what's in the box."

He smiles and removes his clothes, then climbs into bed with me. He sits with his back propped against the headboard, and when I sit up, he pulls me onto his lap. I grab the box for him and watch as he opens it.

"This is everything you missed with the kids. I figure we can start at the beginning."

I tell him about finding out I was pregnant with Adam and how Brian and Kevin took care of me. I show him videos of the doctor's appointments and the game Adam and I would play at night. While I was pregnant, I'd place the TV remote on my stomach, and he would kick it off. We watch the video of Adam's birth and both cry. I tell him how I play his music for them every night before bed and how neither can sleep without it. He loves that and says he can't wait to sing them to sleep.

We have dinner in bed, and I tell him about finding out I was pregnant with Clara and how I refused to let Adam sleep in his own bed until she was born. We watch videos of every doctor's appointment and the birth of Clara. The video of Adam holding Clara and meeting her the first time and him leaning down to give her a kiss. We go through pictures of me snuggling with them both. And Clara sleeping on my chest.

"That's probably why it looks like you gained another cup size. I love these babies," he says, cupping one of my breasts. He brings it to his mouth and sucks hard. My nipples are still super sensitive. He sucks the other one before he pulls out the next item in the box.

We continue through first smiles, first steps, first teeth, and first words. I tell him about their personalities and the funny things they have done. We watch videos of it all. He asks questions, and I answer them, and it's well after midnight before we're done.

He's spooning me, and we are talking about the kids when he grabs my leg and moves it back over his hip and thrusts his cock in me again. He's kissing my neck, and this time, it's slow and passionate lovemaking. His hands are all over my chest, belly, and hips. He's telling me how much he loves my new curves, and every stretch mark reminds him of the beautiful children I gave him. He tells me those kids are the most amazing gift and how he didn't think he could love me anymore until today.

He thanks me for being there for him with that letter and pulling him back from the edge. He thanks me for this time we have together and how his heart feels whole again.

As he starts lazily stroking my clit to match his lazy thrusts, he tells me that he hopes we have a whole litter of kids running around, but he wants to be there for everything, so if I do end up pregnant again, I am to send Brian to tell him. He doesn't want me traveling through the rocks and risking the baby. He withholds my orgasm until I agree, then thrusts into me hard and fast until we both shatter at the same time, and he barely pulls out in time.

He comes all over my back, and then he rubs it in and pulls me into the shower, where he comes all over my chest before fully washing me clean.

We finally tumble into bed and sleep hard that night.

We spend the next few days reconnecting on every level. We relearn each other's bodies, and he loves my stretch marks and memorizes how they fall on my hips. I don't know how he does it, but he makes me fall in love with my body too, and it's just one of the many things I love about him.

We tell each other everything that's happened over the past few years. He tells me about making movies and the concerts and how hard it was to get rumors of him sleeping with people started without actually sleeping with them. Said he had to pay a few of the women to go to the papers and sell the story. They thought it was funny to say he was lousy in bed. I laughed. Let them because I know the truth.

His favorite subject to talk about, by far, is the kids. So, after four days at the cabin, we head home. He insisted on stopping at a store on the way home to buy something for them. He refuses to show up empty-handed.

When we pull in the driveway, I text Brian to let him know we are here, then I turn to David and take his hand. I can tell he's a bit nervous, so I say, "They love you, David, and they are so young they will never know you weren't there. I made sure they know you." I give him a kiss, trying to calm his nerves.

We walk to the door hand in hand, and I open the front door.

David

I'm nervous to meet my kids. More nervous than the first time I played in front of a sold-out crowd. More nervous than when I sang for my record deal.

I'm holding the two toys Ivy assured me they would love, though toys are very different now for sure.

Ivy opens the door, and I hear footsteps and two little voices. "Mommy, Mommy, Mommy!" Ivy bends down and scoops them both into her arms and holds one on each hip. I see Brian beside me.

"Adam, Clara, there is someone I want you to meet." Ivy turns to me.

I watch Adam's eyes light up as he reaches for me. "Daddy!" he yells, and Clara screams and reaches for me too. With tears in my eyes, I pick them up and hold them both just like Ivy was, and she takes my photo, then comes to my side and holds the phone out to Brian.

"We need our first family photo," she tells him.

Brian takes a few photos, and then we head to the living room where I sit on the couch with the kids. Ivy sits beside me, and I realize this is the life I want, here in the house with Ivy and my kids and even Brian and Kevin.

Adam starts patting my shoulder to get my attention. "Daddy, Daddy, sing York!!" I look at Ivy for help.

"He's talking about the song from your New York City movie."

Well, I'll sing all day if it makes them smile, so I start singing. When the kids get down and start dancing in front of me, I can't help my eyes tearing up. I dreamed and prayed for moments like these, but I never thought they'd happen.

When I'm done singing, I give the kids my gifts. For Adam, it was something called *Paw Patrol* with dogs as rescuers. Ivy explained it to me, and I thought it was kind of cute. He has Ivy opening it so he can play with it.

For Clara, it's a lamb stuffed animal from a show called Doc Mc something where the kid can talk to toys and help fix them. She is hugging the lamb so hard, saying, "Yammy, love Yammy."

Ivy puts on each of the shows so I can see them, and I listen as the kids tell me about them. We have dinner as a family, and Ivy snaps so many photos.

I get to help with baths and bedtime and sing them to sleep. Tonight was perfect, and I want every night to be like this, so once the kids are sleeping, Ivy and I head to the living room and join Kevin and Brian.

We are sitting on the couch when I say, "I want this every night. This is the life I want."

"What about singing?" Brian asks.

I shake my head. "Honestly, it holds little appeal for me anymore. I do it because it's expected, not because I enjoy it. The same with acting." I look Brian right in the eye. "Please, I know Ivy said you might have a plan. Please bring me here. This is where my heart is, where I'm happy and feel whole. I'm just a shell back in 1964."

"But you have a kid there too," Kevin says. It's a statement, but I hear the question behind it.

"I will make sure he's taken care of, but Anna keeps him from me. I don't know him, and he doesn't know me. He's never called me daddy, and I know he's mine, but the connection isn't there. I can't prove it, but I think Anna is feeding him lies, so I doubt I'll get much from him."

What I don't admit is how it doesn't break my heart even though it should. I get he's mine, but when I see him, he's a reminder of Anna and that night. I tried to have a relationship with him, but every time I wanted to see him, Anna withheld him unless I agreed to have sex with her, and of course, I wouldn't touch her.

The only time I've seen him is when I've threatened her, and recently when she wanted to visit her dad, who was on his death bed. Can't say I'm not happy. Maybe things will get better when he isn't controlling her. I feel guilty about all this, and when I confess it to Ivy, she says she understands.

"What plans do you have, Brian?"

"Well, we have been working to build you a profile with a social security number, birth certificate, and a small online footprint. I've worked with a friend of mine doing it slowly so as not to flag any systems. I've also been digging into your death. I have a folder downstairs, so we know the details, but I think we can fake it as a drug overdose. I'm working on the plans for that. There is something you will need to handle on your end."

I know Brian works with computers, but I can't quite wrap my head around what he does. Ivy tried to explain it to me—IT, networks, databases—but none of it made sense to me.

"Tell me, and I'll do it," I say with no doubt in my head. I know they can lay out a plan for me, and I'll do it.

This week and a half I get to spend with Ivy and my kids are heaven.

Every morning after breakfast, we watch cartoons, then we go play in the backyard. One morning, Clara had me push her in the swing for an hour. I'd do it all day if I wasn't worried about her being out in the sun.

I've read them every book they own at least four times and learned the name of every stuffed animal they own.

One night when I'm tucking the kids into bed, I realize I need to do my part to make this happen, so Brian, Ivy, and I spend a few long nights going over all the details surrounding my death.

By the end of my time here, we have a solid plan, and I have a bright outlook on life for the first time in 3 years.

∞∞∞

Today is the day I go back to my time. I've been trying to convince Ivy to come with me for a few weeks, but she says she can't while I'm still married. I reminded her I'm married to her and only her. The one with Anna is a piece of paper only.

As I'm packing, Ivy walks up and hands me a few letters. "I figure I need to update the one on if things get too hard, and here are a few extras." She smiles.

I kiss her, and say, "You know I'm not waiting a year to see my family again, right?"

"I figured." She sighs

"I'm going to try to visit every three months and be here for their birthdays and Christmas."

"Okay, but don't let it interfere with the last movies you are making. They still need to happen."

I pull her close and wrap my arms around her waist and kiss her hard. "My whole world is right here in this house. Everything I want. I promise to keep up my life there as I need to, but this is where I want to be and where I will be as often as possible. I love you, Ivy, more and more every day, every time I see you."

I have breakfast with the kids, and Brian stays with them as Ivy walks me to the stones. Saying goodbye to them even for a few months leads to a bunch of tears. We get to the stones, and leaving Ivy and the kids is the last thing I want to do.

For a brief minute, I think about not going back and just staying here. But I need to get things in order, not just for my son and my parents but for Ivy too. I will do this the right way, but I know it will take everything in me to do so.

Knowing the time between seeing her will be much shorter this time gives me a kind of hope I haven't had in the past three years, but it doesn't make walking through the stones any easier.

Chapter 21

July 12, 1964

David,

Congrats on finishing your film. The kids and I are watching it today in celebration. Doing the full movie night with popcorn and staying up late. I'm betting Clara falls asleep at about the halfway point, though. I think it's your voice; it just lulls her to sleep.

I know you coming to visit last month wasn't a part of the plan, but I wouldn't change it for anything.

I'm betting the kids are back to sleeping in my bed again, and I'm not sorry about that.

1 year, 1 month, 26 days. 422 days until you are mine again.

I love you more than I did yesterday.

Ivy

October 18, 1964

My sweet Ivy,

We are under the 1-year mark. The only thing that made it even better was being able to come home and spend your birthday with our family. That part was over the top, and I wouldn't have it any other way. Both kids seemed to light up when I said I'd be there for Christmas.

Having these dates closer and seeing you guys more is making this last year fly by. I know it's not what we planned, beautiful, but it's perfect.

I love you and will see you soon.

David

October 19, 2016

David,

You are spoiling these kids by coming home so often. I know it's for their birthdays, and I love that you are here. They haven't stopped talking about your visit for Adam's birthday, and I want you to know it means the world to them and me that you are here.

10 months, 23 days.

From what I understand, Anna should be filing paperwork any day now if she hasn't already. We are in the home stretch, baby.

We love you.

Ivy, Adam, Clara

October 21, 1964

Ivy,

She did! She filed for divorce. I had the papers when I got home from my last visit! Of course, her first demands are a bit crazy, and a part of me wanted to agree just to be done with this, but we just sent the revised papers back to her. I'm expecting it to be a bit before I hear from her again.

I can't wait to be there for Christmas. Our first Christmas as a family. I hope it's the first of many more.

I love you, my sweet Ivy. I see the light at the end of the tunnel.

David

January 2, 1965

David,

Having you home for Christmas was a dream come true. Our first family Christmas and I promise there will be many more.

We will make our own traditions, and it will be the perfect end to every year.

My love, there are only 8 months, 9 days left. 252 more days!

I love you with all my heart.

Ivy

April 11, 1965

My sweet Ivy,

Today, I start my last movie from this stretch in California. Being this far from you and the kids is killing me. I don't think I will be able to do too much more in California after this. I made the promise for this movie, and I think this will be the last of my movie career.

There is something comforting being at Ivy Hill and being near you, surrounded in you, and the possibility of you walking in the door at any minute.

Exactly five more months.

All my love,

David

July 28, 1965

David,

If you are reading this, then things are hard again. We are so close to the end of this. The kids and I can't wait to see you. I have special plans for when you are mine again. Plans that will make all this waiting worth it.

If you need to take a break and come and see us again, then do it. Even if it's just for a weekend. The kids miss you, and of course I always miss you.

I again feel like I need to say I'm sorry we have to go through all this, but we will come out on the other end of this even stronger than before.

We can do anything together, David. Please hold out for me and for the kids. We need you.

I love you, baby. Come home to me.

Ivy

July 28, 1965

Ivy,

I read your "if things get hard" letter today. Anna won't let me see my son and is making all sorts of threats. I know you say the divorce will be final, but it's just hard to think the end is really less than two months away.

The closer the time gets, the worse Anna gets. I am about to wrap up this movie in the next few days, and then I will be heading back to Ivy Hill. Back to us. I am going to try to hold on until this is over. Spend some time with my mom and dad.

Before I head home, I'm going to go spend some time with your grandparents. They have forgiven me to a point for marrying Anna, and we talk every few months. Your grandfather has given me some great advice.

I love you, Ivy, and these letters mean more to me than you

will ever know.

Your David

Chapter 22

Ivy

September 3, 2017

Eight days. I am on edge. I have been pacing the house for three days now, and Brian says I'm wearing a rut in the carpet. I don't care. I'll replace it if I have to.

I'm already packed for my trip. The guys are excited to have the kids to themselves for two weeks. I'm not looking forward to being away from the kids for two weeks, but David and I need this time too. Then I plan to bring David here and spend some family time together.

But best-laid plans and all that.

∞∞∞

I wish I could say it's been four years since I've been here, but I cheated. Twice, I cheated. As I walk by the familiar newsstand, I check the date once again. September 11, 1965.

I normally get here in the morning, but this time, I wanted to make sure he got the papers, so it's just before dinnertime.

I walk the street to Ivy Hill and take in the changes. A few new houses have gone up on the street. Sad to think they won't be there in fifty years when the museum is built.

One of them across the street has some kids playing on a tire swing with their dad, and I can't help but watch and smile. *Soon*, I tell myself. I have to believe that soon I will have my David with me always. The alternative is something I can't think about right now.

I walk toward Ivy Hill and see a few people out front of the gates taking pictures. Well, this will be fun. As I get closer to the gates, I recognize one of David's security members, Clint. So I take a chance and walk up to him.

"Hello, Clint," I say with my best smile.

His eyes light up. Thank god!

"Miss Ivy, I was starting to think you weren't coming," he says as he opens the side gate for me to walk through.

"Don't tell David, please. I want to surprise him," I say, and he nods. I also notice a few dirty looks from the fans at the gate. I guess I will be spending time inside instead of out in town on this trip.

When I walk in the side door via the kitchen, I can hear the notes from the piano playing in the house.

His parents are in the kitchen. When they see me, I can tell they are about to make a big deal, so I hold my finger to my lips, asking them to be quiet.

They hug me and tell me they are so glad I'm here.

"Did he get the papers today?" I ask because I have to be sure.

"Yes, dear. He got them this morning, and he has been waiting on you ever since. I think he's given up hope that you will be here today," his mom says.

"I didn't know when he'd get the papers. So it's done?" I have to be 100% sure before I truly get my hopes up.

His mom and dad just nod.

I set my bag down on the counter and make my way to the piano room. Stopping just around the corner, I take a moment to watch David play. From here, his back is toward me, and he has the bench perpendicular to the piano just as he always does when I'm in the room with him so I can sit behind him while he plays.

I watch him play, and I can feel his parents observing from behind me. I take in a few changes like the new stained glass of roses over the window with the letter M in it. Roses like the scent of my bath product that he loves so much, and I can't help but smile.

His mom places a hand on my shoulder, and they both head back into the kitchen, leaving me to watch David play.

When the song ends, I clap, and he looks over his shoulder slowly as though he's scared at what he might see. I see him take a deep breath, and his whole body shakes before he stands up and walks over to me. When he's right in front of me, he falls to his knees and wraps his arms around my waist, pressing his head in my belly. I can tell he is crying, even if he's trying to keep it silent.

I rub up the back of his neck and run my hands through his hair. For a few minutes, no one moves, and no one says anything.

"Please don't ever make me do that again," David says just above a whisper.

"Not a chance. You are mine now. Forever and always."

He stands up and pulls me tight against him and kisses me slow but hard, and his tongue makes love to my mouth. His hands are in my hair, pulling me even closer, deepening the kiss until I let out a soft moan. He then pulls back slowly and rests his forehead against mine.

We are both breathing heavily but don't say a word. A moment later, he bends down and swoops me into his arms, bridal style, and starts up the stairs. I can't help but throw my head back and laugh.

He walks into our room, and I see it hasn't changed. There are a few pictures of the kids now, but otherwise, it looks exactly as I remember it. I can't explain how it makes me feel that this room is strictly ours and has been left untouched this whole time.

He lays me down on the bed gently, then sits down on the edge and just looks at me. Leaning in, he kisses me again long and slow.

He then stands. "Clothes off, beautiful," he says with a smirk. I can't get them off fast enough. Once we are both naked, he leans down to kiss me again and wraps one arm around my waist, moving me to the center of the bed while never breaking the kiss.

His kisses trail down my jaw to my neck while his hands travel up my waist and grab my breasts. He nibbles at the pulse point on my neck before his kisses trail down to my nipple, sucking hard and nipping at one then the other.

His kisses head farther down to my stomach, and he kisses each stretch mark, telling me how much he loves them. His kisses continue to travel down until his lips wrap around my clit.

I am already on edge, so it only takes to good tug, and I'm flying over the edge, screaming his name. He doesn't let up and continues making love to my pussy with his mouth, sending me into orgasm two and three before he starts kissing back up my body.

"I've missed you so damn much, beautiful," he says before kissing me. I can still taste myself on his lips. I never thought that would be such a turn-on.

The slick head of his cock is at my entrance before he pauses. I try to arch and angle to get him to slip in, but he just keeps rubbing it over my clit.

"You want my cock, beautiful?" he asks as he is driving me crazy.

"Yes, David, please!" I beg.

"Tell me you will take me home with you so I can spend some time with the kids." He grinds harder on my clit. "Tell me, and you can get the relief you are looking for," he whispers into my ear and then takes my earlobe into his mouth.

I gasp for air. "Yes."

"Yes, what? I need your words, beautiful." He slows his thrusting on my clit before stopping.

"Yes, you can come home with me and spend time with the kids," I say and watch the blinding smile of pure joy stretch across his face right before he slams into me.

He grabs my hands and intertwines our fingers and holds them above my head as he builds a steady rhythm. His face is replaced with pure pleasure, one I know only I get to see.

It doesn't take long for both of us to reach our peaks and tumble over. But David remains hard and starts the buildup all over again. This time, we take time to explore each other's bodies, and we spend the night making love and whispering how much we love each other.

∞∞∞

The next morning, he brings me breakfast in bed, and we just talk about everything and anything. He tells me about his son, and I tell him about the kids and some events that have happened.

"Will you help me redecorate? I want any sign of Anna out of here, and I want it all to be you."

I smile. "This is why I always felt at home at Ivy Hill on the tours."

We spend the next few days going over plans for the décor. We are talking about the plans for the living room when he comes up behind me and wraps his arms around my waist.

"I need you to know I never touched Anna in this house. Not a kiss, not a handhold, not a hug. It didn't feel right. I couldn't tarnish your memory here because I see you in every room. I see the time I took you on the dining room table, or the pool table, or on the piano bench, and I couldn't lose that. She was never in our room. She stayed in her own room on the other side of the house."

I turn in his arms and wrap my arms around his neck. "That takes all the fun out of it."

I laugh as a confused and horrified look passes over his face.

"I was looking forward to making new memories in each room of the house once it's redecorated." I kiss him lightly on the lips and feel his smile against mine, and he deepens the kiss.

He pulls me closer. "I want to go home with you and never come back, beautiful."

"You have to soak up time with your son. Four more years, David, he deserves that time with you."

"I agree, and I will try, but I don't even know my son."

I jerk back to look at him. "What do you mean?"

"Even though I have visitation, Anna holds him from me every chance she gets. She has told me before she would let me see him if I slept with her. I'm sure it's so she can get pregnant again and get more money from me each month."

"David... I don't know how things are here, but where I'm from, she can't do that."

He shrugs. "She's the mother. I don't hold many rights."

"And she has spread many rumors about the drugs she can threaten to use against you."

"And if I prove they aren't true, then I ruin any chance of us being together."

I rest my head against the center of his chest. "This is the most selfish thing I will ever do in my life."

"My sweet Ivy, you are the furthest thing from selfish. Where do you think I want to spend my life? Here without you, with a woman who I can't stand to be around who is poisoning my son against me, and with a kid I don't even know. Or with you, the love of my life, our two kids who know me and love me thanks to their amazing mother, and where I can watch over 100 TV channels in color."

I can't help but laugh. "Well, when it comes to the TV channels."

"I will make sure my son is set up and taken care of. I am working with my lawyer now. My dad will be the trustee, just like you said. He will have everything he will ever need, and as soon as he is old enough to take over, all this will be his. I am going to iron out the details when we head home next week."

I smile again. I love that he calls 2017 home.

Chapter 23

David

"Daddy, Daddy, Daddy! Uncle Brian told us you were coming!" Adam comes running up to me, and I swoop him up in the air, causing him to laugh and squeal.

"And how did Uncle Brian know I'd be here?"

"'Cause Mommy had planned it." Brian comes in laughing with Kevin right behind him with a sleeping Clara in his arms.

She wakes up, rubbing her eyes, and looks at me. "Daddy?"

"Hey, sweet pea." I smile and reach for her. She climbs into my arms and rests her head on my shoulder.

"I missed you, Daddy," she says, and with that simple phrase, I know this is where I am meant to be.

"I missed you too, sweet pea. I missed you too." I kiss the top of her head and hold her just a bit tighter.

The afternoon is filled with me singing songs for the kids, TV, and cuddles. Right here, I truly feel like a father, and I know I have to fight for this life. It isn't going to be easy, and we have a short timeline to figure it out. A little less than four more years. But we *will* figure it out because, in my eyes, there is no other way.

After I help put the kids to bed that night, I sit down with Brian.

"Okay, what do you need?" he asks as he opens his laptop.

"First, I need to know how to set up my will. I want to make sure my son gets everything, and Anna can't touch any of it. I want to have my dad set up to run it for the time being. I also want to make sure my parents are taken care of for the rest of their lives."

"Let's see what the almighty Google can show us first."

I shake my head as the word Google shows across his screen.

"It's a search engine. Think of it as the library reference section, but for everything that's on the internet."

What Brian can pull up in a few minutes blows my mind. There is a copy of my will word for word, showing my father as the trustee until my son turns twenty-five. Once my son turns eighteen, he is to work alongside my father, learning how to manage it all. At the age of twenty-one, he gets half, and at the age of twenty-five, he takes over full management. There is even a section stating at no time is Anna to receive any part of my estate and no increase of her living expenses per the prenup.

Brian prints it off, minus the part with the signatures on it. I should be able to take it to my lawyer and say this is what I want, and he can fix it up pretty for me.

"What else do you need?" He eyes me like he knows what I'm going to say.

"Two more things, but I want you to think about them, and we can work them out before I leave."

"Hit me with it."

"First, I want to make sure Ivy and the kids are taken care of, and I have an idea on how to do so. I just need you to use your fancy computer for the details."

"And the other?"

"Okay, I have an idea as to the how surrounding my death on my end, but again, I need your fancy research."

I head back to our room and hear Ivy taking a shower. I think about joining her, but something in the corner catches my eye. It's a footlocker like the one I had in the Army. I head over and take a look at it. There is a scratch along the side just like mine has. What are the odds?

I open it up, and sure enough, in the top corner in tiny print. *D. Miller*. Shock hits me that she has my footlocker. Does she know? My mind races. I know mine is in the storage in the basement back home, and I haven't pulled it out in years. I smile. This is what I needed.

I'm so distracted I miss being able to get in the shower with Ivy, so I just get ready and wait for her in bed.

She walks out of the bathroom with wet hair, wearing the sexiest little sleep shorts and a tank top, and crawls into bed with me.

"Hey, beautiful." I kiss her forehead. "Where did you get that footlocker in the corner?"

I watch the dreamy smile on her face. "It was my grandpa's. I saw it in their house growing up. My grandma always stored blankets in it. They would tell me it was a special chest, and it would be mine one day. It's like having a piece of them so close to me."

I nod and hold her close as she drifts off to sleep, and my plans slowly fall into place.

∞∞∞

Over the next week, I spend my days getting to be daddy, playing with the kids, and singing songs on demand. I love every minute of it. I spend my nights researching with Brian. There is so much we still have to plan, but we are making great progress.

Sunday comes, and I wake up to Ivy already in the kitchen and amazing smells filling the house.

"Why are you up so early, beautiful?"

"It's football Sunday; we make a day out of it, watching as many games as we can while filling up on tailgate food. It's so much fun."

"I'm betting it's a lot different now than the football I know."

She smiles. "Let's find out."

After just an hour into the first game, I'm amazed at the camera angles and the graphics they can make on the screen. It makes following the game so much easier. These newscasters can pull stats up in a heartbeat, and the instant replay is remarkable.

This is the life I want, and I'm so close to getting it that I can't think of that possibility that stands in the way that this is all just a pipe dream.

Chapter 24

Ivy

It's been six months since I've seen David. It was hard to let him go because I know he has to finish up a tour, so our next visit isn't for four more months, and I'm getting a little antsy. I hate being away from him, but knowing the next time I can see him really helps.

The kids just know Daddy has to go away for work. Because really, how do you explain time travel to someone who isn't even in kindergarten yet?

Brian has been working on David's and his plans to get him here. He tried to explain the geeky side of it to me, and my eyes glazed over. Kevin took mercy on me and distracted him.

I'm lying in bed and having problems sleeping. My gut says something is up, but I can't place it. I get up and go check on the kids and find them both in bed sound asleep. When I get back downstairs, Brian and Kevin are both in the kitchen.

"Can't sleep, either?" I ask as I sit down at the bar top.

"No. I feel like something is up, but I just can't place it." Brian shrugs his shoulders.

I see Kevin making some french fries, our go-to snack, and Brian is mixing up our dip when there is a knock on the door. We all look at the clock and see it is almost midnight. Who the hell is it?

Kevin goes to answer the door, and we are all on edge until we see David on the other side. I run to him and see his face red and tears running down his face. He squeezes me into a bone-crushing hug, and we collapse against the door.

"You weren't there," he mumbles into my neck.

"David, I don't understand."

"She died, and you weren't there!"

"David, baby, who died?" I ask softly.

"My mom."

"What? No, that's next year! Of a brain aneurysm."

"No, I just left her funeral and wake."

I look at Brian with panic in my eyes. He is already on his phone.

"No, we mixed up the dates. It was this year."

"Shit." Panic rips through me as I get him to the couch.

I kneel in front of him and take his face in both hands.

"I am so sorry. I would have been there with you, and I had every intention of doing so. I am so, so sorry."

He hasn't stopped crying, so I wipe the tears from his face.

"Let's go to bed," I whisper and stand. He follows me to the bedroom, and I spend the night holding him as he tells me everything from the past few days down to the funeral. I can't believe we mixed up the dates.

I don't remember falling asleep, but the next thing I know, the kids are bouncing on the bed, squealing that Daddy is here. Despite everything, he wakes up with a smile on his face when he sees them. He holds them a bit tighter as we snuggle in for breakfast in bed and watch morning cartoons.

When Brian comes to get them for lunch, I see the pain all over David's face, so I snuggle up to him.

"What's on your mind?" I run my hand down his chest.

"If my plan doesn't work, if it's really me in that grave at Ivy

Hill, I know the pain they will be feeling. That rips me apart, Ivy. I have to find a way to take care of them."

"You know you can't be associated with us in any way, right?"

"I'm going to find a way, Ivy. You can count on that."

∞∞∞

David has been here for two weeks, and I'm assuming he heads home tomorrow.

"I'm going to miss you when you leave tomorrow." I kiss his neck, which causes him to laugh.

"I'm not leaving tomorrow."

"But it's been two weeks."

"Yeah, but everyone thinks I'm in rehab because I couldn't take my mother dying, so I have four more weeks before I have to go home."

I let that sink in. All those six-week rehab visits where no one saw him. Could it be they are when he is here?

I smile. "So rehab is code for visiting me, huh?"

"Yep." He smiles too.

"I can get on board with that. I still plan to come to visit in four months as we have planned."

He kisses the top of my head. "Good, I will need some Ivy time after the end of that crazy tour. We rescheduled some dates. My manager wasn't happy, but since his contract is up in a few months, he hasn't pushed the issue. He's worried I won't re-sign him, so I'm enjoying that."

"Will you re-sign him?"

"Probably. He can be a pain in the ass, but he has gotten me this far." He sighs. "I'm going to tuck the kids in for their naps, then I need to talk to Brian and see how far he's gotten on our plans.

"What plans?"

"Go get us lunch, and I'll meet you there and explain."

When he joins us at the table, he explains that Brian has been working on setting up an identity for him, but it's a slow process so he doesn't flag any systems. Once it's done, I will be able to add him to the kid's birth certificates, we will be able to get legally married, and he can do simple things like get a driver's license.

"What about people recognizing you?"

"Well, I've been working with a voice coach to learn a more Southern accent; they think it's for a movie. And my natural hair color is blond, not this black, so I will go back to that, and you said you love my beard."

I can't help but smile. David has the sexiest beard, and boy, does it feel great when he wakes me up in the morning with his head between my legs.

"Stop thinking dirty thoughts, woman. I have stuff to do," he jokes, and I laugh.

"Well, if you are working, then so am I."

The routine we fall into over the next few weeks is a slice of the life I send up a prayer every night for.

Chapter 25

Ivy

The past four months have dragged by. I know he had to go back and finish up his tour, but none of us wanted him to leave. The kids drew him pictures to take with him, and while they were sad to see him go, and they didn't want him to leave, they have done great with him being gone. I'm sure watching Daddy on TV helps, and they have every one of his movies memorized by heart.

Today, I am walking past that familiar newsstand again and making my way up to Ivy Hill, September 17, 1966. I give my name to the guard, and he calls Clint to verify it's me.

"Ivy, we have an interesting visitor today." He hugs me and guides me inside.

"Interesting how?"

"Anna showed up out of the blue with his son."

"What does she want?"

"We don't know yet. Supposedly out of the goodness of her heart, she thought to stop by since she was in the area and let David see his son she has been keeping from him for the last year."

"Right. Well, I will take your lead. Do I go in and be friendly, do I go in and be a bitch, or do I go shopping and come back in a few hours?"

Clint laughs. "Ivy, if David finds out I sent you shopping, he will have my head. No, no, let's get you in there."

I stop at the kitchen door. This is the first time I have been back since Helen died. The last time I walked in that door, she wrapped me in a huge hug and was so happy to see me. I should have been here to say goodbye, to hug her one more time, to hear her laugh at the dinner table, and watch her smile so big when we rave over a new recipe she tried out.

I should have been here for James and David. I should have been by their side at her funeral and the wake. I should have been here, and I wasn't. I'm kicking myself even more for that, and I don't think I realized how guilty I truly felt until now.

I know David has forgiven me, but will James? I could have warned him it was his last night with her so he could have spent every second holding her and telling her how much he loves her. Can he ever forgive me for that?

I guess I hesitate long enough because Clint breaks me from my thoughts.

"What's wrong, Miss Ivy?"

"I should have been here, Clint. When Helen died, I should have been here."

"It was a sad day, but you will see they are doing well. We all are."

With a nod and a deep breath, I step into the kitchen as tears fill my eyes. It isn't the same to see James sitting at the bar without Helen. He looks older and sadder, but he still manages a huge smile for me and comes over to hug me.

The moment I'm in his arms, I burst out crying. "I'm so sorry I mixed up the dates. I should have been here."

"Oh Ivy, David came back, and we talked. It's okay, and honestly, I'm glad I didn't know. It would have been so much more painful for me to know. This way, I know she didn't suffer, and while it was hard, we are doing well on this side."

His words don't stop the tears from falling. But he holds me tight until they stop. He kisses my forehead and smiles.

"Now, I'm glad you're here. Did Clint tell you who made a surprise visit today?"

I sigh. "Yes. I don't know what her agenda is, but I guess I'm about to find out."

James holds up his finger and goes to pour me a glass of wine.

I laugh. "If I'm still in there in an hour, send in something stronger."

I make my way to the living room and poke my head in to see his son Scott sitting on the floor playing with some toys, and Anna sitting next to David on the couch. I can't hear what they are saying, but Anna is leaning in, and David looks uncomfortable and is leaning away from her. I smile and head back to the kitchen and get a questioning look from James.

"Let me get a drink for David. From the looks of things, he needs it more than I do." James pours me a drink, and I walk into the living room, not even caring what conversation I am interrupting. David sees me, and his face lights up. He jumps up and rushes over to hug me.

I laugh and hand him the drink. "I was expecting you earlier this morning." David gives a fake pout that makes me laugh.

"Sorry. Kevin got home from a delivery and was telling us about it, and we lost track of time."

"David, we aren't done talking," Anna whines, and it makes my skin crawl. Judging by the look on David's face, it makes his skin crawl too.

"It is anything important?" I whisper.

"She is trying to set up times for Scott to stay with me while she visits her friends back in France."

I nod just as Anna stands up and comes over and tries to grab David's arm, which he yanks away and wraps around my waist.

"Sorry, *Ivy,* but we have parental business to talk about."

I roll my eyes at her and walk over to Scott.

"Hello, I'm Ivy," I introduce myself.

"I'm this many." He holds up four fingers.

"No way! My son Adam is five!"

I smirk because I see Anna catches on right away when her jaw drops, and David smiles.

"You know I was told there is a waterfall here, that true?"

"Yes, it's in the back room!"

"No way! Can you show me so your mom and dad can talk?"

He jumps up and picks up his toys and heads out of the room but stops to look at me.

"Follow me!"

I laugh and follow him, giving David a wink before I leave the room and hear him mumble as I walk by, "Evil woman." He knows what I did.

"Look right there!" he points.

"Wow, I've never seen a waterfall in a house before. It's so cool!"

"Yeah, my dad's house is the bestest house I've ever seen, but my mommy doesn't let me come here much."

I'm sad for this little boy, but I know it's time to change the subject.

"Will you show me your tractor?" I ask as James comes to sit on the couch and watch us play.

A little bit into playing, I find myself humming the tune of "John Deere Green" without realizing it.

"What song is that?" Scott asks.

"Oh, it's one that stuck in my head."

"Sometimes, if I sing a song, it gets unstuck."

I look at James, and he knows I've been caught. This song is one that was popular when I was growing up and not around yet.

Knowing this little boy has a long list of people who disappoint him over the years and not wanting to be one of them, I start softly singing the song for him. He picks it up pretty fast, and by the time David and Anna join us, he is singing the chorus pretty well.

Anna doesn't look too happy, and she snaps when she sees Scott and me laughing.

"It's time to go."

He jumps up and runs over to hug me.

"Thank you for playing with me, Miss Ivy."

Knowing I can give this little boy a small ray of hope, I whisper in his ear, "Things will get better once you're an adult. Don't forget that."

He looks at me with a confused look on his face, so I hold my finger to my lips, showing him it's a secret, and he smiles and nods.

He hugs James and David before running out after his mom.

"Well, isn't she a ray of sunshine," James says as David collapses on to the couch next to him. I get up and sit on his lap.

"I think the trip to France was just an excuse to come here because she knows no dates, and she kept saying I should take her out to dinner to talk about it and let Dad watch Scott."

"She wants to be seen with you so she can sell a story," I say. "Promise me you won't ever drink anything she gives you. I have a weird feeling she'd try to drug you first chance she gets."

"I promise, and I hate to say it wouldn't surprise me one bit because I've already had that thought. I know where her mind is—get another kid, get more money—and I hate that. I wish I could find a way to get Scott away from her. Tell me he's okay?"

I smile. "He learns the truth about her, and they don't talk much now. The only time she was allowed at Ivy Hill was when they put your wedding section in the museum. He allowed her to come in and let the press get photos."

He cringes and shakes his head. "It should be *you* there, not her."

I sigh. "I know, but history is what it is. We know the truth, and that has to be enough."

He rests his head against the back of the couch and looks at the ceiling for a bit before looking back at me.

"That day we toured Ivy Hill; it was the wedding exhibit you pulled me away from, wasn't it?"

"Yeah, I figured you didn't need to know about it until the time came. I told you knowing what is to come isn't a gift; it's a burden." I force a half smile at him.

He rubs my back. "That is a burden I will gladly share with you if you will only let me."

"I know. A few more years and you will know everything." I give a sad smile.

After dinner, we sit down with his dad to work on his will to make sure his son and his dad are taken care of.

"When does he... um, when we will...?" His dad stumbles over the question.

I give him a sad smile. "August 1969. We have a bit yet, but ..." I pause and look at David. "I'd like to have you come home with us to meet your grandkids. I want you to know how to get to us so you can visit if everything works, even if not."

I watch his eyes water, and he nods. David is smiling.

"I will get Clint and Nancy to hold things down here while we are gone," David says, then stands up. "Now, it's time for some alone time with my girl." He takes my hand and pulls me toward the stairs, making his dad laugh.

Chapter 26

David

Two weeks fly by, and before I know it, we are standing in front of the rocks. I see my dad looking skeptical, and I can only imagine it's how I looked when I was here the first time.

"Okay, here are the rocks you need. It only lasts a few seconds."

Dad looks at me. "You have done this?"

I nod. "Several times."

He nods, and Ivy offers her hand to him. He takes a deep breath and takes it. We walk into the center of the stones before stopping. My dad looks at his skin.

"You feel it?" Ivy asks, and my dad nods.

She counts to three, and they both touch the stone, and I watch them be pulled in. I take a deep breath, count to ten, then touch the stone myself.

The familiar sensation of being pulled, then pushed surrounds me before I end up on the other side.

I look up and see my dad looking around and relax when he sees me.

"It doesn't look much different, but it sounds different."

I smile. "Wait until you see the TV."

∞∞∞

Watching my dad with his grandkids was amazing. Anna never lets him do anything with Scott, but with Adam and Clara, he was able to be as hands-on as he wanted, and I caught him crying a few times. He is their only living grandparent, and he wants to spoil them as much as possible, so he was learning everything he could. He hated having to come back here just as much as I did.

That was eight months ago. Today, I am heading back through the rocks, back to my Ivy with a huge surprise for her that I have been putting in motion. This is another time the world thinks I am in rehab, so I have six weeks with not only my girl but also my kids.

Once back in 2019, I take in the new changes on Ivy's street. There is a new house getting ready to be built, but otherwise, it looks almost the same as the first time I was here.

I knock on the door and hear the kids yelling, "Daddy!" and the sound of running feet, making me laugh.

When Ivy opens the door, she takes my breath away. She looks even more beautiful than the day we met; maybe it's because I love her more today. Or maybe it's because she has Clara on her hip and looks like everything I always picture as a mom.

"David, you don't have to knock. This is your home. You are always welcome, announced or not, but keep in mind, I know you are coming most of the time."

"I can tell." I laugh as I swoop Adam in my arms and head inside. I help Ivy put the kids to bed, and Brian and Kevin come home just as we are sitting down on the couch.

"So, I have good news."

Ivy's face gets so hopeful that I almost wonder if she already knows.

"I found a way to take care of you and the kids."

"David, we have everything we need."

"I know, but I can't explain it. There is this need to take care of you three and any future kids we may have. They will never be tied to the Miller name or legacy, and I feel like they are getting gypped because of it. Come on, I want to show you something."

I pull her into our bedroom. Brian and Kevin follow but stop at the door.

"Umm, is this some sexy 'got to show you'? Because we need a ten-minute head start to get downstairs," Brian asks.

I laugh. "Come on."

I walk over to my footlocker. "Remember when I asked you about the footlocker? It's because it drew my eyes. It looks just like the one I had in the Army, scratch on the side and all. I opened it and look." I show them the small D. Miller in the corner, and all three gasp.

"But it belonged to my grandparents!"

"Because I was up there a few months ago and gave it to them with instructions to pass it down to one of their grandkids but not tell them it was mine, knowing they will only have one, you."

"David, that may be so. Now it just means so much more to me, and I could never get rid of it."

"I know, sweet girl, but did you know it has a false bottom?"

I see the confusion on her face, so I know she didn't. I start to pull out the items she has in there and then pull out the false bottom.

"Knowing you had it and about the bottom, I filled it with some things after I talked to Brian last time I was here."

I pull out some signed records, a letter to my son, and the missing gold record album that no one could track down. It included a letter addressed to Ivy's grandparents, thanking them for their hospitality, advice, and home cooking. The names are a bit smudged and no last names were used, so this will eliminate any doubt about why it has gone missing.

I hear three gasps behind me when I pull out the gold record.

"David, is that… is that the missing record?" Ivy whispers.

"Yes, with a letter to your grandparents. Names smudged with no last name as to why I gave it to them. Well, the public reason."

I made sure to smudge the names so if the letter gets in the hands of the public, it can't be traced back to Ivy.

"If Ivy shows up with that anywhere, the press will surround her and dig into her and her family, the kids, us," Brian says with his eyes still on the record.

"I figured, so I have a plan for that too."

"Care to share it with us?" Kevin asks.

I place the items back and close up the footlocker. "Let's go to the living room."

As we sit down, I pull Ivy onto my lap, needing her close.

"I need you guys to trust me on this. My son is getting a letter right now from the trust of the estate. It explains who I gave the album to and why, which will match up to the letter in the footlocker. It says not to ask questions but to come to this address. He will buy the items from you and place them in the museum, and it will be listed as an anonymous source who found it in their grandparents' things they were going through after they died."

"He's going to have questions, and what if he remembers me!"

I laugh. "Ivy, he's five now. Was four when you saw him last." I shake my head. "He's how old now? In his fifties? You think he's going to remember you?"

"He's fifty-seven, and I guess not." She sighs.

"See, trust me, I've thought this out. You will see. Now tell me everything I have missed."

We talk and chat the rest of the night before I take Ivy to bed and make up for lost time.

The rest of my time in 2019 seems to fly by. I fall into a routine helping with the kids, meals, nap times, bath times, bedtimes, and hours of making love to Ivy.

I find out the house being built down the street is Brian and David's in preparation for me coming to live here. This way, they'll be close, but they give us our space. I hear Adam will be starting kindergarten in September, so I make plans to come back to be here for that. I am so excited that it is a first I get to see in person. I'm sure my dad will want to be there for that as well, so we plan to make that happen.

I will be finishing up my last tour. No one knows it's my last, but it will be. I made sure I will be home working on my next album during August of 1969. I am making plans and wrapping things up. It's weird to plan your own fake death, hoping it won't be your real one, but as I watch my kids dance to one of my songs, I know it's the right move for them and me.

Chapter 27

Ivy

A week after David heads home, I hear a knock on my door. I don't think about it, but when I see a grown-up fifty-seven-year-old Scott on the other side, my eyes go wide. He looks so much like his dad and what I picture his dad to look like at that age. Not to mention, he's well known in this town for all his charity work.

"Scott." I smile and watch him force a smile. I can tell he's uncomfortable. Heck, so am I now. "Come in, let's sit."

He's quiet for a minute before he speaks. "What's your name?"

I'm shocked for a minute because I had assumed he knew. "Ivy."

I watch him nod, then he holds out a piece of paper. "This was left by my dad in his trust for me. I got it just over a week ago."

I take the letter and read it. It's just like David has said—he gave the items to my grandparents as thanks for everything they did for him. They were passed down to their only living relative, their granddaughter, me. There is a whole section about how to handle the purchase, so it keeps my family and me out of it, and money has already been set aside for the purchase. There is even a section stating that I am to keep the footlocker and instructions on what to do if at any time I wish to sell it to the museum.

By the time I am done reading the letter, I have tears running down my face. I run a hand over the letter, handwritten by David. I'd recognize his handwriting anywhere. I take a deep breath and hand it back to Scott and wipe my face.

"Is it true? Do you have the missing record?" he asks gently.

I nod. "Yes, and a few other items that were with it."

"How did my dad know it would be at this address? This is his handwriting. I know it."

I look at my hands in my lap. "I don't know. Maybe he assumed my family would stay in this area."

He looks out the window but doesn't push the subject. I take in this man across from me and try to reconcile him with the four-year-old boy I played tractors with just nine short months ago.

"You have the footlocker too?" he asks.

When I nod, he continues, "Can I see it?"

"Yeah, it's in my room." I stop at the foot of the stairs and listen, thankful Adam and Clara are napping, then lead him to my room to show him the footlocker.

He pulls out a photo and looks from the photo to the locker.

"It has the same scratch down the side." He compares them.

"That's what he said," I say without thinking.

"Who said?" Scott asks.

I just smile and shake my head. I open the footlocker and show him where it says D. Miller.

"I never noticed that growing up. My grandma kept blankets in here, so I'd go in and get a blanket and not think about it. They never told me anything about it other than it would be mine someday. My grandpa was in the Army, so I always assumed it was his footlocker and never thought to ask."

I pull everything out and pull open the false bottom like David showed me and start to pull everything out and hand it to Scott. He reads the letter, and then I hand him the record, and I see a slight tremble in his hand. I can understand what he is feeling. After David left, I spent a whole night holding it, just looking at this record. I tried to understand what it means that it was sitting here in my house, in my grandparents' house, long before I even met David. That I touched this footlocker as a little girl, and it was David's.

My head hurt before I finally made it to bed because it doesn't make sense. None of it does from the footlocker, to how I was named after Ivy Hill, but Ivy Hill was named after me. How do you explain that other than this was meant to happen? I'm not changing history. I'm following history. If I never went back, it would have changed everything.

I focus on Scott and see tears running down his face. "My dad and I weren't ever close; that's my mom's fault. But being able to preserve his legacy makes me feel closer to him." He looks up, and I can't hide my anger fast enough.

"Why do you get that look when I talk about my mom?"

I sigh. I know I'm a horrible liar, so I go for a version of the truth. "I just don't like her."

"Ever meet her?"

"Yes."

He laughs. "Then you know not many people like her, but a lot of them sure do suck up to her, thinking she can do something for them."

"She hasn't changed much then." Dammit, I need to watch my mouth.

Thankfully, Scott looks at me a bit weird but doesn't question it.

"I'd like to do a showcase at Ivy Hill. It's coming up on the sixtieth anniversary of when my dad came home from his Army tour. Would you be willing to loan the footlocker for the exhibit?"

Just talking about the day David came back from France has

the tears flowing again. I hide my face in my hands, not that it will hide all those emotions. The moment his eyes locked with mine, the relief of holding him after two years, the heartbreak of that night talking about Anna, and how it all led to him proposing and our wedding.

I remember that day looking out at the memorial garden realizing how hard it was to be away for those two years and then the four years while he was married to Anna. But I knew he was alive, and I'd have him in my arms again. How will I ever get out of bed and put one foot in front of the other if David is really in the ground at Ivy Hill? Then the thought of that being him sends a new wave of tears.

Scott mistakes my breakdown for him asking to showcase the footlocker and places a hand on my arm, which seems to sober me instantly.

"It's okay. I'm sorry I asked." I wipe my face on my sleeve and make a note to change my shirt later. I look at my hands and rub my wedding rings.

"That's not it, Scott. I'd be more than honored to have the footlocker shown in the museum. That footlocker is attached to so many memories that I have kept pushed down for so long, and they have just come to the surface in light of all this."

He takes my hand and looks at my rings. "My dad had a ring just like this that he wore up to the day he died. Even while he was married to my mom. It made her so mad when someone talked about it. My dad left strict instructions he was to be buried with that ring on. I've seen pictures, and it looks exactly like that."

"I don't know what to tell you. Someone special gave it to me. We made promises to each other, and as long as those promises aren't broken, I wear this ring."

We head back to the living room and work out the details of the sale. We are talking for a few hours when Brian and Kevin come home.

"Ivy! Are Adam and Clara up yet? We got them the cutest outfit... Shit," Brian says when he sees Scott.

"Scott, this is my best friend and family, Brian, and his husband, Kevin. They live here and help me with my kids."

Scott is looking at me as though he is trying to work out a puzzle. "Clara was my great-grandma's name. And Adam was my dad's middle name."

I nod. "Would you like to stay for dinner? I'm trying out a new street taco recipe. It's what I do. I tweak recipes, then photograph them and all."

"I'd like that," Scott says with a smile. I know the longer he stays here, the more of a risk it is, but it just feels right.

"I'll go get the kids up from their nap." Brian heads upstairs, followed by Kevin, and a few minutes later, the kids come running downstairs.

They stop when they see Scott, and Adam stares at him before he smiles. "You look like my dad, older though. Do you know my dad?"

My heart stops, and Brian looks at me, but it's Kevin who saves the day.

"No, little man, he doesn't know your dad," Kevin says, and Adam shrugs and runs off to play.

The rest of the evening goes smoothly. And there are lots of laughs and stories. Scott tells us about David, and some about Anna but lots about his grandpa teaching him about the business and how they set up Ivy Hill and funny stories.

When he's getting ready to leave, he turns to me.

"Listen, this might sound weird, but I don't have family in my life. I'm sure you know I don't speak to my mother unless I have to. Or when she wants something. Being here felt like home. I know it's weird, but I'd like to stay friends. Your family meant something to my dad. I don't know why, but it's a thin connection to him."

"Scott, you are welcome any time. I just ask to keep us out of the spotlight. I don't want the attention—things like loaning the footlocker. I don't want my name for the public to see. But we can hang out here at any time."

He laughs. "I normally have to worry about people only wanting to be around me to get in the spotlight, but you want nothing to do with it. It's refreshing. Thank you again."

We exchange phone numbers before he leaves. No sooner does the door close than the tears start pouring down my face. Brian and Kevin wrap me in a hug.

"I'm a horrible person. I have his brother and sister right here, and I can't tell him. He has no family who cares, and with any luck, his dad will be here in a few years, and I can't tell him. He is clinging to me for a slim thread to his dad, but little does he know how big of one I could give him. I could tell him so much about his dad. About how much he loves him. All the things his mom lied about."

"Ivy, do you think he'd believe you? You are doing what's right. Maybe David could write a journal or letters for his son, and you can find them in more of your grandparents' things. But otherwise, this is the best you can do."

I know he's right, but that doesn't soothe my heart or my guilt.

Chapter 28

Ivy

It's been a month since Scott was at the house for the first time, but he's been back twice and is always happy to tell stories over dinner about his time at Ivy Hill. He says he doesn't get to the house much because of all the paperwork at his office in the museum across the street. But he has been working on the exhibit to show off David's time in the Army.

I am putting the kids down for a nap when I hear someone at the door. I know Brian will get it, so I take my time putting Clara to bed and snuggle with her a bit. The more I think about the museum and the possibility of a life without David, the more I think I need to cuddle these little pieces of him, and they love it as much as I do.

I head downstairs to find Scott. He is studying me closely, and it makes me a bit uncomfortable.

"Hey, Scott, is everything okay?"

"I'd like to show you something at Ivy Hill if you have time this afternoon."

I look over at Brian. "Oh, I have the kids. Go, Ivy!"

On the drive over to Ivy Hill, I remember when I brought David here and start to see it a bit through his eyes. I see our Ivy Hill from 1967, not the museum it is now. It feels like coming home.

We make our way to the house, and people stop Scott to talk

about this or that, but as we walk through the front door, I see it with all new eyes. Having sections blocked off and people touring it is just weird. I see our nights on the couch watching TV, I see David practicing music on the piano, I see Helen and James eating dinner with us at the dining room table, and my eyes start to water.

I turn to act like I am looking at the stained glass roses to get my emotions in order before looking back at Scott, who is watching me.

I smile. “I love roses. The stained glass there has always been my favorite.”

“So, you have been here before?”

“Oh, I’ve toured it many times. Brian got me an annual membership for my birthday because I love the house so much.”

“Come on, I want to show you something upstairs.”

He opens the stairs, and I hesitate. The upstairs is blocked off to the public. The family says it’s because David died up there, so it’s a private area. Will it look the same? Will I be able to keep my emotions in check? What if this has to do with his mother?

I offer a timid smile and follow him up the stairs and down the hall to David's room, our room. He opens the door and stands to the side. I slowly walk up to the doorway and have to lean against the doorjamb for support. I couldn’t stop the tears in my eyes this time if I tried. I see the bed and knowing he died there brings tears to my eyes thinking he could have truly died here, and I still don’t know.

I’m shaken from my thoughts when Scott speaks. “I had a feeling you’d been here before.”

My eyes snap to his, and he is watching me. “Go look.” He nods toward the room.

On shaky legs, I take a few steps into what I know as David’s and my bedroom. Not much has changed since the last time I saw it. I guess I expected him to get rid of all of this before that day in August. Knowing this has been here all this time while I was walking around downstairs all these years is enough to blow my mind.

I take in the photos crowding the nightstand and walk over to take a look. Most of them match mine; the birthday cake one is still front and center. There is also the one with us and the kids that Brian took. It starts to sink in that Scott has to have seen all these. I look around the room and, on the wall, across from the bed, is the wood sign I gave him on our wedding day surrounded by photos of us, including the one on our wedding day and one from our honeymoon. There are a few new photos of myself and David that I don't recognize. It's an odd feeling seeing yourself having done something you have yet to do. It's a feeling I'm sure David is familiar with by now.

I take a shaky breath and look at Scott, who has been watching me this whole time. "That's you, isn't it?" He gestures to the wall of photos with his chin, and all I can do is nod.

"How?"

"I found a loophole." I walk over to the photos on the wall and look into David's eyes. To think he might be in this same spot looking at me in 1967 causes more tears to fall. I reach up and trace my finger down the frame of our wedding photo.

Scott walks up and looks over the photos. I wait for the questions on how and why. I am preparing in my head how to explain the time travel. I don't expect the question he finally asks.

"Will you tell me about my dad?"

The shock must have registered on my face, but when I look at him, I see the vulnerability of the little boy I was playing with just a few months ago.

"Please, I've only heard stories from my grandpa and Mom, and she wasn't his biggest fan."

I can't help but laugh. "Well, I guess not if she ever saw this room."

I look back at the photo of David and me by the pool. "We met once, you know. You were about five, and your mom brought you here, trying one of her stunts. While she was talking to your dad, you showed me the waterfall..."

"And you played trucks with me. Grandpa sat on the couch. That's why you looked so familiar to me that first day."

"I can't believe you remember that. Out of curiosity, do you remember the song I taught you that day?"

"No."

"I had 'John Deere Green' stuck in my head, and you suggested if I sang it might help. You loved the chorus."

He chuckles. "To this day, that song makes me think of that room in the house, and I never knew why."

I sigh. "That was only a few months ago for me." I walk over to the nightstand and pick up that first picture we ever took together of me sitting on his lap the morning I left, the one of him and his birthday cake, and the one where he named Ivy Hill.

"I know you're an adult now, and you deserve the truth. You may not like me much after this, and you might blame me for so much of your childhood, and that's okay, but before I start, I need you to promise me you will let me tell you the whole story. You deserve the whole story."

"I want the whole story, good, bad, or ugly. I've always felt like people were keeping things from me and not telling me everything."

"Your grandpa knew the truth. Your mom didn't, though I'm sure she had her own wild version of it."

I walk over to the couch and stare at it and smile for a minute, remembering our wedding night before sitting down. Scott walks over and closes the bedroom door and comes over to sit next to me.

"I met your dad in 1957, just a few months after he bought

this place, but he hadn't named it yet. We spent ten days together and fell madly in love. The kind of love you are lucky if you find once in a lifetime. The love that survives anything. My heart broke the day I had to walk away because I had no idea if I would ever see him again. This photo was taken on my phone the day I left. Three months after I left, he named the house Ivy Hill. Seven months later, I did get to see him again." I show him each picture.

I stop and smile, lost in my thoughts as I remember that day. The look on his face as he stood in the front door and that kiss.

"We spent a month together before he got his draft orders and went to France. We spent every minute together." I walk into the closet, hoping what I'm looking for is still here, and I find it. I walk out and hand it to Scott.

"I wrote to him every day he was gone and gave the letters to him when I saw him two years later after he came back. He did the same. I have the letters at home."

"Why didn't you mail them to him?"

"It's hard to mail letters from 2010 to 1958." I smile and watch his eyes go big. Then I see the wheels turn as he is putting it together.

"He met your mom while in France. The letters at the back of that box hold the truth of what happened if you want to know. The truth of it is she hurt a lot of people—your dad, his parents, and myself included—because of her lies."

He takes the envelopes from the back of the box and looks at me, then opens them. I let him read them, and my eyes wander around the room as he reads. When he is done, he looks at me, his eyes a bit misty.

"This picture with the cake that everyone tries to pin down?"

"You know?"

"I took that photo. It was taken the day after he got back from France. His parents wanted to have a small get-together for his birthday. I took him out for the day, then came home, and his parents had put this all together.

"I knew he would end up marrying your mom, and I wouldn't stop that because you had to be born. I refused to change history, but when I told him he would have to marry Anna... It broke him in a way I have never seen before." I walk over to a spot a few feet from the bed and kneel. "He fell to his knees here, head to the floor, and just cried. He begged me not to make him do it many times. All I could do was hold him and cry with him. He asked me to marry him that night." I rub my rings and show them to Scott.

"You recognized these rings, and for good reason. They are my wedding rings to your dad. We never were able to be married legally, but he always said... says that we are married in every way that matters. Heart, body, and soul. He is my husband. We were married on April 14, 1960."

"Over a year before he married my mom."

I nod. "The ceremony was in the backyard. David's parents, Brian, and Kevin were there, and his dad married us. We went on a honeymoon in Hawaii and California." I point at the honeymoon photos. "Then he did the most amazing thing. He took me to Maryland where we met my grandparents, who raised me but are no longer alive. We had dinner with them, and I can't describe the feeling of having that with them after thinking I'd never see them again. He kept in contact with them, and that is how they ended up with his footlocker. Though I didn't know until last month that it was his. When I left that time, he made me promise to come back before he got married. I found out just after that I was pregnant with Adam."

I watch Scott's eyes water. "He's my brother?" I nod. "And Clara?" I nod and watch him wipe the tears from his eyes.

"I chose not to tell him about Adam because those four years would be too hard as it was, and I was terrified of him turning to drugs. It was the hardest secret I ever kept when I saw him before he married your mom. I met her on that trip. I guess she saw how David looked at me, knowing he never looked at her that way, and things got bad. He lied to her and said he was working, but we went away to a cabin he had in the woods just to get away from her. That trip was the first time I saw your dad perform. It was at the concert here in Nashville with Johnny Cash. He put it on for me because I wanted to see Johnny Cash perform. He had a way of captivating his audience in a way I've never seen before. Leaving that time, pushing him to her arms, it felt wrong. But I knew you had to be born, and I wasn't going to stop that. I found out I was pregnant with Clara a few weeks after I got home that time."

I place my hand on his arm. I try to convey I did it for him, and I don't regret that one bit.

"I want you to know that I stayed away the entire time he was married to your mom. There was a time he was in rehab about the time your mom filed divorce papers? He came to visit me. Your mom was withholding you from him and making everything really hard. He wasn't in rehab. He hadn't taken drugs up to that point even though your mom tried to supply him with plenty. I want you to know your dad fought for you as much as he could. He had so few rights back then, it makes me sick."

Scott nods. "I know that now. Grandpa explained it."

"I was back at Ivy Hill the day the divorce was final from your mom. He was broken and just not himself. It took a while for him to be David Miller again. I need to know you want to hear the rest because it will change everything, and I still don't know the outcome."

"I want to know everything," he says, his voice shaking.

I pause and send up a silent prayer David will forgive me for this, and that it won't all backfire in my face. He seems to be soaking in the information, but I expected him to walk out on me and tell me I was crazy long before now. I take the leap of faith and continue my story.

"As I said, your mom was the one trying to supply him with the drugs. He promised me several years before he'd never take them, but it was about this time we had an idea. Let the public think he was taking them and doing the rehab visits because we can't change history. Rehab then turned into time with me and the kids."

"He's been here to visit?"

"Yes, see my David... isn't dead yet. When I go to visit him, it's 1967." I point at a few photos I don't recognize. "These photos haven't happened yet for me. We are hoping the rumors and whispers of the cover-up and all are because his death was a cover-up and allows us to be together. So, you realize this story can never leave this room. It can never be told."

"Then why tell me?"

I point at the pictures. "How else would I explain this? Plus, you are his son. You deserve to know him, the real him. He is an amazing man, but he gets painted in a bad light because of what your mom did, and what she keeps trying to do to his reputation."

Scott stands up and looks at the photos on the walls again. "God, you must hate my mom!"

I laugh. "Some days, yes but in general, no. I knew from day one he would marry her, and this would be our story because you had to be born. Look at everything you have done to this place. Knowing a piece of him is walking around is calming in a way I can't explain. You are half her and half him, and I love him more than I hate her, if that makes sense. Knowing he will live on in your kids and their kids. I wouldn't change that." There are tears in my eyes again.

Scott walks over and stops in front of me and hesitantly reaches out and then pulls me into a hug. After a moment, I step back and pull out my cell phone. "Can I take a picture with all this in the background to show your dad when I see him next?"

This time Scott's eyes water. “You are going to see him again?” I nod. We take the picture of us with the wall of photos behind us.

“I don’t know when I will see him again.”

“I want to write him a letter. Will you give it to him?”

“Of course.”

“I can meet my brother and sister formally as my brother and sister?”

I laugh. “I’d love nothing more. We just can’t tell them quite yet. They can’t keep a secret to save their life.”

I look at the bathroom door and walk over, taking a deep breath before walking in. My bath products are still on the counter mixed with his, and I lose it. Scott comes up and rubs my back.

“We left everything in this room untouched, down to the dirty laundry in the hamper there.”

“It’s hard to see my bath products still mixed with his. It’s why he loved roses so much.” I walk out to the hallway to try to get myself in order. “I want to see the memorial garden before we go, please.”

Scott nods, and I follow him down. He has security block the area off and halts the tours to give us a few minutes of privacy. I walk up to the graves and stop at Helen's. It’s the first time I’ve been to her graveside since she passed.

“I’m so sorry I wasn’t there, Helen. I should have been there that day, for you, for James, for David. I still haven’t forgiven myself for mixing up those dates. You were like a mother to me and the most amazing woman I’ve ever known. You accepted me with open arms, and I’m so sorry you never got to meet your grandkids. I love you, Helen, only you know the truth now and how this story ends. I love you.”

Next is James’s grave. “I’ll see you in a few months, old man.

We have the fight of our lives coming up."

Last is David's grave. August 29, 1969. Just over two years from now. We will know the truth if it's truly David in this grave. I kneel next to the gravesite.

"You listen to me, David Adam Miller. It better not be you in there. You better fight because I need you, your kids need you. All three of them. Do you hear me? If it is you in that grave, I won't be far behind. We have a love like Johnny and June, baby, only our story is ours alone. I love you."

Standing, I wipe my tears and try to smile for Scott. Not a word is spoken on the way back to my house, but once there, the whole mood shifts. Watching Scott interact with Adam and Clara, I tell Brian and Kevin he knows the truth and is welcomed into our little circle. After dinner, he spends time and writes David a five-page letter, front and back.

Before he leaves, we make a promise to get together weekly for family dinner. He wants to hear every story I have about his father, and the kids love hearing about their dad too. It's a weekly tradition I can't wait to start.

Chapter 29

Ivy

Today is David's birthday. It's the first time I've been back at Ivy Hill in my time since I was here with Scott a year and seven months ago. I've seen David several times, but he comes to me more now because he wants the time with his kids.

I told him about Scott and my time at Ivy Hill that first time back, and he cried. I gave him the letter Scott wrote him, and his hands trembled the whole time he read it, then he sat down and wrote him back a letter twice as long. They haven't met face-to-face. David thinks it's best to wait until we know if he makes it to my time for good or not. He figures Scott lost his dad once; he doesn't want to do it to him again.

They talk about everything in their letters. I think it's been healing for both because when David has to deal with Anna now, he's a lot less on edge knowing as bad as he thought it was not having the time with his son, that his son saw through her, and he has some time with him now.

Scott listens and wants every detail from every visit and has remained a part of our family with weekly dinners unless David is with us. Then I meet him at his place.

Brian dragged me to this birthday celebration at Ivy Hill, saying I needed to get out of the house, and since Scott invited us, it seemed perfect. The place is busy, but then again, it always is. I wander around Ivy Hill this time watching everyone take it in and listening to the comments people make. I hear a lady ask what made David choose the roses for the stained glass over the door, and the attendant said they didn't know.

"Ma'am, I'm sorry I heard your question about the roses. David picked the roses because they held a special significance in his family, and it was a family tribute."

"Oh, thank you, dear. You don't happen to know the details on it, do you?"

"No, I'm sorry."

The piano room catches my eye, and I smile, remembering all our times there.

"Can you imagine the songs that must have been written and sang on that piano?" I hear a couple next to me talking.

"He wrote his famous 'Stay With Me Now' while sitting at that piano. Fun fact: David would sit with the piano bench perpendicular to the piano and not parallel like you see there."

I smile and move through the house. I end up next to the same couple again in the back room with the waterfall and just smile.

"Scott loved to play with his cars here next to the waterfall when he visited. He said it was his favorite place."

"Are you a tour guide here?" the gentleman asks.

Scott walks up then. "No, she is a friend of the family who has heard all the stories." He has a big smile on his face. "Come on, Brian said you were getting yourself into trouble."

He leads me to the backyard where a local cover band has set up to play a few of his songs. I hang out in the back, away from most of the people, and listen to David's songs once again fill Ivy Hill. When they start to play "Stay With Me Now," an older man stands beside me.

"They are playing our song."

My eyes snap to him and take him in. This is my David, I have no doubt. I'd know those blue eyes anywhere. He looks to be the eighty-five years old we are celebrating for his birthday today.

He's in good shape and still makes my heart race.

"David..." I whisper.

"My sweet Ivy. Walk with me?"

Tears are falling down my face now as I follow him farther into the backyard where there are fewer people. Once we hit a part of the garden where we are alone, he turns back to me with a huge smile.

He reaches up to wipe away my tears. "Don't cry, my sweet girl." Which of course only makes me cry harder and makes him chuckle.

"Does this mean our plan worked? It's not you in that grave?"

He smiles and gets a faraway look on his face. "You once told me knowing the future is a burden, and I hated how you carried it alone. Well, my sweet girl, it's time for me to carry that burden for you. I'm standing here today at age eighty-five, staring at the only girl I have ever loved. That's all you need to know."

More tears fall down my face, and he wipes them away again.

"I'm so scared, David, scared we are tempting fate, that something will go wrong. That I'm going to lose you for good."

"Remember there *is* one other person who knows exactly how you feel. I felt it too. I was just as scared as you are now. Lean on me, talk to me, tell me this, and let me comfort you, while you in turn, comfort me. Remember this day and this meeting. My love for you is as strong as ever, beautiful."

With that, he smiles and walks away. I want to chase him and demand he tell me everything, but I know he's right. It's better this way. I just have to hold on to the fact that it's not him in that grave. Yet a nagging part of me says something could still happen. That we could slip up and change everything, and he could truly end up in the grave.

I go and find Brian, who takes one look at me and just wraps his arm around my shoulder and lets me bury my head in his chest.

"Do you want to go home?"

"Please, Brian."

We say goodbye to Scott and head out. I don't say a word until we get home. Kevin has the kids down for a nap when we get there.

"How did it go?"

"I saw David." I turn to look at them.

"What? Like he's here? Why did he go there?"

"Not my David, eighty-five-year-old David."

"What?" Kevin asks.

"Future David was there. He wouldn't tell me any details but said he's alive and loves me just as much now. He told me to talk to him about my fears for all this and open up because he's scared too."

"Then what?!" Brian asks.

"Then he left. I have always asked him not to push so I don't have to tell him stuff from the future, so how would it be fair for me to push now?"

"So, our plan works?" I can tell Brian is getting excited.

"I guess, but there is still a worry in my gut that it won't, or we mess it up and it doesn't work this time. I can't explain it."

"We are here, Ivy, and we aren't going anywhere. Now go snuggle with your babies. Tomorrow is another day." Kevin gives me a small hug, and I know he's right.

Chapter 30

David

Two months. Two more months until the date of my death. How weird is it to think that, to know it with such certainty? I'm scared something is going to go wrong. So scared. I'm scared to leave my Ivy alone and my kids without a dad for good. I'm scared all this was for nothing.

I try to shake the thoughts away and get ready to step through the rocks. Today is my last rehab visit, and I'm looking forward to six weeks with my family. My dad is going to join us next week for a few days, but he's busy helping me line everything up as well.

Before I know it, I'm through the stones and walking up Ivy's driveway, our driveway. I open the door, and call out, "Honey, I'm home!"

Both kids come running. "Daddy!!" I catch them but hear chairs in the dining room and "Oh shit, Ivy."

"Dammit, I mixed up the dates!"

I smile. My Ivy is so cute when she is flustered, but I won't tell her that.

"Daddy, Adam said I'm his little sister, but I'm not. I'm a big girl!" Clara gives me her pout lip.

"You are a big girl, sweet pea, but you are also Adam's little sister because he's older than you. But that just means his job is to protect you always."

"See, I told you that!" Adam sighs but puts his arm over Clara's shoulder.

"Good, then *you* can check for the monster under my bed tonight."

"I got this, Dad," Adam says and runs off to check under Clara's bed.

I stand up to see Ivy watching me with a worried look on her face next to an older man I don't know.

"Hey, sweet girl." I walk over and pull her into my arms because it's been too long, and I just need to reconnect. She melts against me.

When she looks up at me, I can't help but lean in for a kiss. Ivy kisses me before pulling back, making the kiss too short, in my opinion.

"What's wrong, beautiful?"

"I'm sorry I mixed up the dates."

"What do you mean?"

She takes a deep breath and looks up at the other man whose eyes are wide, and I realize he hasn't stopped staring at me.

"David, this is Scott."

Scott, like my son Scott? I do a calculation, and this man looks to be the right age.

"My son Scott?"

Ivy nods, and what I can't vocalize is this is the best gift she could give me. I know I've said I didn't want to meet him in case this whole plan backfires, but what I haven't said is I was scared too.

I reach out and pull him into a hug, and no sooner does he start crying. We stand there for a few minutes, just taking in the moment.

"He's been having dinner with us every week. He loves spending time with the kids and having another piece of you here helps me through the dark days."

"Ivy, Ivy, Ivy, this is a gift I can't ever say thank you enough for. Did I miss dinner? I'd kill for your cooking right now."

She laughs. "No, we were just sitting down."

I spend the evening talking to my son over dinner with Adam or Clara on my lap. Ivy makes a dessert as we talk the night away, and it is perfect.

As we wind down and he gets ready to leave, I ask him. "You will be here next weekend, too right?"

"Yeah, I'd like to."

"Well, I'm here for six weeks, and my dad will be here next weekend."

I watch his eyes mist over. "I wouldn't miss it for the world."

"You understand this can't leave this house. You can't even tell your best friend about it."

"I understand, not that anyone would believe me."

We hug, and he whispers in my ear, "I love you, Dad. Thank you for this life you gave me." I hug him a bit tighter. That right there makes it all worth it. The time away from Ivy, having to deal with Anna, all of it was worth it for this moment right here.

"I love you, Scott, I'd do anything for you. All you ever need to do is ask. And Scott?"

"Yeah, Dad?"

I smile. "I heard I have a few grandkids?" He nods. "Maybe bring them around next time. I know Dad would love to meet them too."

"I'd like that too."

When he leaves, I walk up to Ivy and wrap her in a hug and cry.

She walks me to our room, and when she closes the door, she

asks, "What did he say?"

"He thanked me for the life I gave him. Ivy, everything we went through, the years apart and my time with Anna, it wasn't because history said so. It was for him. That makes it all worth it."

"It does make it all worth it. When I visited Ivy Hill with him the first time, the time I told him everything. At one point, he was worried about how I felt about him because of Anna. I said to know that a piece of you, your name is out there in the world, carrying on your name, your legacy means the world to me."

I lie down in bed and pull her with me.

"Tell me everything I have missed, my sweet girl, and let me hold you."

"Brian dragged me to Ivy Hill for your birthday. Since it was your eighty-fifth birthday and guess who I talked to there?"

"Who?" I send up a silent prayer it's not Anna.

"You."

"What?"

She smiles. "I talked to eighty-five-year-old you."

"Me... Does that mean...?"

I can't seem to voice the hope I have right now.

"I don't know. I want to think it means everything is going to be okay, but I don't know. I'm still scared things won't go as planned. I'm still scared to lose you because other than those five minutes with older you, I have no proof this worked. I had proof you would come back from your Army time fine. I had proof we would survive your time with Anna. I could see it. This is the first event I can't see what is going to happen, and I'm so scared."

I nuzzle her ear and close my eyes and just breathe her in. Her rose scent that is distinctly Ivy fills my soul and settles me.

"I'm scared too, beautiful. I'm scared to leave my kids without a father. I'm scared to leave you to raise them all on your own, and I'm scared of not getting to hold you again. But I am also scared of it working too."

"What?"

"I'm scared it all works, but when I get here, I'm found out, or that I'm too late and my kids won't want me. I'm scared that once you are around me all the time, you won't love me like you think you do. I'm scared I won't be able to take care of my family, which includes Scott, Brian, and Kevin."

Ivy turns to face me and pulls me in for a tight hug, and we just lie there holding each other in our warm bubble.

"You have more than taken care of us, David. Do you know what that lost album was worth? We won't change our lifestyle, and our grandkids will be set for life. You took care of Scott, and he has done amazing things in your name, and his kids will continue to do so."

Then she leans in and kisses me soft and slow. When I try to push further, she pulls back, forcing me to let her have control. After several minutes, she pulls away and looks me in the eye.

"Most importantly, David Miller, I love you. Do you hear me? This isn't an 'I love you when you are around' or an 'I love you because I can't have you' kind of love. This is a soul-crushing, can't function when I'm not with you, I can't survive without you kind of love. If you don't make it back to me, I won't be far behind you in the grave. This is a Johnny and June kind of love. Do you understand me?"

I remember her telling me Johnny and June's love story, and how they were together for so long when June died, Johnny wasn't far behind. I know that's how I'd feel, too, if I ever lost her.

"Yes. But can you make me a promise?"

"Depends on what it is."

"After all this and I'm here for good, will you consider having another child with me? I missed you being pregnant, and I want to go through it all with you."

"If we make it through this, I would love nothing more than to have another child with you, David. As many children as you want."

"When, not if," I whisper against her lips before I roll on top of her and kiss her hard and thoroughly. There is a knock on the door and little Clara's sleepy voice sounds from the other side. "Mommy?"

"Yes, baby?"

I slide off Ivy to lie beside her before the door opens, and Clara comes in.

"I don't think Adam got all the monsters from under my bed tonight. Can I sleep with you and Daddy?"

I know she is thinking the same thing I am. We won't deny these kids any time with me because this is the last time I will be here before August.

"Come here, sweet pea." I scoot to the side and make room for Clara in the middle. Just as we are cuddling, Adam walks in.

"She woke me up coming down the stairs."

"Climb on in, there is plenty of room." Ivy smiles as she turns off the light.

I reach across the kids and take her hand, rubbing my thumb over her wedding ring.

"I love you," I whisper.

"Love you too, Daddy."

"Love you too, Dad."

"I love you too, David. With everything that I am."

With any luck, there are many more nights like this. I just didn't know the fight it would take to get there.

Chapter 31

Ivy

It's August. That's what I have been saying every day since August 1st.

For the past twenty-five days, I have woken up and thought, *It's August.*

My stomach has been churning daily as I try to keep myself calm for the kid's sake.

Today, I go to see my David. We will have three days together. I tried for two weeks, but he is sure this is going to work that he wanted to make sure everything was tied up. He was giving a few last concerts and appearances for his fans and then going to try to go see Scott one last time. We both doubt Anna will allow him any time, but he was going to try.

The more I think about the days to come, the heavier the weight on my chest gets, so I try not to think about it. I try to think about taking in Ivy Hill one last time where it's just ours and not filled with tourists. I try to think about one last swim in the pool and making sure I get a few of Nancy's recipes.

Once through the stones, I try to take it all in. I will have no reason to come back here after this because my whole world will be in my house. My family.

I take in the perfectly landscaped homes. Homes that won't be there once they start buying the land for the museum. I take in the families getting ready for work on this Monday morning. I take in the kids who are enjoying the last few days of summer vacation.

As I pass the familiar newsstand, I stop and buy a cup of coffee this time and leave the guy a big tip. He has been such an intricate part of my journey here, and he has no idea. He won't be written about in history books as part of the David Miller legacy, but he should be.

I watch the vintage to me cars drive down the road and take in the Brady Bunch-style clothes as the country enters the height of the hippie years. This is a country that is getting ready to see the World Trade Centers completed.

They just had the first man walk on the moon, and soon, Disney World will open for the first time. Life is simpler, and the pace is slower. I take my time and take it all in on my way to Ivy Hill this morning.

I don't even make it up to the gate before Clint greets me.

"Hello again, Miss Ivy. He's expecting you." He walks me to the side gate, guarding me from the large number of fans waiting for even the slightest glimpse of him. The dirty looks I get from them amuse me. If they only knew.

As I enter the kitchen, David is sitting at the bar drinking coffee and reading the newspaper. When he sees me, he smiles, but there is such a look of sadness too. He looks tired, and his eyes are bloodshot, and my heart drops.

"David..." I can't move.

"I swear it's just from lack of sleep. What's up there is to back the story after."

My heart races as I look at Clint.

"I can vouch. He hasn't slept; he has kept my men up as he paces the living room, plays the piano, and goes for three a.m. swims, trying to tire himself out."

His words don't calm me, but when David wraps me in his arms and holds me tight, I know I have to trust him. To believe in us.

"Let's go upstairs. I know how to tire you out, and I can use some sleep too."

He gives me that famous crooked half-smile, and I laugh.

Once in our bedroom, I take a look around, and it looks just like it did that day at Ivy Hill with Scott. Every photo in place of me, of us, and of the kids. I run my finger down the frame of our wedding photo and smile. Our memories would live on here only for David's family to know the truth. That is enough.

"Your grandfather is going back to school. I paid for his schooling via a scholarship."

I laugh. "Good lord, that scholarship bugged him until the day he died. He always went on how he never applied, but it covered everything, and he had no idea who to thank for it."

"I also added in my will that Clint is to be moved to Scott's detail and his salary paid from the trust. Clint knows how Anna is, and I know he will keep an eye on Scott. My dad is going to keep Nancy on to cook for him. They have become good friends over the years. I set up her paycheck to come from the trust too. Made sure my dad will be taken care of as well."

"You are an amazing man, David. I wish people could see how deeply you care about those around you. But then I'm selfish and glad this is a side only I get to see."

"I'm leaving this room the same. Our story needs to be told even if they have no idea what it is. I refuse to pack you away like a dirty secret."

"I saw our room with Scott, remember? It looks just like this. I had walked around Ivy Hill so many times, not knowing the key to my future was right above my head."

His eyes look a bit misty, and he looks down at his feet before looking back at me.

"So, we have three days. What do you want to do while here?"

"I think you mean *where* do I want to do it."

I watch him relax, and his eyes sparkle. "Well, can I have the first choice?"

"Of course. Where are you thinking?"

He just smiles and takes my hand. He leads me out to the garage to that blue Cadillac that means so much to us. I remember the last time we had sex in this car when his voice snaps me out of it.

"Clothes off, beautiful." His tone is firm and leaves no room for arguing. I don't break eye contact as I remove each item of clothing, and he does the same. When I'm completely naked, he just takes me in. His eyes travel over my breasts and make my nipples tighten. As his eyes travel down past my hips, my wetness slicks my thighs. When he sees me rubbing my thighs together, trying to find relief, his eyes snap back to mine.

"On the hood of the car," he orders.

I lie down on that iconic sky-blue hood and watch him walk over to me. He grips my hips, and his knees spread my thighs as far as he can before he kneels, and his mouth attacks my clit. I yell out his name and feel his smile as his assault continues. My hips try to move to get him in just the right spot, but he has them pinned to the hood. He slows his licks, causing me to moan and reach down to grab his hair and pull him closer. The harder I pull, the faster he goes. My back arches, and I let out a silent scream as my nerves are set on fire, and my climax washes over me.

I don't get time to catch my breath before he stands and thrusts into me. His body covers mine as he buries his head in my neck.

"Every time with you feels like the first time when I was so happy to see you again after months of being terrified I never would."

He leans up to look at me. "I'm getting you pregnant tonight, my sweet Ivy. You think taking me from this time is the most selfish thing you have ever done. This is the most selfish thing I have ever done. I want you pregnant, so if I make it to your time, I can watch you grow. I want you pregnant, so if I don't make it, you have another piece of me to live for because I need you to promise to live, Ivy." He thrusts into me harder, causing me to cry out.

"Promise me if anything happens to me, you will live for our babies." *Thrust.* "Promise me!" Then he stills completely.

I feel the tears running down my face, and I nod. "I promise, David. I don't know how I will live without you, but I will try for our kids."

He slams into me again, this time changing the angle of his thrusts and sending me over the edge and following with me. I feel his hot release deep inside me.

We spend the next few days making love everywhere in the house again. How he has that much stamina and energy I will never know, but the night before I have to go back, we are lying in bed, neither of us willing to sleep, and I can't seem to stop the steady stream of tears running down my face. Neither one of us wants to voice the obvious; this could be our last morning together.

"Talk to me about your plan," I say to him. I haven't heard much of the details, but right now, I want to hear him talk.

"We found a doctor who, according to Brian, will die of a heart attack just weeks after he finishes my autopsy. We paid him well in a roundabout way that isn't linked to me. He gave my dad a drug that will still my heartbeat and breathing so slow everyone who sees me will think I'm dead. Nancy will find me. The doctor will rush over, pronounce me dead on the spot, and then do some shifting around to get another body in the bag to be taken out. He and my dad worked out the details. He does his report, saying it was the drugs, my dad gets the funeral done quickly, and I rush to you. Once the dust dies down, my dad will come to visit."

"You know the dosage to give, right? You trust the doctor to keep his mouth shut and do as promised?" So many questions fly through my head; so many things could go wrong. He could take the wrong dosage, the doctor could flake and reveal the whole plan, or it could get out that he isn't really dead.

"We are doing it all per plan like Brian says to. He researched every detail around my death down to the doctor and who found me. I have to trust that this will work."

As the sun starts to shine into the room that has held every important part of us, we get up and have our morning shower like every time before, except this time, both of us are crying. We let the water wash our tears away as we make love in the shower. We take our time with each other, not saying a word. I don't think I could speak if I tried. My throat is raw, trying to hold back the river of tears that want to swallow me whole.

We eat breakfast, and he walks me to the stones. Once there, he pulls me into a hug and stops trying to hold back and starts sobbing uncontrollably.

"I love you. You were completely unexpected and unexplainable, and you changed me and changed the world in ways most will never know. You are the light in the darkest hour. I will fight my way back to you."

"I love you too, David. This is *not* goodbye. Do you hear me? I will see you in five days, okay?"

He smiles and nods. "Five days. Now go before I go with you."

I smile, but as I step through the stones, my heart breaks.

Chapter 32

Ivy

As I open my eyes, I check the bed next to me.

Still empty.

I stayed up all night and don't even remember falling asleep. David was supposed to be here yesterday, but he's not. I know something could have come up, but my heart is breaking anyway. I promised David I'd find a way to go on but not today. Brian and Kevin bring the kids in, and we curl up and watch movies all day and even eat breakfast and lunch in bed.

"Hey kiddos, Kevin has dinner. Go see what he made!" Brian says, and the kids run out of the room. He sits on the side of the bed and rubs my arms, and I just start crying.

Brian lies down beside me and just holds me, rubbing my back, and lets me cry.

"I've been online all morning; no history has changed." This causes me to cry harder because if he isn't here, the only other option is it's truly him at Ivy Hill.

"Anything could have held him up, Ivy. Just give it time."

Nodding, I wait for my babies to finish dinner and snuggle with them for another night.

∞∞∞

It's now been seven days since the day David died. He should have been here three days ago, and my whole body is numb. Scott has been over every day, and today is no different. He is sitting in the living room when I walk out, and everyone walks out.

"Ivy, what's wrong?" Brian asks with concern on his face.

"What do you mean, what's wrong?"

"Well, you are dressed."

"I am. I need to go out. I will be back by dinner. Will you watch the kids?"

All three of them exchange a look.

"Of course, we will, but do you want one of us to go with you?" Kevin asks.

I force a smile. "Nope."

"You aren't, you know, going back, are you?" Brian asks.

I drop the smile. "No."

"Okay, sorry, I had to make sure."

I eat a banana and then head out the door and drive straight to Ivy Hill. I walk the house first, taking in every detail, no matter how small, wondering if he left me a sign or I missed something. Nothing is out of place, no small sign for me, nothing. My heart shatters as I start to try to comprehend that he didn't make it. He truly died in that bed on August 29, 1969. How do you live after that? I feel empty, and even though I made David a promise, I don't know how I am going to be the mother my kids need me to be.

I follow the crowds out to the memorial garden, and when I'm in front of David's grave, I sink to my knees and just let the tears fall. I don't know how long I am there for, but I know I get many confused looks, many weird looks, and several people ask me if I'm okay. After the third person checks on me, I figure I've made enough of a scene, and I get up and walk away without a word.

I drive home on autopilot, and when I walk in the door, there is a buzz in the air, and for a moment, I have a ray of hope as I walk to the living room.

Scott jumps up. “No, he isn’t here, but I did something for you that might help.”

I sit on the couch and don’t bother telling him nothing will help unless it’s my David in my arms or me lying in the grave next to him.

“My mother did another interview and went on and on because it’s the anniversary of... well, you know. So, I decided it was time the world knows her as we do. I leaked her letters to David, admitting she lied to her parents and the ones of her parents threatening him. I said her lies took him from the love of his life, which led him down his spiral of drugs that eventually killed him. His fans have turned on her, and she can’t leave her house. People are pissed.”

A sick part of me does get joy from this. That woman has been making money off David ever since he died with books, interviews, magazine spreads, and who knows what else. I hope this is the end of it.

Scott gets up and sits next to me and wraps me in a hug. “I warned her to stop this many years ago, but I never had anything to use against her until now. I wasn’t going to put the letters out, but in light of everything... I figure it’s time the world sees my dad for who he is.”

“Was.” I stand up. “Who he was. Let’s call a spade a spade.” I walk off to my room and let the tears flow. Even my David Miller playlist doesn’t soothe me to sleep; it just makes me cry harder.

Two weeks.

It's been two weeks since the day David was supposed to be here in my arms. Since our family was supposed to be complete. I haven't been able to pull myself out of bed. Thank goodness for Brian, Kevin, and Scott and their help with the kids.

This morning I've been replaying my last few days with David over and over in my head. What did I miss? What could I have done differently? I know I promised him I'd get up and go on for the kids. What he didn't tell me is *how* to do that.

How do I move on?

How do I stop the pain?

How do I keep breathing when every breath without him hurts?

I love my kids. They are a part of him, and that helps, but he was my heart and soul. Now that he is gone, the motivation and ability to go on is as well. But I know I have to keep my promise for him. I want my kids to have an amazing childhood, to know their dad loved them with his whole heart, and everything he did was for them. I can give them that, and to do that, I have to get out of bed.

I get up and get in the shower, which brings back memories of our shower together that last morning. I can still feel his hands on me, rubbing the soap all over me and lovingly washing my hair. I can feel his lips on mine and that moment when he slid into me.

The emotions overwhelm me, and I lose it, crying for the man I love and not just all I lost but all my kids have lost, and they don't even know it. I sink to the shower floor and let the water wash away my tears. I cry until the water turns cold. The icy water running over my skin is the push I need to get up and get dressed.

When I walk into the kitchen, all three guys look at me. I know they can tell I've been crying, and I don't know when that will stop, so I'm not even going to try to hide it.

"I made David a promise to keep going for our kids and live for them. I don't know how to live without him, but I have to try. Scott, will you take me to Ivy Hill? I need to say goodbye, and to do so, I need the grounds people free."

"Of course, Ivy, the house isn't open for tours for two more hours. If we go now, you will have plenty of quiet."

I nod and let Scott drive me there while I contemplate how to move on with my new normal.

He talks to a few people and clears out the house grounds for us.

"You have free rein of the house. I'll be by the front door to keep everyone out until you're done."

I smile at him as best as I can and step inside Ivy Hill for what will be the last time. I know someday I will have to tell the kids, and they will be brought here, but I don't think I will be able to do it. I have to shut the door on this part of my life if I have any chance of being a mom to our kids.

As I walk into the living room, I remove my shoes and duck under the rope to make my way across the white carpet to the piano. I turn the bench perpendicular to the keys and sit down.

I close my eyes, and I see David sitting here playing "Stay With Me Now" and singing to me.

I see him laughing and carefree, his eyes full of love, and I know that's how I always want to remember him.

I stand up and put my shoes back on and head up to our room. I take in each photo and the memories behind them. I stop and remember the newest photos. The ones that were strange for me to see when I was here with Scott the first time. One of us in the pool and another of us backstage after one of his shows.

I remember the many nights I got to lay in his arms in this very bed. Knowing I will never feel his arms around me again makes it hard to breathe, and the tears keep falling.

I walk to the bathroom and take in the bath products and just try to catch a scent of him again. I turn back to the bedroom and look at the bed where his body was found.

Was he scared?

Did he suffer?

Was he thinking of me?

I fall to my knees and cry for him, for my David, who I know was so scared this would be the outcome. I should have stayed. Once again, I should have been there. When I think I have cried all the tears I possibly can, I stand up and make my way out to the memorial garden. I kneel beside David's grave, and the tears I thought I were done with start flowing again.

"I'm so sorry I wasn't there. I should have insisted I was there with you. I made you a promise, and I'm here because I will keep that promise. To do that, I have to close the door on us. I have to lock you in the depth of my heart and keep you safe there to have a fighting chance to be the mother I promised you I would be to our kids. I won't be back here, but I promise Brian, Kevin, and even Scott will bring the kids to you often. They will know what an amazing man you were and how much I loved you."

I double over in tears, my heart shattering at this moment of truly admitting to myself he's gone. My David died that day on August 29, 1969, and I couldn't stop it.

I cry for everything lost and every person this affected. I cry for his dad, having to lose his son, and I cry for his mom who had blind faith in me, and I failed her.

"I'm so sorry. God, I love you so much..."

Strong arms wrap around me from behind, and assuming they are Scott's, I try to stop the tears; he's seen me cry enough already.

"I love you too, my sweet Ivy, and I have no plans to ever leave you again." I think I'm imagining it, but the warm breath on my ear says otherwise.

My body collapses again, and my body is being turned in his arms as I look up into those stunning blue eyes I'd know anywhere even if his iconic black hair is replaced with his natural blond, and there is a two-week-old beard across his face.

"David..." I choke out. For a moment, I think I'm seeing a ghost, but a ghost wouldn't be able to wrap his arms around me; a ghost wouldn't leave hot breath on my ear.

"I'm here, my sweet girl. I'm sorry I'm late. I'm sorry I worried you."

I throw my arms around him and hold him tight. He's here, I can hold him, and my body relaxes, but my mind hasn't grasped that he is really here. He's really here. At that thought, I cry even harder, and his grip on me tightens.

He rubs my back and whispers how much he loves me over and over again until the tears finally stop.

"I will explain everything, but I think it's best we head home, okay?" he whispers in my ear but never lets go of me.

I nod. He puts his sunglasses back on, and we head out front to greet Scott, who has a huge smile on his face.

"No more tears, Ivy. Tonight, we celebrate," Scott says, never taking his eyes off his dad.

"No more tears, Scott, only happy ones."

When we walk through the door, Brian and Kevin are grinning too, so I guess David stopped by here first to find out where I was.

We all sit down in the living room, and he pulls me onto his lap. I rest my head on his shoulder, just soaking him in and letting his woodsy scent surround me.

"So, what happened?" Brian asks, almost bouncing in his seat.

"Well, everything went as planned, but as the news broke, fans surrounded the house on all four sides. Poor Clint had to bring in more people from other companies to help with the crowd. The Nashville police even showed up to help. I've never seen anything like it. Dad asked everyone out of the house, Nancy, Clint, everyone, so it was just him and me. We thought maybe at night I could sneak out, but these people never left, and the crowd got bigger each day."

I watch him shake his head with a sad look on his face. "Nothing you could have done would have prepared me for it. Anna showed up on day four, claiming she had a right to mourn at the house as did Scott, but my dad had my will and the divorce order ready, stating she wasn't allowed access to any part of Ivy Hill. To say she was pissed was an understatement. I guess she thought everything would go to Scott when I died, and she was right. What pissed her off is that I left my dad as the trust holder for him and not her being his mother."

"I remember reading about her taking it to court and trying to fight it, but she dropped it and never said why," Scott adds.

"Yeah, Brian found a record of that, so I prepared for it in my will, leaving a handwritten letter to explain why I chose my dad along with copies of the letters from Anna and her dad with the threats and her admitting to lying. My dad was ready with proof Anna had supplied me with the drugs and would accuse her of purposely trying to kill me off to grab hold of the estate. I'm sure my dad will let us know how it ends. He plans to visit in a few months, but he doesn't want to come for more than a long weekend in the event Anna tries to pull anything."

"So how did you eventually get out?" Kevin asks.

David smiles. "After about ten days, people finally started to go home. My dad went out and made a statement that he was overwhelmed by all the support and love shown, but he asked to be allowed to mourn in peace as funeral arrangements were being made. He would hold a private service for the family and then a public one and announce where they could come to mourn at my grave. That seemed to appease people. He also asked that they keep to the front wall for mourning, so that allowed him to get me out through the back. We circled Nashville twice to make sure we weren't followed to the rocks."

He squeezes my hip. "When I came through, I came straight here, but Brian and Kevin said you were at Ivy Hill, so Brian drove me there. When Scott saw me, he knew I was there for you. He said you have been a mess and made me head right to you. It broke my heart to see you so broken, beautiful. I promise it won't happen again. You are stuck with me now."

"As much as I want to tell the kids, I'm going to be selfish and steal you away for a bit. You guys got the kids?"

Scott laughs. "That's my cue to go. I will be back tonight for dinner."

"Go, go, go!" Brian shoos us away as I pull David toward our room. As soon as the door is closed, he has me pinned to it and his lips on mine, devouring me.

"No more nights apart," he whispers against my lips, then trails kisses across my jaw to my neck. "No more saying good-bye." He nips at my earlobe. "Just us." His hands trail to my ass as he lifts me. I wrap my legs around him, but instead of heading to the bed, he heads to the bathroom.

"What are you doing?"

"I know you, and I'm willing to bet every time you stepped into this shower, you thought about our last shower together. About our morning goodbye showers. Then you would burst into tears and collapse on the floor. Am I right?"

I shake my head. "Of course, you're right."

"Then we are going to make a happy memory and turn showers together into a fun, positive thing."

"I can get on board with that." He sets me down so gently and starts the water. As he removes my clothes, he is kissing every spot on my body. My shoulders, my elbows, my wrists, my breasts, my belly button, my knees, my feet. Then he leads me into the warm shower.

As the warm water washes over me, he kisses me with so much passion that it heals all the broken pieces of my heart.

"I'm so sorry for every tear I caused you. I knew what you were thinking and feeling, and it tore me apart every minute I was away. Knowing the pain I was causing you killed me. Knowing the tears you were shedding and I couldn't stop it was my undoing. I knew I was doing the right thing then."

He takes my body wash and gently washes every part of me. As he kneels, he kisses my belly just below my belly button. Then he looks up at me.

"Too soon to tell," I whisper, knowing he wants to know if I'm pregnant.

"So I get to be there through everything." His smile is so big.

"Every minute of it."

This time, he isn't so gentle when he kisses me and slams me up against the shower wall. It's frantic need as I wrap my legs around him, and he thrusts into me, causing us to moan. I hold him a little tighter and enjoy his body heat in a moment that just this morning I thought I'd never have again.

Feeling him stretch me and fill me is a relief, and after the past few weeks, my climax builds quickly, and I can tell his does as well.

"You are mine for good now, Ivy, and I have a feeling I'm going to be needing you a lot. You are going to take care of me, aren't you, sweet girl?"

"Yes," I moan. This dominant side of him has my nerves tightening and ready to go off.

"Good. You thought I needed you before, but that was nothing. The thought of you pregnant with my child... I will never get enough of you. But I will take care of you too, Ivy. Anything you ever want or need will be yours all you ever need to do is ask."

He rubs his thumb across my clit, and I shatter just as his warm cum coats every inch inside me.

Lying in bed later that night, I sit up and look down at him and smile.

“We get to live it out now.” I smile at him.

“What's that, beautiful?”

“You get to stay with me now.”

Epilogue

Ivy

One Year Later

Brian has been watching things closely, and in the past year, there haven't been any changes to history, further confirming to us this was our destiny. Too many things just don't add up otherwise.

A few weeks after David came home to me, we found out I was pregnant. I don't think I've ever seen him so happy. A few weeks later, we tested the waters and applied for a marriage license and had no issues. We were married on the same day we said our vows all those years ago. It killed David to wait six months, but when I reminded him that I would be visibly pregnant in our wedding photos, he was all for it.

His name is still David. Brian gave him David as a middle name and my last name. So, he is officially Astor David Collins. Brian gave him a weird first name so people would understand why he went by his middle name. We decided to give him my last name for a few reasons.

One, less paperwork with me not having to change my name. Two, my last name is pretty common. But most importantly, we now don't have to worry about changing the kid's last names. It was a quick process to add him to the kid's birth certificates.

So, by the time we had baby James Scott Collins, everything

was in order. He was born at home, surrounded by David Miller, just like his brother and sister were. Scott took care of the kids for us and cried like a baby when he heard the name of his newest sibling.

David loved every moment of my pregnancy, and just like he said, he couldn't keep his hands off me. Brian, Kevin, and Scott laugh it off now, and even the kids find it funny when he starts pulling me toward the bedroom even though they have no idea what is going on.

Brian and Kevin have moved into the house they built down the road, but they are over here daily. Brian and Kevin have been with our kids so much and can't seem to stay away. They adopted twin girls whose parents died in a car accident. Kevin was on call that night and delivered them via emergency C section at thirty-one weeks. They had no family, so while still in the hospital, they started the process to adopt them, and it was finalized before they were released four months ago. There are plenty of babies to love on around the house now.

James comes to visit every few months for a long weekend and updates us on what's happening. It seems Anna has crawled away and is leaving him alone, and Clint has been keeping a good eye on Scott. He has the museum starting and has this glint in his eye when he talks about all of David's accomplishments. I can tell he loves being able to show them off.

David had gone back with his dad twice just to help with this or that for the museum, and the dates he has gone back match when the rumors of the sightings have happened, so that is always a running joke now.

We attended little Clara's school play last month, and there were so many people there. David was nervous; it was his first big gathering, but he refused to miss her play. He said he missed so much already. He had been working with Brian and picked up a bit of a Southern accent to mask his famous voice.

One older lady stopped him and mentioned that he looks

a lot like David Miller. He thanked her and said he has been told that before, but he's checked, and there is no relation. She laughed and told him about seeing one of his concerts when she was younger. David loved to hear it.

I asked him that night if he missed singing and performing. He said he does a little but when he was there singing and performing, he missed me and the kids a whole lot more, so he doesn't regret giving it up even for one moment. I smile at myself in the mirror at that before heading out to find David and the kids.

They are watching cartoons in the living room and still their PJs being the first one up. When David sees me up and dressed, he smiles.

"Where are you going, beautiful?"

"Well, first, Happy Birthday, and second, I'm going to Ivy Hill. Remember that Ivy Hill on what would be your eighty-seventh birthday. Got it?"

"I'll be there, Ivy, always." He smiles, knowing exactly what I mean.

I meet Scott at his office, and he walks over to the grounds with me. Ivy Hill always does a celebration for David's birthday. This year it isn't as big as his eighty-fifth was, but it's still busier than a normal day.

We walk in and notice the piano bench is perpendicular to the piano.

"What's going on there?" I ask him.

Scott smiles. "We found some new information that my dad would sit with the bench perpendicular to the piano when he was writing music or playing, but only here at Ivy Hill. Interesting, isn't it?"

I laugh. "Yeah, his small quirks helped make some great music."

I follow him to the backyard and off to the side where there are fewer people, and I start scanning the crowds.

"Calm down, Ivy, he will be here. Dad would never let you down."

That's something else that makes me smile. Scott has started to call David dad, and the first time he did, David cried. Now he still smiles every time.

Finally, over by a bench, I see him. I smile when my eyes lock with his. He nods his head to the part of the garden where we talked the last time we met here. An area that gets us away from the crowd.

When we are out of sight of the public, I reach over and hug him. He holds me tight and laughs.

"I never get tired of seeing that smile on your face, my beautiful girl."

He hugs Scott too and smiles. "Thank you for being there for her when I couldn't be. I don't think I ever thanked you for that."

"Of course, Dad, she is family."

David smiles when he says dad and to know that one little thing still makes him smile means everything.

"You found your way back to me." I smile at him.

"I did. I'd never leave you, my sweet Ivy."

Just then, the opening chords to our song starts from the stage.

"Dance with me, beautiful?"

"Of course."

He holds me close, and when the chorus starts, he sings, "Stay with me now, it's now or never..." in my ear, and it makes me smile.

"You didn't answer me last time, but I'm going to ask again. Are we happy?"

He smiles. "Deliriously happy. This isn't the life I pictured growing up. I never thought I'd be a famous movie star or a singer. All I wanted was a wife who loved me as much as I loved her and kids to spoil. You gave me that with a twist. This life is so much better."

Want More Kaci Rose?

She's Still The One: A Brother's Best Friend, Rockstar Romance

Bro Code Rule #1 – You can't have your best friend's younger sister.

Austin

What is it that guys I date don't seem to understand what a causal relationship is?

That doesn't mean to propose to me. This is why I packed up everything into my car and I'm now heading to my brothers.

Only he's not there. His best friend Dallas is.

Dammit, he's the reason none of my relationships have worked out. I compare them all to how he treats me.

When they go on tour and drag me along it's hard to hide feelings in the small space of a tour bus. But my brother has made it very clear.

Dallas is no good for me. We both risk losing my brother if we go any further.

Dallas

It sucks when you can't have the one girl you love.

When the band I started with Austin's brother took off girls were easy. It was less messy having flings.

Then she moves into the house with us.

Even when her brother has made it perfectly clear she is off limits I can't seem to stay away.

She is still the only one who makes my heart race.

When her life is on the line because of the band's fame can we put our differences aside long enough to save her?

Can I convince them both I've changed, and I will be a one-

woman man the rest of my days if she just chooses me?

This is a Steamy, Rockstar, Brother's Best Friend Romance. No Cliffhangers.
As always there is a satisfying Happy Ever After.
If you love steamy romances with hot love scenes, and rock-stars, then this one is for you.

Mailing List, Website, & Social

Want to get to know the whole Rock Springs Texas gang from the beginning? Grab the FREE Novella *Sage & Colt The Beginning* by joining my newsletter!

Get Sage & Colt: The Beginning Now!

https://kacirose.com/SageandColt

Connect with Kaci Rose

Website

Facebook

Kaci Rose Reader's Facebook Group

Instagram

Twitter

Goodreads

Book Bub

Amazon

Join Kaci Rose's VIP List (Newsletter)

Other Books By Kaci Rose

See all of Kaci Rose's Books

Oakside Military Heroes Series

Saving Noah – Lexi and Noah

Saving Easton – Easton and Paisley

Saving Teddy – Teddy and Mia

Chasing the Sun Duet

Sunrise

Sunset

Rock Springs Texas Series

The Cowboy and His Runaway – Blaze and Riley

The Cowboy and His Best Friend – Sage and Colt

The Cowboy and His Obsession – Megan and Hunter

The Cowboy and His Sweetheart – Jason and Ella

The Cowboy and His Secret – Mac and Sarah

Rock Springs Weddings Novella

Rock Springs Box Set 1-5 + Bonus Content

The Cowboy and His Mistletoe Kiss – Lilly and Mike

The Cowboy and His Valentine – Maggie and Nick

The Cowboy and His Vegas Wedding – Royce and Anna Mae

The Cowboy and His Angel – Abby and Greg

Standalone Books

Stay With Me Now

Texting Titan

Accidental Sugar Daddy

She's Still The One

Take Me To The River

Please Leave a Review!

I love to hear from my readers! Please head over to Amazon and leave a review of what you thought of this book!

Made in the USA
Columbia, SC
23 September 2024